THE NIGHT BLINDER

A HARRIET HARPER THRILLER

DOMINIKA BEST

THE NIGHT BLINDER
HARRIET HARPER THRILLER SERIES - BOOK 4

Copyright © 2021 by Dominika Best

ISBN: 978-1-949674-12-5

www.dominikabest.com
First Edition

For Dave
without you, none of this would be possible

DAY 1 - FRIDAY, NOVEMBER 30, 2018

Detective Harri Harper pulled up to the swanky home right off of Pacific Coast Highway just on the border of Malibu. This had to be a very special case because RHD was rarely called out to Malibu. She'd received a phone call from her Lieutenant, Violet Howard, the night before with the exciting news that she'd been transferred into RHD, the Robbery-Homicide division of the Los Angeles Police Department.

Harri had been trying to get into the division for well over four years and she wasn't entirely sure what had happened to finally get her placed in the storied division. RHD, as it was known around the department, handled cases of a sensitive nature: political, serial, or cases that would most likely make the evening news.

An old colleague of hers, Richard Byrne, ran RHD and had continually made sure she couldn't transfer because he didn't want to work with her. She had settled into the Cold Case unit thinking that's where she could make the most difference, and she'd made peace with that. Then the phone call came and here she was driving up to a multimillion-dollar house.

Harri drove past the address on the wrong side of the divider and then flipped a U-turn to pull up to the gate. The address was emblazoned on a gate surrounded by trees. This must be one of those modern mansions perched right on the beach that have a long drive from the main road.

She pressed the call button and announced her arrival.

She didn't have to wait long for the gates to open. She'd been wrong about the house. The property had both a front lawn with a circular drive and a backyard from what she could see so far. The drive was filled with the Coroner's van, an unmarked sedan, two Malibu police cruisers, and a paneled van. She assumed the crime scene techs had to be here already. She parked behind the Coroner's van.

Detective Tom Bards stepped out of the sedan and smiled at her.

"Harri, welcome to RHD," he said and shook her hand. "How's the voice box feeling?"

Harri had most recently been involved in a case where a Hollywood director had tried to strangle her. She was still recovering her voice and was careful not to strain her vocal cords or worsen the internal bruising on her neck. She'd been in the hospital for close to five days and her inability to speak above a whisper was the reason she'd been on leave for the last two weeks. It was also the reason why she was not in Berlin with Jake Tepesky, tracking down her sister's killer.

Jake was striking out though and seeing as she had gotten such a big promotion, her staying behind was the logical choice, no matter how much she wished she could be with him.

"It's still not fun for me to talk," Harri said. Her voice sounded a hundred times better than it did the week before but still came out strained.

"It's coming back and increasingly fast," Tom said.

"I'm pleased with my recovery. Thank you for asking," Harri said. She was aiming for polite but also a let's-not-talk-about-it tone. In case he didn't catch her meaning, she changed the subject.

"Do you know anything about my assignment to RHD?" she asked as they headed up the front stairs of the mansion.

Loud music blared from somewhere inside. The sound was ear-splitting even from outside the home.

"Someone put in a good word for you," Tom said. "Could have been me."

This surprised Harri. She had been on the Creek Killer task force with him earlier in the fall and had been integral in bringing the killers to justice. But she hadn't worked that closely with Tom himself on the case even though they were part of the same task force. She'd been sidelined early on and happened upon the key to the entire case, totally by happenstance.

"I very much appreciate that," she said. "I'd given up trying."

"I know," Tom said.

Harri smiled. She'd already solved that mystery and it was still early. Hopefully, the rest of the day would be as easy.

She'd tried getting a transfer into the unit for the last four years and failed miserably. Tom Bards had the kind of pull that comes with close to twenty years of experience as a homicide detective.

"Thank you," Harri said.

Her doctor told her to whisper instead of speaking in her normal range to protect her voice, but she wanted to appear totally well and fit to handle whatever happened on the case.

"You deserved it," Tom said. "You've solved the last two major cases thrown your way. You have sharp instincts and an impressive record. We need more people like you on the team."

Harri nodded and felt her cheeks burn. A compliment coming from him meant a lot.

They had reached the front door and the music was blaring.

"Is this how the body was found?" Harri asked, pointing to her ears.

"The music?" Tom asked, raising his voice to be heard over it.

Harri nodded.

"Neighbors called it in," Tom shouted. His voice reverberated around the courtyard as someone inside turned off the music.

""I'm Sitting on Top of the World" by Al Jolson," Tom said in his normal voice. "Haven't heard that one in years. Was a huge hit during the Roaring Twenties."

She'd never heard the song before.

Tom opened the massive double door, and they stepped into an immaculate all-white living room. The owner had definitely used a decorator.

Crime scene techs blended right in with their all-white coveralls and were busy collecting evidence throughout the large open plan room.

The victim hadn't been killed in the living room apparently.

"And who is our vic?" Harri asked.

"His name was Miles Davidson. Some hotshot wealth manager who helped keep all the Hollywood elites rich in this town."

"Where is he?" Harri asked.

The hive of crime scene techs was going over every surface of the luxury interiors. Harri pulled on the plastic booties and latex gloves she carried to every crime scene. Tom did the same beside her.

"His body is outside," Tom said and pointed to the deck outside of the glass doors.

Harri could see the back of a man sitting on a chair on a patio overlooking the expanse of the Pacific Ocean. The coroner, Dr. Grimley, was already out there with her assistants assessing the body.

Tom and Harri walked across the oversized living room to the wall of glass doors. The cool, salty air hit her face as soon as she opened the door. This was some kind of house.

"Good to see you again, Detective Harper," Dr. Grimley said. "And Tom. How are the kids?"

"Good, good. What do you have for us, Dr. Grimley?" he asked.

"As you know, I won't put anything on the record without getting him on the table. But my preliminaries are this: time of death is anywhere between midnight and four this morning. The body is just starting to go into rigor now."

Harri stepped over to Dr. Grimley and looked at the disfigured face of the man in front of them.

"What happened to his eyes?" she asked.

"Scooped out. Judging by the amount of blood coming out of the sockets, I'd say it happened while he was still alive," Dr. Grimley said.

"Birds love soft tissue. Could it have been them? Lots

of seagulls around."

"I don't see any pecking marks around the eyes. He was alive when he lost them, I'm pretty sure. I'll know for certain during autopsy," she said.

"And would the cause of death be that really nasty cut on his throat?" Tom asked.

The man's throat was slit from ear to ear. His head leaned back on the chair. Miles Davidson's ankles and wrists were secured to the arms and legs of the chair he died in with zip-ties.

"Most likely," Dr. Grimley replied.

Dr. Grimley pointed at the pool of blood underneath the sitting man.

"This looks about right for the amount of blood that would pump out if the carotid artery had been sliced through," Dr. Grimley said.

"Any idea about the murder weapon?" Harri asked.

"Something very sharp. And small, almost like a scalpel," Dr. Grimley said. "But don't quote me on that just yet."

Harri's brain analyzed the scene for things that were out of place. What was there that shouldn't be? What was obviously missing?

Harri looked through the wall of glass into the living room and dining room space. The chair he sat in was from the dining room. The killer most likely brought the zip-ties. Judging from the look of the place, she doubted Miles Davidson had any use for zip-ties.

"He was killed out here?" Tom asked.

The chair was from inside, but all the blood was out on the patio.

"My educated guess would be yes," Dr. Grimley said.

The victim had to be at least six-foot-two and by the looks of his body, he spent a lot of time exercising.

"Did he put up a fight?" Harri asked.

Joanna Wood, Dr. Grimley's assistant, was kneeling in front of the dead man placing bags on his hands.

"I'm not really seeing any skin under his nails," she said and stood back up again.

"Could have been drugged first," Tom remarked. "Have you found any punctures?"

"Not at first glance," Dr. Grimley said and waved two of her staff over to bag the body. "Can I take him now?"

"Yes. How soon can you do an autopsy?" Tom asked.

"I'll squeeze you in tomorrow. I'll let you know what time," Dr. Grimley said.

Tom and Harri turned away from the body and Harri scanned the sides of the house. Privacy hedges blocked the view to either neighbor's property.

"I doubt there are going to be cameras pointed at this porch," Harri said.

"Uniforms are checking with the neighbors about getting their camera footage for the last forty-eight hours. I wouldn't hold my breath though," he said.

"The victim was supposed to have died last night between midnight and four. And the neighbors called it in around eight-thirty in the morning because of the music. Does that mean that the music was not playing when he died?"

"The music playing gives us two available scenarios." Tom nodded. "The killer left and came back in the early morning hours to set the scene the way he wanted Miles Davidson to be found. This scenario is the riskier of the two because our killer would be seen coming and going from the residence multiple times. The more likely scenario was that he stayed with the victim all night and turned the music up on his way out the door."

"So that bears the question, what was he doing all

night? And if he did stay here, he must have left some trace of him behind for us to find," Harri said.

"And if he didn't," Tom said and stopped. "We'll deal with that when the time comes. Between you and me, I hope it never does."

"If it's that clean, we have an expert killer on our hands?" Harri asked.

"Something like that. But I don't want to go anywhere near that idea yet," Tom said. "If there's something to find the techs will find it."

They both entered the living room again. The place was even more glaring white.

Harri could not see any smudges on the shiny white surfaces of the dining table and entertainment system, except for where the crime scene techs were dusting for fingerprints. The white tiled floor looked spotless.

"What if he spent all night cleaning?" she asked.

"Or Miles Davidson was a clean freak."

"That's either going to make our investigation easy or super hard," she said.

"Do you smell bleach?" Tom asked.

"No, I don't."

"Excuse me, detectives." A crime scene technician in goggles and latex gloves ambled up to them. "We're probably gonna be here for the rest of the day. So far, we've found several fingerprints on windowsills and fibers in the bathroom. Otherwise, it's been clean. We're starting on the upstairs now and it's going to take a while."

"Have you found his computer? Or his cellphone? I haven't been able to locate either of them," Tom said.

The tech pointed to a door to his left. "That was his office, but no computer equipment is there. Only the cords. Same goes for his phone. We found his cords and docking station but no phone."

"Have you gone through it already?" Tom asked.

"We have. It's been wiped and cleaned. We found nothing. No prints. No trace. Killer had to have vacuumed. It's thorough."

Tom opened the door.

The room was indeed an office. Built-in shelving took up two walls, while the third wall was all glass, overlooking the beach and the Pacific Ocean. A massive wooden desk was anchored to the shelving on the left and jutted out into the small space. Harri could see the tangle of cords that must have been plugged into a computer. His printer was still sitting on the shelf. Harri didn't see any filing cabinets.

She got busy checking the drawers while Tom went to a shelf holding a pair of Bose Bluetooth headphones and nothing else. "I see a cord snaking behind these books for an iPhone."

Harri scanned the cords and recognized a Mac power cord. "This looks like a MacBook Pro cord. I have one at home," she said. "I'm not seeing any filing cabinets."

"It's all probably on the cloud somewhere," Tom said.

Harri found a business card on the floor. It said Miles Davidson, Wealth Management & Financial Planning. The card listed a phone number and the address of the property they were currently inspecting.

"I don't think he worked out of an office," she said.

"A lot of these guys don't. They like working from home," Tom said. "We'll be able to pull the cellphone records at least. Hopefully, they'll shed some light on a client list or what he was up to for the last twenty-four hours."

"You don't think this was a random killing, do you?"

"I'm not sure yet. I doubt we'll find a planner or calendar. Knowing these kinds of guys, everything would have been on his devices."

They searched the room for any other electronics or paper planners but came up empty. They gave up and walked back into the living room.

Tom nodded and looked at Harri. "Are you ready for this?"

"You mean RHD? Or dealing with people as wealthy as this? Or the media that's going to hit us any minute?" she asked.

"All of that and more. I know you've been on high-profile cases before, but rich people can be a pain in the ass. They always claim to have friends in high places, and often actually do," he said.

"I'm ready. I also want to thank you again for getting me into RHD," Harri said.

"It was my absolute pleasure and I look forward to bringing whoever did this to justice with you," he said with a grin. "Cases like this, especially with a dead rich guy, revolve around money. Who has it, who doesn't, and who is willing to do whatever it takes to take it. I'm not seeing this as a crime of passion."

"Neither am I unless we count greed as passion. But the eyes?" Harri fought back a shudder as the image of the dead man's bloody and empty eye sockets came into her mind.

"Maybe our killer got creative with the body trying to hide that his motive was money."

"I'm trying not to put too much emphasis on the eyes, but the body's presentation makes me think something else is at play. Especially with how meticulous this crime scene is," Harri said.

"The overkill could be a ruse," Tom said. "Why don't

we start by looking into his financials? I've a feeling we're going to find some very interesting things in there."

"You don't trust the finance guys, do you?" Harri asked.

"Honestly, there's always something fishy to find when it comes to the wealthy and their money. And when somebody can afford a place like this and is found like that? I always think it's a good place to start," he said.

"Money and politics bring out the worst in people," Harri said.

"Every time," Tom said.

"Are the uniforms going door-to-door right now?" Harri asked.

"Yes. Hopefully, they'll get us those security tapes. There aren't that many ways in and out of this place. I do hope all these fancy gates have good enough cameras to see a couple of doors down," he said.

They walked out of the front door.

"I'll see you back at the PAB?" she asked.

"I bet you'll get there faster than I can," Tom said with a wink and turned to his unmarked vehicle.

Harri knew she would enjoy the ride back to the office. She'd probably be stuck in traffic but her stereo system was stellar.

She climbed into the driver's seat. "Here we go," she whispered under her breath and started the car.

Harri had wanted to join RHD for such a long time and here she was on her first RHD case. She almost couldn't shake off the wonder that it had finally happened and that her partner was the legendary Tom Bards.

She pulled out onto PCH, turned on the radio, and

worked through the traffic at a decent pace. Her mind wandered to Jake and how he was doing in Berlin.

They'd spoken the night before, and Harri was disappointed to hear that all the leads they had so hoped would go somewhere had fallen apart on him. He would be heading back home in the next few days which made her happy. She didn't like staying in his place all by herself and missed her things.

Harri put her own house on the market and had left most of the furniture there to help sell the place. It felt weird being surrounded by all of Jake's things and none of her own, but she was thankful she had a place to stay. Her home had been permanently tainted when the murderer she'd exposed on her last case had broken in and nearly murdered her in her bed some weeks back. The changes in her life over the last three months were astonishing.

She shook off those thoughts and turned back to the case. She considered the staging of the crime scene and how the body was positioned in that particular way outside.

Why was the body put outside? Why was he staring out at the ocean with no eyes?

The killer took a huge risk leaving the dead guy out like that. Was he making some sort of statement about privacy?

Or private beaches?

That was dumb, she thought.

She hadn't often been to an active crime scene in close to five years. The Cold Case unit obviously worked differently because the murders they investigated were long dormant. The team re-investigated the cases mainly through the murder book the original detectives created with their notes and evidence.

Many of them were fifteen to twenty years old. Some of the crime scenes had been so altered, they weren't even standing anymore. Other crime scenes had been extensively changed or completely lost the character they had at the time the crime occurred. But time moved on.

Los Angeles was gentrifying so fast that neighborhoods that had been gang-infested and crime centers were quickly becoming the hottest neighborhoods for investors who renovated properties quickly to flip them for fast cash. Desperate first-time buyers rushed to move in and claim the neighborhoods as the trendy new destinations, but all Harri could see were the crime statistics the sellers and buyers tried to ignore.

RHD had jurisdiction over the entire city. Anything that was high-profile, political, and would come with a lot of media RHD took over.

She was finally in. And all thanks to Tom Bards.

Harri pulled on to the I–10 and was happy to see there wasn't that much traffic. It was close to eleven o'clock, and the roads had cleared. She was going to get back to the PAB in record time.

2

DAY 1 - FRIDAY, NOVEMBER 30, 2018
BEL AIR HOTEL - NOON

Philip Townsend sat at the bar in the lounge of the Bel Air Hotel, scowling. He hated this time of year. All the palm trees were decked out in lights and cheesy Christmas music played in every store, restaurant, or elevator he went into.

At least here the pianist was playing tasteful, jazzy Christmas carols. It was the best he was going to get.

He took a sip of his water and watched Lucas Reinhart, one of his oldest friends and his wealthiest client, weave his way through the tables. Lucas had lost most of his hair in the last ten years, but he still had that old-money-I-haven't-a-care-in-the-world swagger. Philip noticed several women watching him walk to their table with hunger in their eyes.

Every wealth manager needed a client like Lucas Reinhart. They made life easy. Lucas had never worked for a living and his fortune was large enough that he had no problem living a lavish lifestyle on the interest alone. Lucas knew the golden rule of never touching the principal.

"So good to see you man," Lucas said. His wispy blonde hair was all over the place and he wore his aviators even inside. He had that classic rich look, bronzed skin, soft white button-down shirt, and gray slacks.

Lucas dropped into the leather seat and waved over to the waiter, his silver rings flashing in the light.

"Are you drinking?" Lucas asked.

Philip shook his head no.

"I'm watching the market carefully and I have a small window of time, so nothing for me," he said.

"I need a scotch," Lucas said.

As the waiter came over and took his order, Philip's eyes wandered to the wall behind Lucas.

"Did you hear?" Lucas asked.

Philip tore his eyes away from the massive John Belushi photograph that was hanging behind Lucas' head to respond to him. The photograph was so detailed that he could see John Belushi's pores.

"Hear what?" Philip asked as his phone buzzed with a text. He flipped it over to see it was from Chandler.

Chandler: Miles is dead.

"Were you going to tell me that Miles Davidson is dead?" Philip asked.

"Not just dead. Murdered," Lucas said as he leaned over. "I have sources who told me his eyes were gouged out."

"You're lying," Philip said in disgust.

"Gruesome, right?" Lucas shook his head. "Miles is gonna be all over the news."

"Yeah, well. Miles Davidson had some famous clients," Philip said.

"Not only that," Lucas said.

Philip cocked his head and waited. Lucas took another sip of his scotch.

"Are you going to spit it out or what?"

"You're in the same game he was. You would know better than me. Haven't you heard of him doing shady stuff?" he asked.

"Shady? Like how?" Philip asked.

Typically, when financial people went down, it was for one of two things: embezzling their client's money or insider trading. Philip knew Miles had embezzled his client's money because he'd told him so last night.

"I heard he'd lost all of his clients' money. Remember that friend of mine who works with all the big Hollywood people? Freddie?"

Philip nodded. "I remember him."

"He told me he's heard that some of the biggest stars who worked with Miles lost a lot of money. A lot of money. He's hearing that Miles was running some sort of Ponzi scheme while he gambled their money away in high-stakes underground poker rooms. Miles had some huge losses in the last two months. Allegedly."

"I never thought his gambling habit was as bad as that," Philip said. "I also never thought Miles would have been that stupid."

Not until last night, that is.

Philip's fund, although worth close to a quarter of a billion dollars, had only seven investors. Those seven men made Philip a very good living. He was a value investor along the lines of Warren Buffett and Charlie Munger and knew his way around both options trading as well as the valuation of companies.

Philip knew what he was good at and didn't venture beyond it. No reason to get cocky or flashy. Good research, discipline, and instincts are how Philip kept the money machine going for his clients.

Miles Davidson, who had never been the sharpest knife in the drawer, did not run his fund in the same way, which Philip had truly been shocked to discover the night before.

"It will come out he lost all their money. And then got murdered in a brutal way. This is like a bad movie on TV," Lucas said.

"All those clients will be first in line as suspects," Philip added as he wondered if he would show up on any security cameras at Miles' house.

"It's going to be a wild holiday season," Lucas said with a wicked smile as he sipped his scotch.

"I don't know why anyone with any sense would have trusted Miles with their money," Philip admitted. "He always came off as a risk-taker to me. Why would you want a guy like that managing your portfolio?"

"All of us guys bet on football games and stuff. Who would have thought he had such a problem?" Lucas shrugged.

Of course, you didn't, Philip thought. Men born into wealth like Lucas simply couldn't wrap their heads around how easy it could be for someone to lose it all. They had no concept of how one false move could wipe away every achievement a man had made in his life. Their inherited wealth protected them from so much, even from thinking of the disaster a gambling addiction could cause.

"I knew he'd lost some of his client's money, but I didn't know exactly how. He wouldn't tell me," Philip said carefully.

"He actually told you he lost all the money?" Lucas asked, leaning forward again.

Philip studied his client and his friend. Should he tell him? Surely it was going to come out that he had seen Miles last night. The police would find their texts and phone calls. And Lucas was his client. He couldn't lose him.

"He told me last night," Philip confessed.

"You saw him last night?" Lucas asked in a whispered awe.

"I left him alive," he said quickly. "He asked me to stop by and then he asked me for a massive loan."

Lucas's eyes slit and he reminded Philip of a snake about to strike.

"He asked you for money?" Lucas asked. "What kind of money would you have to give him? Not any of mine?"

Philip tried hard not to roll his eyes. He did very well for himself, making millions off the profit from the fund. Lucas should know that. He got statements every quarter. For Lucas though, Philip's kind of money was peanuts.

"He wanted me to give him a loan against the fund. I told him absolutely not. No way was I going to put any of my clients' money in jeopardy," Philip said.

"And this is why you are my money guy," Lucas said with a smile. "He must have been desperate."

"I told him no way. I couldn't do anything for him." Philip shook his head at the memory. "He lost his shit, started yelling, threw me out of his house."

"How much did he want?" Lucas asked.

"Forty-five million," Philip said and watched Lucas shrug as if it was a reasonable amount. "He acted like I'd write him a check on the spot. I don't know why he thought I'd even entertain the idea."

"Well, our fund is doing fantastic. That twenty percent must be going far for you," Lucas said.

"You know I only get paid when you make gains," Philip reminded him. "Would you rather I fee you to death like all the other guys in town?"

Lucas didn't say anything for a moment. He took another sip of his scotch and watched Philip from across the table before cocking his head and asking, "So all he asked you for was money? Did anything else happen?"

"He asked me for a personal loan. That's it." Philip shook his head in disbelief. "Like I would throw good money after bad on a risk monkey like him?"

"You never really did like to gamble, did you?" Lucas asked. "Remember that time we all put a hundred on that women's curling team in the Olympics? You lectured us about the negative odds, the impropriety of betting on the Olympics. Then we won, and I thought you'd be pissed, but you weren't."

"You risked big and won big. Usually doesn't work out like that. I'm more about the sure thing," Philip said.

"What time did you leave him?" Lucas asked.

"Around nine-thirty, I think. I was only there for about twenty minutes before it went south. I left him pretty upset, so I got out of there fast."

"You know you're a suspect now. Right?" Lucas asked.

"He was alive when I left him. So, no. I shouldn't be. He was alive when I left."

"Do you have an alibi?" Lucas asked.

Philip wished he had a drink. His face flushed as he thought back to the night before and how pissed he was at Miles. He hadn't made any phone calls, though.

"I put some trades in around one a.m. I could give them my IP address I guess for that," Philip said.

"Looks like you'll be having some visitors soon. This bad publicity won't affect the fund, will it?" Lucas asked.

"Why should anyone know about me?" Philip muttered.

"This will be all over the news," Lucas said with another wicked smile.

He sounded like such a damn gossip. Philip wondered why he'd even said anything to him.

Because he had nothing to hide.

Lucas sat back in his seat and drank his scotch.

"This is all so wild," he said.

"That's one word for it," Philip said, his heart starting to beat a little faster. "Miles was our friend. And he's been murdered."

He wished he had a better alibi for last night.

Why did Miles have to call him for help? He was the least rich guy of all in their group of friends. What in the world was Miles thinking?

Lucas finished his drink and turned back to Philip.

"Are you going to the party tomorrow?" he asked cheerfully.

Philip nodded. "Can't miss Chandler's party, can we?"

Chandler James Robert III, king of their frat and wealthier than all of them, held his annual Christmas party the weekend after Thanksgiving. It was the event that started off the Christmas social season every year. Chandler opened his palatial home to everybody that was anybody in town and the gathering was a great place to make deals. Philip had met several of his clients at the party four years ago and he'd managed to parlay those clients into a fund that was worth close to 450 million dollars. It wasn't in the billions yet, but he'd get there.

Lucas grinned.

"All right, tell me what's happening with my money," he said, and Philip got down to business.

3

DAY 1- PAB (POLICE ADMINISTRATION BUILDING)

Harri Harper stared out the window of her sixth-floor cubicle at the PAB (Police Administration Building). The RHD bullpen had much nicer views than the Cold Case bullpen had. She turned back to her desk. She'd been working on getting Miles Davidson's phone records sent over and had started the application process to get into his bank and brokerage accounts. It was too early to find any financial troubles since they had no access to his paperwork yet.

Tom had called the next of kin and dealt with the notification. He spoke with Miles Davidson's mother, who lived in Massachusetts, about any problems or issues her son had in the last month. The mother didn't know of anything and believed her son had been doing great. Tom had said that he could hear the father in the background complaining loudly about something, but he couldn't exactly understand the words.

Harri had done a basic search on Miles Davidson and put together a preliminary dossier on him. Miles had gone to Philips Academy in New Hampshire which was

22

a fancy East Coast boarding school. His father had donated quite a bit to the school per one of the alumni newsletters from back then.

Miles had then gone off to Cornell University where he studied finance. He'd been a brother at Sigma Phi Delta and graduated in 2008. He was single and didn't have any girlfriends that Harri could find from her searches. It looked like he was into socializing and making appearances at charity events. The image services showed him at most of the really big events in LA in the last two years and he always had a different young thing on his arm.

His parents lived on Beacon Street in Boston and from a quick real estate service search their house was worth millions. When she searched for the father, Montgomery Davidson, she found articles detailing the family tree and how they were descended from the Mayflower. If Miles Davidson had embezzled his clients' money, it was quite the fall from grace, Harri thought.

Tom waved her over to where he was standing.

"Lieutenant Byrne wants to speak to us," Tom said.

Harri's heart skipped a beat.

She and Richard Byrne had a long, unpleasant history. Harri was convinced he was the reason it took her so many years to get into RHD. They normally tried to avoid each other as best as they could and even though the Cold Case unit was in the same building, they had managed to see each other as rarely as possible.

Now that Harri was in this unit and Lieutenant Richard Byrne was her direct boss, they would have to interact.

"Something wrong?" Tom asked as Harri shoved her chair back and got to her feet.

"You know how it is with us," Harri said.

"All water under the bridge. You're part of RHD now. You belong here," he said as she followed him toward Richard's office.

Her heart thumped against her chest and sweat broke out along her hairline. Why did she get so nervous around the guy?

He was an asshole, but she had met a lot of assholes in her life.

Tom knocked on the solid wood door and a voice from inside called, "Come in."

Tom opened the door. Lieutenant Richard Byrne sat behind his desk with a scowl on his face.

"Where are you at?" Lieutenant Byrne demanded.

Tom ambled to the chair directly in front of Byrne and Harri took the chair to his right. She sat back and decided to let Tom do all the speaking.

"At the very beginning," Tom said.

"You two are the only detectives on this for now," Richard began. "We have another gang shooting down on Crenshaw and I have another unit out in East LA. So far, this is a single murder and, even though it's a prominent member of the community, I think you two can handle it."

"Thanks for the vote of confidence, Richard," Tom said.

He had a smile on his face and, though his comment could be construed as defensive, it came off as good-natured.

"Sylvia Lambert will be dealing with the media on your behalf. I already have calls from every reporter, gossip column, and online blog that have the number to this office. A reporter from the LA Times named Aguilar has been haunting the front door waiting to ambush me. Either of you heard of him?"

Harri had heard of him but decided not to say anything. Richard was avoiding making eye contact with her.

"He's a bulldog," Tom said.

"I was hoping we'd be able to keep this out of the news for at least twenty-four hours, but Miles Davidson pissed off too many people," Richard said.

"Expound on that," Tom said.

"I've gotten several phone calls from lawyers about Miles Davidson doing something with his client's money."

"Are we talking about embezzlement?" Tom asked.

"Sounds like it," Richard said,

"Well, that's a motive," Tom said.

"Agreed. You've done finance crimes before so I'm hoping you won't need too much help. If you hit a dead-end, guys from the finance unit can help you out."

"We could use a forensic accountant to see exactly what he did. I'm good but I'm not a professional," Tom said.

"Have anyone in mind?" Richard asked.

"I do, in fact." Tom nodded. "He worked that same finance case I did years ago. I'll give him a call and see what kind of time he has."

"Do that," Richard said dismissively. "And welcome to the unit, Detective Harper," he said, finally looking over to her.

His blue eyes were cold and flat, but he had a smile on his face.

Harri smiled back. "Thank you, Lieutenant. I'm happy to be here and back at it," she said, her voice cracking. Her voice was almost back to normal now, but she noticed when she was nervous it was unreliable.

"Is there anything else?" Tom asked.

"That's it for now," Richard said. "Let me know when you uncover the embezzlement. This case is high profile enough with connections to Hollywood. You know rich people don't like talking with us. There'll be a lot of white-shoe lawyers involved. Keep on top of everything, but don't overstep."

Tom nodded.

Harri stood up to go.

"Thank you, Lieutenant," Tom said.

Richard nodded and Harri followed Tom out the door. She hadn't realized she'd been holding her breath in until she got out of his office and exhaled deeply. That didn't go as bad as she thought it would.

"He's worried," Tom said after he closed the door behind him.

"Why?" Harri said.

"Richard's a political animal and doesn't like flapping in the wind. This case is high-profile because of the rich clients. Rich people hate to be inconvenienced and they have expensive lawyers to do their bidding. We're just gonna have to make sure we play nice with everyone. If he hears a complaint, he's gonna come down hard on us."

"But you're such a congenial guy," Harri said with a grin.

"Sure, that's me. Miss Congeniality." Tom chuckled. "This one is going to be a doozy. I want it to be about his finances. That makes it pretty simple. I'm worried about how clean that place was."

"All the orders are in for his financial paperwork. We should be getting the files by the end of the day. I've also done some research on who Miles was as a person," she said. "I've put that into the murder book."

"Thanks for that. The mother might be coming out

here to bring the body back once it's been released. Sounds like Miles didn't have any family here in Los Angeles."

"We'll be able to talk to her then," she said.

Tom nodded.

"What's bothering you?" Harri asked.

"The crime scene. It's too clean. Where's the blood splatter? Guy gets his throat slit and eyes gouged out, where's the arterial spray? Techs haven't found squat on that. How come?"

Tom was known as a DNA expert and had created the Cold Case Special Section over ten years ago utilizing new DNA technology to bring killers to justice years after their crimes. He knew how killers left DNA behind. Or how they didn't. If he was worried, that meant there was something to be worried about.

"Are you thinking he used plastic sheeting and then took it all away?" Harri asked.

"There's always some sort of DNA evidence left behind. Especially in such a messy killing. Even if the killer took it all with him, it shows an understanding of forensics and how to clean up after himself. This scene was as premeditated as I've ever seen."

A chill ran down Harri's spine.

Killers tended not to be calculated like this. They were messy, filled with rage and passion. The organized ones that kept the crime scenes clean tended to be either professional killers or worse, the kind of killer murder mystery novels were written about. The organized ones never stopped at one victim.

"We haven't found any others yet, though?" Harri said.

He ran his fingers through his gray hair and pursed his thin lips.

"Not yet," he said. "I'll call Garth. He's the forensic accountant. Fill him in on what we have so far."

"I have calls into Apple to see if we can access his cloud. I have a call out to a judge for a warrant for that, too," Harri said.

They might not have his computers and phone, but all Miles Davidson's info was stored in the cloud. They just needed to access it.

Tom nodded and went back to his desk.

Harri watched him go and ignored the tightening of her neck muscles and the beginning of a tension headache. Her first case in RHD would be a big one if it was worrying Detective Tom Bards.

4

DAY 1

Harri parked the car right behind the beginning of the gnarly stairs leading up to Jake's front door. She grunted as she eyed the flight of stairs ahead of her. It was close to one in the morning and the last thing she wanted to do was climb those stairs. They were the number one problem with Jake's place. Each time she climbed them, she was winded by the middle and sucking air hard by the end. She ran a couple of times a week but somehow the stairs just killed her every time.

She took a deep breath, hoisted her heavy computer bag over her shoulder, and started climbing.

Gasping for air at the top of the stairs, she limped to the front door and opened it. She quickly punched in the numbers of the security code so the alarm wouldn't go off and turned on the lights.

The house was beautiful and rustic with a double-height ceiling to the right and a smaller dining room and kitchen to the left. Since Jake had left for Berlin, she'd mostly stayed in the dining room to do her work and slept in the bedroom upstairs. She didn't venture into the remainder of the house. Jake had been gone for a week and she wasn't comfortable using the rest of the house.

She dumped her computer on the dining room table and walked through the doorway to the kitchen. She had gotten pizza the night before and grabbed the slices from the refrigerator and put them into the toaster oven.

She was debating what she wanted to drink when her cell phone rang from her computer bag. She left the pizza warming up and raced to the dining room to grab the phone before she missed the call.

Could Tom have gotten footage from the neighbor's security camera already? Or had Jake finally caught Jerome Wexler in Berlin? Her heart pounded in her chest as she flung the cover over her bag and pulled out the phone.

Jake's face and name filled the screen. She swiped to answer the call.

"Jake! I didn't think I'd hear from you today. Any news?" she asked.

"You sound out of breath. Did you get home recently?" he asked.

"You caught me. Those damn stairs are going to be the death of me," she said.

"You're sounding a little hoarse," he said.

"I talked all day and used my normal voice. I couldn't keep whispering. My vocal cords need the practice, right?"

She didn't want anyone to know she still suffered any effects of her attack. The shrink had cleared her. She didn't have any acute signs of PTSD and she would go to therapy once a week to make sure she kept it that way. She wasn't going to let anything stand in her way of succeeding at RHD.

"I don't think that's the way it works," he said.

"How are you doing?"

She did not want to have this discussion.

"Did you find Jerome Wexler?" she asked.

"We've hit another dead end. I'm not even sure the alias my contact at Interpol had was for Jerome Wexler. The picture he showed me was of a much younger guy. I stayed because they were about to raid a home on the outskirts they had traced to a large cache of pornography. They arrested a lot of Russians, no Americans in the lot."

"He's in the wind then."

"If he was ever here. They didn't have a photo of Gunter Schmidt, the alias that Jerome Wexler was supposed to be using when I came here. Alec, the Interpol agent I've been dealing with, tracked one down for me. It was a grainy surveillance photo, but the man looked to be in his 50s. Jerome should be well into his 70s by now."

"I guess this means you can come home," Harri said.

"Missing me?"

"I don't like your home without you in it. Or the stairs." Harri sighed.

"I've already booked a flight. Should be home by Sunday evening. We can officially start the Christmas season. We should get a tree."

Harri smiled. She hadn't put up a Christmas tree in ages and loved that idea.

"That's a plan. We could start looking at houses. Maybe we can find a deal somewhere," Harri said.

"You don't like my house?" Jake teased.

"It's the stairs, Jake. I can't even with those stairs."

"How was RHD today? What's the case? Have you seen Richard yet?" Jake asked.

Harri launched into a retelling of her meeting with Lieutenant Richard Byrne and the discovery of Miles Davidson without going into a lot of detail. She could tell Jake everything when he got home.

"Sounds like you're busy and tired so I'll let you go. I can't wait to see you," he said.

"I hate that you hit such a dead end, but we'll find him," she said.

"I know we will," Jake said. "You have a good night sweetheart and I'll talk to you tomorrow."

They hung up and Harri sniffed the air.

Something was burning.

Her pizza dinner.

She rushed to the kitchen and pulled out the slices of pizza. They were the only thing she had in the house to eat so she sat at the dining room table munching crispy burned pizza as she checked the news sites to see what info had come out on Miles Davidson.

That reporter at the LA times had already put together a short bio and somehow had quite a bit of detail about what the crime scene looked like. He mentioned the eyes that Harri knew Tom had wanted to keep out of the news. A victim this high profile and with mutilation this grotesque, it was only a matter of time before someone in the chain of the investigation talked to the LA Times. Or any of the gossip rags for that matter. It could have been anyone from the crime scene techs to the coroner's assistants. This was LA and money for information flowed freely.

She rubbed the bleariness from her eyes. It was time for bed.

Harri grabbed her cell phone and went up the stairs to the master bedroom. She brushed her teeth, washed her face, and pulled on her pajamas. She crawled under the covers and flicked off the light.

Then she lay there, staring up at the dark ceiling. What had happened to her exhaustion?

Thoughts rushed through her mind in a jumble.

The island where they found her sister's remains.

Bryan Mortimer attacking her in her own bedroom.

She touched her neck with her fingers. The bruises were barely visible on her skin from the attack. Maybe she should call her therapist Jeanine tomorrow. Make sure the PTSD wasn't going to rear its ugly head. She'd been in and out of therapy since her sister disappeared and was always vigilant if she felt herself slipping down into the darkness. The last few months had been life-changing in many ways. And now was the time to make sure she was handling it all okay.

She turned over and squeezed her eyes shut. Miles Davidson's all-white living room flashed on her eyelids.

Harri opened her eyes again and watched the moonlight shimmer on the ceiling.

There was a problem with the crime scene.

Something was off and her mind was working the puzzle out.

Was it the lack of blood?

The staging outside?

What was the significance of taking the eyes? And had the killer kept them? Harri shuddered inwardly at the thought. Why hadn't they found them on the scene? Or could it have been the birds? What if the eyes had been left at the scene but taken by the seagulls? She'd have to ask Tom about that possibility.

Her eyes closed again.

Her sister's voice called out to her as she slipped into sleep.

5

DAY 1

Philip Townsend did not get home until the early evening. He'd finished up his lunch meeting with Lucas Reinhardt, gone to the gym, ran some errands, and grabbed some takeout for dinner, all the while pushing thoughts of Miles Davidson and the last twenty-four hours out of his mind.

It was dark and damp in the North of Montana neighborhood of Santa Monica and he was starving. He drove his BMW into the alleyway and clicked the garage door opener.

He'd splurged on this house when it came onto the market and put pretty much everything he had into it. It came with a hefty price tag upwards of four million dollars, even though it was only a three-bedroom built in the 1930s.

The home was worth it, though, and had become his oasis. He'd lived in a condo in Brentwood before that and had been over sharing walls with neighbors.

When his fund made him a seven-figure income in its

second year, he decided he would finally splurge on himself.

He hadn't found someone to share his life with yet and it wasn't like he was getting any younger. He knew he had to purchase a home before getting serious with anyone. He'd even chosen an interior decorator. Miles had spoken so highly of his decorator, Daniele Luxembourg, Philip hired her before even seeing what Miles' place looked like. If he had seen the way she'd outfitted Miles' Malibu home, he would've never hired her.

Daniele had listened to his requests and designed his home with comfort and color in mind. Plush sofas and chairs were tastefully centered in the living room. She understood that everything had to have multiple purposes of comfort, style, and value. She understood that and chose a pleasing palette of color, unlike Miles' place which was white, sterile, and so cold.

When Miles had invited everyone over after the Malibu house was finished, Philip's mouth fell open at the sight of it. The place looked like something out of a glossy ad for a hospital or a high-end hotel.

He pulled into the garage and the door closed behind him. Philip grabbed his takeout, locked the car, and walked through the decently-sized backyard. His yard featured a lap pool and a grassy area surrounded by trees where he'd set up a grill and a seating nook.

The walk was artfully lit with border snapdragons running alongside to the backdoor. Every time he saw it, he smiled. He had the thing he'd always wanted most, his own home.

Philip took the steps two at a time and unlocked the French door. The door swung open and his security alarm blared. He punched in the code on the security console and the alarm fell silent. He set his takeout on the dining room table and walked through the house turning on lights.

As was his custom, he checked the mailbox outside on the left side of his front door. He pulled out some bills and a large manila envelope. His name was written in black marker but there were no stamps or postage showing it had gone through the mail. Maybe one of his neighbors had dropped it off for him.

He looked up and down the street as if he'd spot who'd left the envelope. His street was a mixture of charming older homes and newer, larger mansions. At least, the newer builds kept a decent front yard as the land parcels here were generous. He also loved that all the garages were accessed from the back alleyway leaving the front yards room for paths to the sidewalk and gardens. It was one of the reasons he'd wanted to buy here.

He studied the envelope as he went back inside. He placed the rest of the mail on the dining room table and dug into his takeout Chinese food. After the first few bites, the curiosity got the best of him and he opened the manila envelope.

The smell of photography chemicals wafted off the newly developed photograph. He recognized the smell immediately. He had a stint in college where he'd become obsessed with photography. His obsession with medium-format cameras started then, too. He bought his first medium-format camera as a reward for himself from the initial profit he'd made right out of college. That was when he was still at the finance firm on Wall Street before Chandler called him to come to Hollywood with the rest of the guys.

He'd collected eleven more medium-format cameras since then. His prized possession was a Hasselblad 500

C/M 6 x 6. He hadn't taken photos in close to five years, but before then he'd rented a studio downtown that he'd converted into a dark room. The smell filled him with such good memories.

He shook out the contents of the envelope and choked on the lo mein he was chewing.

Miles' contorted face, eye sockets empty and bleeding, screamed at him.

He dropped the photo on the table and spat the food back into the container. His stomach twisted in knots and he felt faint. He grabbed the counter to balance himself and dropped into the dining chair, fighting not to hyperventilate.

What the hell was this doing in his mailbox?

Who brought it here?

Why to him?

Then his heart sank, and he vomited his dinner onto the plush carpet.

He wanted to push away the photo. Flip it over. Not look at it.

Then he saw it.

The red line along the bottom of the photo made his heart sink even further. He knew exactly what that was.

Whoever had used the medium format camera to take this photo hadn't tightly rolled the film. That red line showed up when the camera wasn't winding properly. His camera did that. The Hasselblad. It was the reason he'd stopped shooting with film.

His camera.

Was his camera still here? His Hasselblad 500 C/M 6 x 6 normally sat in its prime location in the middle of his mantel in the living room.

He raced into the living room and looked at the mantel. There were eleven cameras there. His Hasselblad. His prized camera, the one with the winding problem, was gone.

"Oh, no," he cried. "Oh, god. Oh, shit."

He clutched his chest and sank to the ground. His heart raced in his chest and he wondered if he was having a heart attack. His breathing was tight, only coming in small gasps as waves of panic crashed over him.

His mind raced. Should he call the police?

What would they say? He had a photo of his dead friend. The one he'd been with at the crime scene the night he died. He had a photo of his dead friend, taken with his vintage camera.

Sharp prickles ran up and down his arms and legs and he felt again as if he would pass out. Sweat dripped down his back even though the place was frigid. He crawled to his couch and pulled himself onto it. He would not die on the floor.

He lay there, in a fetal position, unsure of what to do. He should call the police.

That was the right thing to do.

But then what?

Finally, after what could have been twenty minutes, but felt like hours, his heart didn't feel like it was going to fly out of his chest. He unfurled himself and sat up. He waited a few moments to make sure he wouldn't black out and then stumbled back to the table and that gruesome photo. He flipped it over and sat back. What the hell did it mean?

'Keep all of your fortunes' was scrawled on the back in black ink.

He reached for his phone. The police had to see this.

His finger hovered on the 9 to call 9-1-1.

Was that the number he needed to call?

This wasn't an emergency like that. Nobody was dying. He'd just gotten some mail. Philip had no idea of who to call. What kind of position was he in?

He sat back unsure of what he should do. He'd seen him that night. The night of his death. Miles had called him in a panic at around seven that evening, begging him to come over immediately. Miles tended to be cool even when he was in deep shit. Philip had never heard him lose it like that and told him he'd be right over.

He canceled two appointments and a dinner date to meet up with him. Philip arrived at Miles' Malibu home at around eight-thirty that night and their meeting had been brief.

Miles had a gambling problem. It was an unspoken truth all their friends knew about. It started their sophomore year in college. They all gambled, mainly on poker, but sometimes the bigger horse races. Philip had been spared because he had no allowance to squander. He had no disposable income to waste on whims and entertainment like the thrill of betting on long odds.

Everyone had wins and losses, but Miles spiraled fast after he won twenty thousand at a high-stakes poker game. He wasn't very good at it but kept trying to make those kinds of winnings again. Philip suspected that first huge win was a plant by the operators of the underground games, intended to keep someone like Miles coming back for more, desperate for the high of another windfall.

That was Miles in a nutshell. Naïve, overly confident, privileged, and not the brightest crayon in the box. He was decent looking, though, knew how to fit in and stand out, and came from a Mayflower family, so that was all the entrée he needed to be accepted into the money tribes.

When Miles had confessed to him he'd lost forty-five million dollars of his clients' money, Philip's first thought was, of course, he had. Then he asked Philip if he could borrow forty-five million in cash against Philip's fund, swearing on his mother's life he would repay it within three months.

Philip couldn't believe it. How dare he?

He knew there was no way Miles could get that amount back to him. Not in a million years. And only God knew what kind of people he owed the money too. Whoever they were, they had to be criminals. Why else would Miles have done such a stupid, desperate thing?

Philip accused Miles of trying to drag him into a mess he'd made himself. They yelled and hurled accusations and insults at each other until Philip took a deep breath and simply said no with a finality that seemed to fill the large open space that was Miles' living room. Miles responded by throwing some heavy glass art object at his head.

Philip had left then.

Miles had security cameras all around the house and Philip knew he'd be on them. Both coming and going. He couldn't have been there for longer than twenty minutes. Miles was alive and furious when he left him.

The police would come knocking on his door. Would he tell them about the photo then? They would ask why he hadn't called them immediately.

Because the photo was of Miles alive and not dead. Because it was taken with his own camera which he'd only just discovered was missing from his mantel. In a home that had security cameras and an alarm, too.

He hadn't been alerted to any alarm activity at the house. The police wouldn't believe his story. It sounded ridiculous. Even if it was the truth.

And if he didn't call the police, and they did eventually find out about the photo?

He was withholding evidence.

What if there was a clue in the photo? Or something in that weird message on the back? They could use their forensic stuff to maybe catch who did kill Miles.

If he called them.

And why did the killer send him the photo?

Was he next?

His brain turned out scenarios of what would happen to him.

The killer or the police?

And how in the hell did his camera get stolen?

DAY 2 - FRIDAY, NOVEMBER 30, 2018

H arri pulled onto Sunset Boulevard as the pink-red dawn lightened the sky. The streets were empty except for early morning joggers taking advantage of the cleaner air. She took her time driving downtown and still made it to the PAB parking garage in under thirty minutes. Living in LA meant spending too much time in your car. The city sprawled in every direction and with the population nearing thirteen million people, the roads were jammed at most hours. The peaceful morning was refreshing and put her in the mood to work.

She'd received the email that the documents she'd requested from Miles Davidson's various brokerage firms and banks had arrived. Harri was relieved. She was anticipating a struggle, but it had been less than a full twenty-four hours since the requests. Sometimes, miracles did happen, especially with the help of the digital age. She couldn't wait to start drilling into them. Harri parked her car and walked briskly into the PAB.

On her way up to the RHD floor, she waved at some

colleagues coming up from early morning workouts and walked into her new bullpen with a smile on her face. Maybe her luck would last. Maybe it was going to be a good day.

She settled into her chair and opened up her email. Before retiring for the night, Harri had worked with Tom Bards and his forensic accountant to lay out a game plan to approach the financial angle of this case. They'd decided she would be in charge of assembling the list of Miles Davidson's clients, past and present. That client list would give them their initial list of potential suspects.

Their team hadn't received the footage they needed from the numerous cameras in Miles Davidson's neighborhood yet. Harri didn't think they would need court orders for the neighbors' camera footage as many of the residents were cooperative with the uniforms who'd done the initial canvas. No one in such a wealthy enclave wanted a murderer loose in their neighborhood. Still, she'd expected some footage by now and was surprised they hadn't gotten anything yet.

Harri clicked on the first statement and groaned. This account consisted of long strings of numbers. She'd have to cross-reference those somehow to his other bank accounts and incoming and outgoing transfers. She hoped that would work.

She whistled at the first large outgoing transfer. Twenty million dollars on Friday, November 23rd. Before that another twenty million dollars taken out on Monday, November 19th. And close to five million dollars was first taken out on Friday November 16th.

Miles Davidson had emptied his accounts in the two weeks preceding his murder. That was a massive red flag.

Were there any other red flags in these statements?

She scanned through them once more. The brokerage files had nothing other than the numbers she'd already jotted down. Tom had received the same email, and she knew he'd already forwarded the information to the forensic accountant as well. When she checked the bank statements, she didn't see any names, either. Just more account numbers. That wasn't going to help her get names.

She called one of her contacts at a mobile phone provider to access Miles Davidson's call logs. Even though they hadn't found his cell phone or his computer, everything had to be stored in some sort of cloud in this day and age. After promising her that a warrant for the data was on the way, her contact came through and sent over his last month's statement. She jotted down the nine numbers that Miles was in contact with the last forty-eight hours of his life. She called back her contact and got lucky. Six of them were the mobile provider's customers, and she was able to get their names. Harri's heart soared. Her luck was lasting.

The list contained some famous Hollywood people. Harri didn't keep up with that side of town, but even she'd heard of most of these people.

The first name was Mirabella Youngston, an actress starring in the latest superhero movie. Her director husband, Steven Whitney, had called several times as well.

The other names included Harold Walters, a big name who'd produced the latest Oscar winner for best film, Jeremy Williams, another A-list actor, Jessica Livingston, another big-time producer, and Matthew Shakenon, another well-known director.

Harri imagined she'd have a harder time than usual interviewing these people. She thought back to her last case. So many Hollywood elites had closed ranks and allowed the horrific abuse and trafficking of young women to continue.

It was going to be quite interesting speaking with such people. She wondered if she'd need to deal with someone in PR to make sure their names weren't leaked to the public. Now she had a list of six decent suspects. Some of them had called Miles multiple times. It was a start.

How much did she want to bet they were calling about what happened to their money? She accessed each of their DMV records and jotted down the addresses on file. Some of them she recognized as corporate buildings. They were probably masked because of concerns about stalkers. She'd have to reach out to DMV for the physical addresses.

She picked up the phone to call Mirabella and saw that it was still only nine-thirty in the morning. Would a top Hollywood actress be up so early? She doubted it.

Some of the other detectives in RHD had slowly started to come in for their shift. She'd been so engrossed in her work she hadn't even noticed Tom Bards had arrived. He was busy at work at his desk. She grabbed her notebook and walked over to his cubicle.

"Hope you got some sleep last night," Tom said as she appeared at his elbow.

"I did. Were you here late last night?" she asked.

"I stayed until about two in the morning. The bank records arrived so Garth and I got started on those. Miles transferred out all of the funds within two weeks to the same bank account in the Caymans. The account wasn't in his name, so it doesn't look like he was stealing it from his clients for himself."

"And there's no way to get the name of whose account it is?"

"No way," Tom said with a laugh.

"Then how do we know it's not Miles Davidson's?" Harri asked.

"We don't know that for sure. We're just guessing that if he was cutting and running, he'd have stashed it somewhere other than the Caymans."

"Oh, why is that?" Harri was intrigued. She didn't know anything about this side of crime.

"The Caymans have to disclose account owners by 2023. So why even bother? Plus, he'd have to have opened an IBC, and so far, we don't see that," Tom explained.

"What's an IBC?"

"International Business Account. It's the first step to hiding financial assets offshore. With all of Davidson's associations with Europe, we're guessing he would have gone to Isle of Jersey to do his dirty work, but the account numbers don't match up with anything over there."

"New Jersey? He went to school on the East Coast," Harri asked.

"No." Tom chuckled. "Isle of Jersey. It's in the British Channel Islands."

"You're enjoying this, aren't you?"

"The game is afoot," Tom said in a terrible Sherlock Holmes accent.

"That was awful." Harri laughed. "Don't ever do that again. Okay, I did find out the six people who called him the most in the days up to his murder. I'm assuming they were his clients since they called numerous times."

"Are they going to be difficult people to reach?" Tom asked. He must've noticed the look on her face.

"It's A-list Hollywood," she said.

"Oh, them again," Tom said with a sigh.

"If we keep their names under the radar, maybe we'll be able to interview them before the media circus begins."

"That's not gonna happen," Tom said.

"Why not?"

"Have you seen the news today?" Tom opened a browser to the Los Angeles Times. Miles Davidson's face was splashed above the fold.

She scanned the article and saw Mirabella Youngston's, Steven Whitney's, and Harold Walter's names mentioned in the article.

"How did he get that information so fast?" she exclaimed.

"Which information?" Tom asked dryly.

"The names of his clients! I've been going through his phone records all morning and three of the names are already in the article," she said.

She read the byline. Javier Aguilar was listed as the sole reporter.

"I'd love to know where he's getting his info from."

"Good luck with that," Tom said.

"I wonder if his client list was common knowledge. And now, the media will pounce on them as prime suspects. And I wonder…" she drifted off.

"Yes?" Tom prompted.

"Would they be so obvious?"

"As to kill the man who lost all their money?" Tom asked.

"Exactly," Harri said. "They would know we'd look at them first."

"I don't know, Harri. He lost them a ton of money," Tom said.

"Lost?" Harri said with an arched eyebrow. "Looks like he moved most of it offshore. I wonder how they could have found out so fast. Even so, which of them would have the brains or the guts to actually do something like that?"

"Good point. Rich people have other people do their dirty work for them. We could be looking at a hired killer situation. That might make sense with the eyes being gouged out. Some kind of signature," Tom said.

"I'll run that through VICAP and see if we have a match with any other crimes," she said.

"We'd get lucky if he was national and had left his mark before," Tom said.

"I'll start calling these six I've been able to get off his phone to schedule interviews with them," Harri said.

A ding sounded from Tom's computer. He opened his email tab and checked the message. It was from Dr. Grimley.

"Looks like the coroner is ready for us. That was fast," he said.

"Dr. Grimley was true to her word. She said she'd expedite, and she did," Harri said.

"I'll drive," Tom said.

As they headed out of the PAB, Harri couldn't help but think about what Tom had said about the killer being so well-versed in forensics. It would have taken an expert not to leave anything behind. No hair, no saliva, no skin, or even blood from the victim that he'd so brutally killed.

Dr. Grimley might have some answers for them but it was still early in the investigation and she wouldn't have toxicology or any sort of DNA analysis if she'd found skin under the victim's fingernails. At the crime scene, she hadn't seen any, but the true examination happened at the autopsy. They could only hope the body would give them a clue.

7

DAY 2 - CORONER'S OFFICE

Detective Harri Harper and Detective Tom Bards entered exam room three, wearing white paper coveralls, hairnets, goggles, plastic gloves, and booties over their shoes. Dr. Grimley stood next to a silver slab table with Miles Davidson's naked body stretched out before her. His privates were covered with a white sheet, but as soon as they walked in, Dr. Grimley took the sheet off the body.

"Good morning Detective Harper, Detective Bards," Dr. Grimley said.

"Thank you so much for expediting this autopsy," Tom said.

"I'm glad I could. It's going to be a high-profile case I'm sure," Dr. Grimley said. "The sooner we get some answers the quicker you can stop whatever is starting."

What an interesting choice of words Dr. Grimley had used, Harri thought. She had been a deputy coroner and then coroner for over twenty years. Harri suspected she was having the same uneasy suspicions Tom was having.

"I started a little bit before you got here. I've been examining the main neck wound."

She turned around and pressed record on the audio recorder hanging from the ceiling. All coroners kept copious audio recordings of each autopsy in case anything they said was disputed or referenced in court. These recordings were included with all the paperwork she put together in the official file.

"This appears to be death by severe throat laceration," Dr. Grimley began. "The incision starts below the ear on the left lateral upper third of the victim's neck. The laceration deepens gradually and severs the victim's left carotid artery. The incision ends near the medial third of the neck and has a slight abrasion at the weapons' exit point. I see no hesitation or defense injuries. His blood-alcohol level is .05, so he wasn't inebriated by any means. He'd been drinking but not enough to not be able to fight off his attacker. I found no skin under his fingernails. He has hematomas on his wrists and his ankles. They appear to be similar in size to the plastic zip-ties that were used to restrain him to the chair."

She looked over to Harri and Tom. "The zip-ties have been sent to the forensic lab for testing. As have the clothes he was wearing and the chair he was found in."

"Was he restrained besides the zip-ties?" Tom asked.

"Someone held his head back to slice his throat easier," Dr. Grimley said.

"I was thinking maybe we might get lucky on his forehead with foreign DNA," Tom said.

"I'll swab for that. He hasn't been washed yet." Dr. Grimley nodded.

She took out a swab and proceeded to wipe it across his forehead. It took six swabs to cover the entire area above where the victim's eyes had been. She put the swabs into small plastic test tubes filled with water. When Dr. Grimley was done with that, she turned back them.

"As you correctly asked, Tom. I believe his head was pulled back, and a right-handed killer made the laceration. He sliced from left to right, indicating he's right-handed. Or she. The lungs do show aspiration of blood, so he was alive when the cut was made. I'll be listing throat laceration with severed carotid artery as the cause of death."

"Have you done the eyes yet?" Harri asked.

"Let's do that now," Dr. Grimley said.

She put her glasses on, took tweezers from her neatly laid out instruments, and bent over the ravaged eye sockets of Miles Davidson.

"It looks like the ligament that attaches the eyeball to the skull has been cut. I am also seeing a groove that makes me think that a rounded object was used to scoop out this eyeball. I'm also seeing silver material here."

She delicately pulled the metallic slivers out of the brutalized eye socket with the tweezers and placed them into a clean test tube. She labeled where the slivers came from and put them in an evidence bag.

"I'll send this off to forensics, as well."

"So, scooped out like an ice cream scoop?" Harri asked. "Or a spoon?

She knew it was a weird reference, but she didn't have another way of visualizing what Dr. Grimley was saying.

"It could be a spoon. There have been cases in history where eyes have been scooped out with a spoon," Dr. Grimley said.

"Seriously?" Harri asked.

It never occurred to her that someone could so easily take another human beings' eyes out.

"Are you thinking this happened peri or post-mortem?" Tom asked.

"Before he died. He was alive for that part, too. I can tell by all the blood."

She took out the tools to crack the ribs open to get to the organs. Harri did not want to be there for the entire autopsy and wondered if they would get any other important information from on observation of his organs and his brain.

"Do you have a better idea as to the time of death?" Harri asked.

"Due to the rigor changes in his body, I'm now thinking death was somewhere between 1 a.m. and 3 a.m. on November 30th."

Tom nodded and glanced at Harri.

"Would you like to stay for the full autopsy?" Dr. Grimley asked.

Harri assumed Dr. Grimley was directing the question to her seeing as Tom didn't seem phased by what was about to come. Harri had been to several autopsies before she joined the cold case unit, but it was a part of the job that she'd never really gotten used to. Especially with the opening of the skull to get to the brain and the cracking of the ribs to get to the lungs and heart.

"I'll defer to my colleague," Harri said.

"I think we're good as far as what we need. Let us know when the tox screen comes back. From what you've told us, it sounds like he was drugged. Did you find any punctures?" Tom asked.

"Punctures. Haven't looked for those yet. Let's do that now," Dr. Grimley said.

She pulled out a magnifying glass and focused on

Miles Davidson's hairline. She traveled down his body with the glass. Looked between his fingers and toes and straightened.

"I'm not finding any punctures," Dr. Grimley said. "Drug could have been ingested."

"How long for the toxicology report then? Forty-eight hours? Longer?" Tom asked.

"We should have it by tomorrow," Dr. Grimley said. "With these metallic slivers, it might take a few days longer. I know an expert in metals at the forensic lab that I'll send it to."

Dr. Grimley pulled out a scalpel and made the Y incision in the chest to open up his cavity. Harri had to turn away as bile rose up into her throat.

"And the murder weapon?" Tom asked as he glanced at Harri without turning away from Dr. Grimley at work.

"Has to be something incredibly sharp," Dr. Grimley said. "I'm not seeing any serrated edges and both the entry and exit points of the wound are clean. It could be a very sharp knife, but also strong and thin. It could be a scalpel," Dr. Grimley said as she pulled up her scalpel and turned it around. "It would have to be something as sharp as this to make such a clean cut."

"Could our killer be a doctor or someone who has medical knowledge of the body? I'm wondering about the no hesitation marks. It was like one long clean slice."

"The laceration looks like it was done by a professional," Dr. Grimley said. "It was fast, and deep, and clean. It couldn't have been their first time. They used a weapon that was strong and sharp. Now, what kind of professional is your job to figure out. But whoever cut this man's throat knew exactly what he was doing. He knew how much pressure he needed to give, and exactly the point of entry and exit to get that carotid artery."

"So, someone who really knows how to cut a throat," Tom said. "Someone who's done it before."

"It could be someone in the medical profession or someone who practiced," Dr. Grimley said. "He could have used pigs. Could be a butcher, but this killer didn't use a butcher's tools. It's someone who knows human anatomy and knew his way around the blade."

Dr. Grimley peeled the skin back to reveal the ribs and Harri wanted to make a run for the door.

"I think we have enough now," Tom said. "Thank you Dr. Grimley for allowing us to join this part of the autopsy."

"I hope I've given you enough to get going," she said.

"You gave us plenty," Tom said.

He nodded one more time with Dr. Grimley and Harri moved as slowly as she could to not make it seem like she was running out the door.

Tom was right behind her.

Just as the door was closing behind them, Harri heard the crack of the ribs. She shuddered and took a deep breath.

"You okay?" Tom asked.

"It's been a while since I've been at one of those," Harri said.

"You were turning a little pale in there," Tom said.

They walked down the hall to a room where they could remove all of the protective gear.

"I think what you were saying before is correct," Harri said.

"Which part? Seems like I'm always right, don't you think," Tom said with a grin.

"Well, that's because you are."

"Are you talking about the cleanliness of the scene?" Tom asked as they stripped off the booties, the white protective coveralls, and the goggles. They placed the paper products into the garbage and the goggles in a marked bin.

"There were no hesitation marks, and he used the right tools to get the job done. None of these Hollywood big shots could do something like that," Harri said. "Now, I can imagine one of them throwing something at his head, or hitting him, or you know stabbing him with a knife in a rage. But something as clinical and clean and perfect like this?"

"My thoughts exactly. We are dealing with a professional as Dr. Grimley said. I'm leaning towards hired pro at this point and I'm hoping we'll get something from VICAP. Maybe the throat laceration is a signature? Or the gouging of the eyes? That's a strange detail in this killing."

"I agree. A signature maybe? The slashed throat is like oh I have to kill this guy. Lemme cut his throat. It's the fastest," Harri said.

"The fastest would be a shot to the head," Tom said. "With a silencer, of course."

"There was no arterial spray," Harri said. "Where did all that blood go?"

"Was he killed inside? And the body staged for discovery for whatever reason?" Tom conjectured.

"Are you thinking he could have maybe been killed inside in an area easy to clean? Then the killer wheeled him out and staged the scene?"

"The lack of blood outside is really bothering me. If he killed him inside, then he added extra time and effort to the whole enterprise. The staging then had a purpose," Tom said.

"And that's not typical for a one-off, is it?" Harri asked.

"No, it's not. But so far, we only have the one. We don't want to think this is the beginning of some diabolical madman going around killing wealthy people case."

"Are you serious?" Harri asked.

"Do I look like I make jokes," Tom said with a grin.

"Of course. So, what now? We go and interview a lot of fabulously wealthy Hollywood people," Harri said.

"It's the perks of this job that I love so much," Tom said. "I don't think you should call them. Let's see if we can find them at home. Surprise them so they can't get their stories straight."

"They all had masked addresses. I'll check if the physical addresses have come in. Shall we start with Mirabella Youngston?" Harri asked.

"Sounds perfect. She's in town. I saw she just wrapped up filming overseas," Tom said.

"Are you a fan?" Harri asked.

"Maybe?" Tom said shooting her a grin.

"Is that going to be a problem, Detective?" Harri teased.

"We shall see, won't we?"

"Let's hope she's home then." Harri smiled.

Her stomach fluttered with butterflies and Harri hoped the good luck she'd had since the early morning wasn't about to run out.

8

DAY 2

D etective Tom Bards pulled off Sunset Boulevard into a driveway leading to a gate in the expensive Brentwood neighborhood on the west side of Los Angeles. Many wealthy Hollywood stars lived in gated communities within the tony neighborhoods of Malibu, Brentwood, Santa Monica, and Beverly Hills. Harri had only crossed the gate into these exclusive communities a few times.

She and Tom had discussed the possibility of their visit not being a surprise if Mirabella Youngston lived in one of these communities. No way would a security guard let them in without calling her.

"You were right," Harri said. Tom had surmised they would be living in one of these communities.

"She's married to Stephen Whitney who's a huge director. I would imagine they'd want to sequester away from fans. They can have all the privacy they could wish for behind these gates," Tom said.

Tom pulled up to the gate, took out his credentials, and flashed them to the security guard on duty.

"Good afternoon, Detective," the security guard said. "What can I help you with?"

"Here to see Mirabella Youngston," Tom said.

"Is she expecting you?" he asked.

"We're here on official business," Tom said.

"Uh, so then she's not expecting you?" the security guard asked.

Harri looked over at him. She guessed he was in his mid-twenties. He was tan, blue-eyed, blonde. She wondered if he was one of the guys who surfed in Ocean Park or Topanga every morning and evening.

"That is correct," Tom said.

"Oh, sorry dude." The security guard shook his head. "No can do. Gotta have her permission. Or, you know, like a warrant or whatever."

"I am aware," Tom said tightly. "Call her."

The security guard looked at Harri and smiled. She flashed him her credentials as well. He went to the gatehouse to make the call. They couldn't hear what he said but the gate opened for them. Mirabella had been alerted. The security guard smiled and saluted Tom as they drove past. Harri braced for Tom's rude comment about the security guard, but it didn't come.

"Have the address?" he asked.

Harri checked her phone.

"Go up the street and at the first stop, take a right. At the next stop, take a left and it should be the fourth gate on the road."

"All right, then. We are on our way," Tom said as they drove down the quiet tree-lined streets.

Many of the houses were also gated but others had open yards and the properties were as impressive as they had expected.

"Welcome to the wealthy and famous," Harri said under her breath.

"Harri, I've seen the house you live in," Tom said.

"That was my family's money," Harri said. "I would've never been able to afford the place on a cop's salary."

"That's why I live in the valley," Tom said. "Deep in the valley."

They followed the instructions to Mirabella Youngston's and Stephen Whitney's home. The gates opened immediately after they buzzed the callbox. They drove up the curved driveway bordering a brilliant green lawn and parked in front of a stunning Tudor home.

"Imagine having this much green space," Harri said.

"We could if we moved out of this city," Tom said.

"Why would you ever want to move from the city of Angels?"

"Exactly," Tom said.

They exited the car and made their way up the bricked walk. They didn't have to knock as Mirabella Youngston opened the door before they had a chance to announce themselves. Her hair was in a messy bun and her bright blue eyes shined behind reading glasses. She wore a lounge-type of pajama top and matching short bottoms. On her feet were the ubiquitous UGG slippers.

"This is about Miles Davidson?" she asked.

"Good afternoon, Ms. Youngston. I'm Detective Tom Bards and this is Detective Harriet Harper," Tom began. "And yes. To answer your question, we are here to ask you about Miles Davidson."

"You should come in," Mirabella said.

As Harri passed by Mirabella, she noticed her

streaked cheeks and red nose. Mirabella Youngston had been recently crying.

Mirabella led them into a massive living room. Two oversized gray tufted sofas flanked a stone fireplace, a glass coffee table between them, and two armchairs finished off the seating area. The room looked lived in although it was cavernous and not entirely comfortable. The smell of roses wafted in from the garden through the open back doors.

"Is your husband home?" Tom asked.

"He's in his studio out back, should I get him too?" she asked.

She had kicked off her UGG slippers and settled on one of the sofas, tucking her feet underneath her and nervously pulling at the bottom of her pajama shirt.

"If you could please," Tom said.

"How did you know I was one of Miles Davidson's clients?" Mirabella asked. "It's so terrible what happened to him. Is it true the killer took his eyes?"

"How do you know about the eyes?" Harri asked.

Harri sat down in one of the armchairs. Tom took the other.

"It was in the LA Times this morning," Mirabella said.

"Your name as one of his clients was in the paper as well, Ms. Youngston," Tom said.

"I saw that," Mirabella said. "Why did they do that?"

She picked up a cellphone from the coffee table and texted someone.

"How did you meet Miles Davidson? Did you know him long?" Harri asked.

"I've known him for years." She shrugged. "We ran in the same social circles. I was his first client actually," she said with pride. Her smile faded, and she stopped speaking.

Harri wondered if she remembered that he'd taken all her money. Harri didn't push it and Tom took the opportunity.

"You called Miles four times on November 29th. That was the day he died. Why were you so anxious to speak with him?" Tom asked.

A tall man with sandy blonde hair walked through the back door. He looked at Tom and Harri and then to his wife. His eyebrows raised. He knew exactly who they were.

"Who are your guests, Mirabella?" he asked.

"I'm Detective Tom Bards and this is Detective Harriet Harper with the LAPD RHD unit," Tom said.

He stood up and held out his hand to Stephen Whitney.

"I'm Stephen Whitney, Mirabella's husband," Stephen said as he shook Tom's hand.

"We need to speak with you as well," Tom said.

"This about Miles?" Stephen asked.

"Yes. We are here about the murder of Miles Davidson," Tom said.

Stephen joined Mirabella on the sofa and Harri noticed that she shifted away from him. Harri guessed the fairytale marriage wasn't as happy as it seemed in all the photos of them together on various red carpets.

Tom sat back down in the armchair.

"Mr. Whitney, you called Miles Davidson five times on November 29th." Tom said.

"You don't have his phone then?" Stephen asked.

"Why would you ask that?" Tom asked.

"You would've seen the texts I sent him," Stephen

said. "Reading them would have been obvious why I was calling him."

"What did the texts say?" Harri asked.

Harri had been jotting down notes since they'd started the interview.

"We heard rumors he'd lost all of the cash in his fund," Stephen explained. "Mirabella has her entire portfolio managed by him. When we first started hearing he wasn't able to make the payments he'd promised, we all started calling. His phone records should show all of his clients calling him frantically that day."

"Where were you on the night of November 29th?" Tom asked.

"I was here," Stephen said.

"And were you here too, Ms. Youngston?" Harri asked.

Mirabella's stature changed. She slumped forward, then straightened back up when she noticed she was slumped forward. She swiped at her glasses and Harri noticed her cheeks were very flushed.

"I was with my friend Caroline Danbury," Mirabella said.

"And where were you and Caroline?" Tom asked.

"You can't possibly think that my wife had anything to do with Miles' murder?" Stephen demanded. "Do we need to get a lawyer?"

"If you feel that is necessary. Miles Davidson did lose your wife's money, as you just said yourself. It's important we get your statements down now. We want to bring whoever did this to justice and need to make sure we can rule you out," Tom explained.

"I was home," Stephen reiterated.

"How much did your wife invest with Mr. Davidson?"

"It doesn't matter since it's all gone," Stephen hissed. "It sounds like we are on your suspect list anyway. Do your worst. You can leave now."

Mirabella shrank into the sofa and this time Stephen noticed as well.

"What are you not telling us?" Tom asked.

"I told you to leave," Stephen said.

"As you wish," Tom said and stood up.

Their interview was over. Harri followed suit.

"If you try speaking to us again, go through our lawyer. And make an appointment," Stephen said.

"Do you have a name and number?" Tom asked.

Stephen gave them the contact information of his lawyer and Harri wrote it down.

"These are standard questions, Mr. Whitney," Tom reiterated.

"We lost a dear friend in a horrific crime," Stephen began. "My wife has been crying all morning because of the news. This same friend lost all of her hard-earned money. It's an exceedingly difficult time for us and we would appreciate your understanding."

Harri stifled an eye roll.

This same friend was brutally murdered, and they were here to find out who did it. Surprisingly enough, that didn't seem to be one of Stephen Whitney's priorities.

"Thank you for seeing us," Tom said, and they both walked to the door. The interview lasted ten minutes, tops.

"That went well," Harri said the moment the door closed behind them. They headed down the brick walk toward the unmarked car.

"She wasn't with Caroline Danbury the night that Miles Davidson died," Tom said.

"And her husband doesn't know where she was, either," Harri added.

"We need to get Caroline Danbury's phone number," Tom said.

"Let me go ask her," Harri said. "Maybe a female detective will soften her up enough to talk."

Tom nodded and kept walking to the car as Harri doubled back and knocked on the door again. Mirabella opened the door on the second knock.

"My husband said I shouldn't talk to you without a lawyer," Mirabella said.

"I understand. Where is he now?" Harri asked trying to look over Mirabella's shoulder.

"He went back into his study," Mirabella said with a tone of disgust.

This marriage was definitely not a good one.

"So sorry to bother you again. I need Caroline Danbury's number so we can corroborate that you were with her that night."

"Do you have to do that?" Mirabella asked.

Her silky blonde hair was slipping out of the messy bun and she looked gorgeous even disheveled, Harri thought.

"Wait, you're the cop that was attacked," Mirabella said. "You're the one that sicko Bryan Mortimer tried to kill. I can't believe you exposed him. I worked with him and he was such an asshole."

"It was a close call," Harri said.

"I'm so sorry, Detective Harper," Mirabella said, lowering her voice. "What if I told you I wasn't with Caroline Danbury?"

"Who were you actually with?" Harri asked, lowering her voice to match.

"My husband doesn't know where I was. I told him I

was out with Caroline, but I wasn't. I was with Tanner Asperson," Mirabella said. "He's my agent at CAA. It was just dinner and drinks. Stephen really wants me to drop him as an agent and I don't think I want to do that. Tanner found out about Stephen and wanted to make sure I wasn't about to decamp to another agent. My career is in a transition and Stephen's upset. He thinks I should be getting more offers. Anyway, now I don't have any money."

With those words, the waterworks began again.

"We'll need Tanner Asperson's number. I'll call him personally to make sure you were with him," Harri said.

Mirabella managed to get herself together to give her the phone number.

"I'm so sorry Miles is dead, but I still can't believe he lost all my money. I trusted that man with everything. Everything I've worked for since I was fifteen-years-old. And now it's all gone," she said.

Harri heard a door's slam somewhere behind Mirabella and the woman's eyes grew big.

"I have to go," she said and slammed the door in Harri's face.

Harri stepped back in surprise. For someone so successful, beautiful, and well-loved as this woman was, she seemed to be living a desperately unhappy domestic life.

Harri walked back to the car and got into the passenger seat.

"We were right about her lying," Harri said.

"She opened up?" Tom asked.

"She recognized me as the cop attacked by Bryan Mortimer. She opened up to me after that. She told me she was not with Carolyn Danbury but with Tanner Asperson who is her CAA agent. Her husband wants her to drop him and Tanner found out about it. He was wining and dining her without her Whitney's knowledge."

"Did you get his phone number?" he asked.

"I did. Then Stephen came back inside, and Mirabella slammed the door on me so her husband wouldn't see that we were speaking," Harri said.

"He's definitely capable of hiring a hitman," Tom remarked "I have him as suspect number one. And he has no alibi for the night Miles was killed. Would he be capable of constructing such a crime scene though?"

"He is a director. They're known to be controlling," Harri said.

"Stephen Whitney had motive and opportunity. We should see what kind of car he drives and send that information to Lawrence. He's the officer in charge of looking through all the surveillance footage."

"That would be too easy to put him at the scene of the crime," Harri said. "He's way smarter than that."

"Too smart for his own good? What does he get out of killing Miles Davidson? This wasn't a crime of passion. The guy has a temper and if Miles had been shot or bludgeoned to death, I'd be more inclined to look his way. He would definitely hire someone," Tom said again as he pulled out of the driveway and back onto the road.

"What is it with these jerk male directors and the women around them?" Harri asked.

"Are you talking about our happily married couple?"

"Not so happily married," Harri said.

"You noticed too," Tom said.

"It couldn't be more obvious. He's such an ass," Harri said.

"You didn't like him much?" Tom asked.

"I didn't like the way Mirabella acted around him. He cowed her," Harri said.

"Women love powerful men," Tom said.

"These women could have anyone in the world, and they choose jerks to be with. It makes absolutely no sense to me," Harri said.

She fell silent then as Tom drove out of the gated community and headed back onto Sunset. They got stuck in traffic on the way to the next name on Harri's list.

Next to interview was Harold Walters, a producer who'd won several Oscars in the last ten years. His address was listed in Beverly Hills and it would only be about a twenty-minute drive to his home.

Harri could feel the investigation taking off. They were putting together Miles Davidson's last movements and were moving forward. Harri didn't get the feeling Mirabella was calculating enough to perpetrate Miles Davidson's death. Her husband though. He was fully capable, Harri thought. She agreed with Tom about him.

9

DAY 2

Harold Walters lived in the flats of Beverly Hills in a white colonial with gray shutters. It wasn't as impressive as Mirabella Youngston's and Stephen Whitney's house and, to their relief, it was not in a gated community either. They would be able to use the element of surprise with him.

Tom parked in front of the house. Harold Walters' street had large oaks towering over the sidewalks. The homes were spaced out and the yards well-manicured and lush. Harri wished these kinds of green spaces existed further east. The poorer the neighborhood the less green anyone had. There were pop-up community gardens in some neighborhoods to the east but many times the yards were paved over with concrete, or the lawns were brown. Water was expensive, and this climate was not wet enough to have verdant green yards or exotic flower gardens. The zinnia's along Harold Walters' walk made quite a picture-postcard effect.

Harri inhaled deeply. Beverly Hills smelled so good.

It was in the middle of Los Angeles and yet had the sweetest rose flower smell all the time.

"It does smell good, doesn't it?" Tom chuckled as they walked up to the front door.

"It's in the middle of the city and gets smog like everybody else," Harri said.

"It must be because of all the trees they have here on these wide boulevards," Tom said. "Or maybe they import it in."

That was actually a good point, Harri thought. The Beverly Hills flats, as they were called by the locals, featured long wide boulevards extending from Santa Monica Blvd. to Sunset Blvd. Each street had a specific type of old-growth trees that towered over the stately homes. Some streets were lined with palm trees but many of them had Linden, Maple, and Oak trees.

Tom rang the doorbell and a man in his fifties came to the door.

"May I help you?" he asked. "You guys look like cops."

"We're looking for Mr. Harold Walters," Harri said.

"And who's asking?"

"We are with the Robbery-Homicide Division of the LAPD. My name is Detective Tom Bards, and this is Detective Harriet Harper," Tom said.

"I know that name," the man said. "Where do I know your name from Detective Harper?"

"I'm not sure," Harri said.

The man snapped his fingers. "You were in the papers. That whole Mortimer incident. I thought you'd still be in the hospital," he said.

Harri's hand drifted up to her neck before she could catch herself. She pulled her hand back down to her side when she noticed it.

"You've made quite the recovery," the man smiled.

"Can I assume you are Harold Walters?" Tom asked in an even tone. "You have time to answer some questions for us?"

"Can I assume your questions are about Miles Davidson?" Harold smirked as he waved them inside. "Come on in. I'll answer whatever questions you have for me."

Harri and Tom followed him into a nondescript living room filled with flowery decor. Harri didn't imagine Harold had used a decorator.

Harold noticed Harri's scrutiny.

"The decor is not one of my choosing. This is my mother's house actually. I've been living here since she died," he said. "I never bothered bringing in my furniture. Wouldn't really go. I'd have to redo everything, and I don't want to make changes. It makes me think of her and that makes me happy."

Harri sat down on a chintz armchair and took a good look at Harold. She put him in his mid to late fifties. His graying wavy hair was swept back in a flamboyant way. He wore a blue dress shirt, three buttons opened strategically showing a darkly tanned chest underneath. He finished off the look with slacks and leather loafers. His look and demeanor screamed West Coast money. Harri knew the term producer meant a whole lot of things in the Hollywood industry and wondered if he was the money guy.

"What would you like to know about Miles Davidson?" he asked.

Harold sat down in the middle of the couch and leaned back comfortably.

"How do you know Miles Davidson?" Tom began.

"Oh boy. Where should I start? I met Miles Davidson

with the rest of the crew about I would say nine years ago."

"The crew?" Tom asked.

"The crew is a bunch of young hotshots from the East Coast. They came into town and started throwing a lot of money around. Most of them had trust funds and were from established families. They wanted to conquer Hollywood, meet celebrities, impress their friends who were slaving away on Wall Street."

"And Miles Davidson was part of this crew?" Tom asked.

"He was." Harold nodded.

"You're a producer, correct?" Harri asked.

Harold waved her off.

"I was born into this business. My father was a director of TV shows in the fifties and sixties. My mother was a costume designer who hosted lots of the stars here back then. I thought I was going to be an actor for a while and then played around with directing. I always had connections, and I kept up with them. Becoming a producer is easy enough when you know everyone in town."

"You've won some Oscars, haven't you?" Harri asked.

"Oscars are just big popularity contests. I've gotten lucky," he said.

"Who else was in this crew?" Tom asked.

"Where do I begin?" Harold rolled his eyes. "Let me tell you about the king of this little group. His name is Chandler James Robert III. Don't you forget to use the full name and make sure to say 'the third' or he will correct you. He's the kid of some real estate scion back in New York City. I thought he was full of crap at first, but he had loads of money in a trust fund that's still burning holes in his pockets. He's the golden boy and expects the world to know about it. He was the one who decided that Hollywood would be theirs for the taking," Harold said with some disgust in his voice.

He obviously didn't think much of Chandler James Robert III.

"And the rest of the crew?" Harri asked.

"Let me see, okay so there was Miles Davidson. I never really thought he did have a lot of money himself. His dad was some finance guy. Jasper Sanders was more of a local boy but knew the others from prep school. Tanner Asperson, another trust fund guy, played around with producing but then decided it would be more lucrative to be an agent. He's at CAA right now. Lucas Reinhart matched the old money vibe Chandler oozed. Lucas put his money in one of my earlier pictures. I did get him his return, but he decided to date a bunch of Hollywood starlets instead. Impossible to have a meeting with. Lucas has the attention span of a flea. The last of the crew is Philip Townsend. He seems to have a good head on his shoulders. He didn't come from a lot of money but was really good with it. He understands value and persistence. He's a wealth manager now with a strong fund. His biggest client is Lucas Reinhart, which helps a lot, of course."

"And they all came out here around nine years ago?" Tom asked.

"Around that time. Chandler wanted to put three million into a picture I was making. And then Lucas Reinhart decided to put another five or six million in. That's how I got to know those guys," Harold said.

"And did you hear of any problems Miles might have been having recently?" Harri asked.

"You mean the embezzlement? That rumor has been streaking through town this last week," Harold said.

"Is that the reason you called him seven times on November 29th?" Tom asked.

"Oh, of course. I wanted to see what happened to my money. I didn't entirely trust the guy, but I wanted to keep in good with Chandler and Lucas. You never know when you need guys like that. I gave him four million to play around with. It's a small percentage of my portfolio. I'm not as out as Mirabella Youngston."

Harold had dropped his voice and said that in a conspiratorial whisper.

"You know about Mirabella Youngston?" Harri asked.

"She's having a hell of a week," Harold said.

"Tell me more," Harri said.

She leaned in, taking notes as inconspicuously as she could.

"Have you talked with them yet?" Harold asked.

"We've spoken with numerous people connected to Miles Davidson," Tom said diplomatically.

"That Stephen Whitney is quite the character. He has a temper and has cost his productions millions with his bad behavior. He, by the way, has all the money in that situation. Mirabella has been washed up for the last two years. Her roles have almost completely dried up, and she had invested all her money with Miles Davidson."

"She's lost the most?" Harri asked.

"All of it, from what I hear. He wiped her out. Rumor is they have an ironclad prenup, and she doesn't get a dime if she steps out on him, which is going to be a problem for her."

Harri tried not to smile. She loved the gossipy witnesses.

"She's stepping out on Stephen?" she asked.

"With one of those young Turks. Tanner Asperson, who is also her agent. I mean it's happened before numerous times."

"Does Stephen know about this?" Tom asked.

"How could he not? Stephen has some girl ensconced at the Château Marmont he keeps as a mistress. I wouldn't refer to her as a call girl exactly. She's one of those types that has everything paid for in exchange for certain favors she bestows. He had the money before the marriage so the prenup doesn't put his funds in jeopardy if he steps out. It very much matters if Mirabella does."

"Who else knows about this?" Harri asked.

Harold leaned forward and smiled. "You mean besides the three of us?"

Harri nodded.

"Everyone knows. It's not a well-hidden secret," Harold said.

He'd just given them a decent motive to move on. Miles Davidson lost all of Mirabella's money and she was in danger of her marriage being finished. She had a motive to kill, but the victim should be her husband more than Miles Davidson. If he pulled the plug on their marriage, she was ruined.

"Tanner Asperson is one of these original guys from the crew?" Tom asked.

"Once you get to a certain level here in Hollywood, everyone knows everyone else. They go to the same parties, sleep with the same people." Harold shrugged.

"And what were you doing on November 29th? In the evening between nine and eight in the morning?" Tom asked.

"Oh well, that's easy. I have a going poker game with some of the other producers that have been kicking around this town for some thirty-odd years. I was there probably until two o'clock in the morning. I had a car service bring me home because I'd had quite a bit of scotch."

He then proceeded to give them the names of the four other men that had been at his poker game as well as the car service he used to get home.

Harold Walters was no longer a suspect, but he had been a fount of information. They would be able to widen their search for who had motive, opportunity, and access to Miles Davidson in those last hours. They'd interview all of Miles Davidson's crew in the upcoming days along with the rest of his clients.

"Do you know exactly how Miles Davidson lost all this money?"

"The rumor mill is saying he had a gambling problem and took out loans from some very bad people. High, high-interest loans. I suspect the only way he could satisfy those debts was with his client's money."

"Those would have been some hefty gambling debts," Harri said.

"I think it's the interest that hurt him," Harold said. "I should've pulled all my money from him. I didn't think he had a good head on his shoulders and well, you live and learn. I knew in my gut that money would be a loss."

Harri wanted to ask why he'd gone ahead anyway but didn't think it was relevant.

"Is there anything else you need from me?" he asked.

"In your opinion, who would want to harm Miles Davidson?" Harri asked.

"Mirabella Youngston, for one. His loan sharks got their money. Maybe one of his other clients? Mirabella lost the most and now she's trapped."

"Do you think she's capable of doing something like this?" Harri asked.

"An actress will do anything to survive in this town," Harold said.

"Even kill?" Tom asked, skeptically.

"She's a famous, gorgeous woman. I'm not saying she did it herself. But there would be plenty of men lining up to help her do whatever she needed to do," Harold said.

"You don't think very much of Mirabella?" Harri asked.

Harold waved his hands again. "I've been around these people all my life. There's a special type of personality that makes it here in Hollywood. That personality tends to be disordered in more than one way. And that's putting it kindly."

"But you're in this business," Tom reminded him.

"As I said, I was born into it. I wouldn't know how to do anything else," Harold said. "But I also have a healthy skepticism for all the people that come to this town to make their fortunes and become famous."

There was a pause and Harri shifted in her seat. It felt like the interview was over.

"Thank you very much for your time, Harold. You've given us a lot to go on," Tom said as he stood up.

"When was the last time you saw Miles Davidson?" Harri asked.

Harold looked up at the ceiling and counted back.

"About a month ago," he said. "I saw him at some party and asked him how my millions of dollars were doing. I hadn't gotten any statements from him recently and was beginning to worry. See that was my gut telling me something was off."

"Was he acting like something was off?"

"Miles was a nervous fellow on a good day. He never

looked calm. But he was acting his typical neurotic self," he said.

"Thank you again," Tom said.

Harold walked them to the door and bade them farewell.

"He was a chatty fellow," Tom said when they got back into the car. "It was nice of him to give us a whole new list of suspects."

"Once we get those camera feeds of the neighbors, we'll be able to match them with this new round," Harri said. "His last twenty-four hours is still eluding us."

"I haven't gotten any updates from the officer working on that," Tom said.

Harri checked her email as he started the car.

"Neither have I."

"Let's go back to the PAB. Finish up the paperwork on these two interviews and start putting together what we can on our happy couple," Tom said.

"If they're both having affairs, their marriage is in shambles and they have this prenup, then Mirabella has everything to lose," Harri said.

"I want to get everything we can on her," he said.

Harri nodded and started checking up on any messages that had come in while they'd been at Harold's. The forensics hadn't come in yet, nor any information on the security footage and the door-to-doors had produced no new information.

"Nothing new so far. It's Malibu. How hard is it to get people to spy on their neighbors?" she asked with a laugh.

"It's those privacy hedges. They get what they pay for," Tom said.

The car slowed as he joined the traffic going east on Santa Monica Blvd.

"It's gonna take us an hour or so to get back to the PAB," Tom grumbled.

"We hit rush-hour," Harri said.

"I'm wondering if we're going in the wrong direction. I mean definitely having a hired killer take Miles Davidson out is a working theory right now. The eyes, though. That is really bothering me," Tom said.

"We haven't gotten any hits from VICAP yet, either," Harri said.

"Something would have come up already," Tom said.

"Then we keep digging," Harri said.

10

DAY 2

Philip Townsend had hardly slept at all since he'd received the manila envelope with the horrifying picture the day before. He'd passed out from sheer exhaustion for a few hours and then tore through his entire house looking for the missing Hasselblad camera. He could not find it. He'd also called his security company and found no evidence of a break-in, so how had the camera disappeared?

There had only been a few people in his home in the last couple of weeks and he trusted them. One was his housekeeper, Matilda, and the other was Tanner Asperson, a longtime friend of his who had absolutely no interest in cameras whatsoever.

Philip gripped the steering wheel until his knuckles turned white. He didn't want to be going to Chandler's annual Christmas party tonight but when Chandler caught wind he wouldn't be showing up, he called him personally to convince him. He hadn't done that in years, Philip thought.

Philip only lived about twenty-five minutes away

from Chandler's home in Brentwood, but it felt like an eternity for him to make the drive. There had been traffic on San Vicente and on Bundy. When he was driving, Philip had a short fuse, and tonight he ended up honking way more on that drive than he had probably that entire year. He was in a bad mood.

He turned left off Sunset to the awaiting gates of Pinewood Manor, the gated community where Chandler's home was located. Chandler lived on Saltair Drive which ran from the hills above Santa Monica in Brentwood to San Vicente and Wilshire beyond. Philip usually enjoyed this pleasant drive, but tonight all he could see were ridiculous exotic cars and the ridiculously rich people driving them.

Chandler had grown up in gated communities. Philip remembered his bragging in college that he'd never lived outside of a gated community unless he was at school. Chandler needed seclusion from the masses. He didn't like his world view penetrated in any way. Philip would never live in one. He thought all the people sequestering themselves behind the gates were elitist cowards trying to keep away from the general riffraff they considered the rest of Los Angeles. He pushed away those thoughts and realized he shouldn't be going tonight. He worried he might say something he would later regret.

He'd gone back and forth in his mind on who to call for advice and several times he'd called his lawyer. He always hung up before Martin, his lawyer, got on the line. What could he tell him? That he was the last person to see Miles Davidson before he was brutally murdered? And then he received an envelope with a photo of the man still alive with his eyes gouged out? And the photo was taken with his missing camera? Someone was setting him up and he didn't know who, or why, or even how.

He had no idea who he could trust.

Philip wondered how the case was unfolding. He'd heard the rumors about Mirabella Youngston. She sounded like the perfect suspect. He knew about her and Tanner Asperson. Maybe he'd have some new information on the case. Philip would be sure to ask him about it.

He slowed his BMW down when he saw the valet booth outside the gates of Chandler's house. No other cars were waiting. He wished there were. He was not ready for this party.

He got out of the car, handed the valet a twenty and his car keys, and started up the drive to Chandler's home.

It was a ten thousand plus square-foot mansion which had been completely renovated in 2007 from a smaller, more normal-looking home to this ostentatious one. Chandler had a pool and a tennis court behind a separate servant's quarters and a rolling green lawn with a stunning view of the city. Even still, this home was nothing compared to the estate Chandler's parents lived on in New Jersey.

Chandler had been known to complain about the size of his estate. He didn't have his own family and Philip couldn't understand why he needed so much house. Truth be told, Philip found Chandler insufferable and had since they'd known each other at Cornell their freshman year. How he'd even gotten involved with these guys he sometimes couldn't fathom.

Philip had gone to Hotchkins, a prep school in Connecticut, and had always been surrounded by trust fund kids. They were the children of wealthy jetsetters and behaved accordingly. He remembered one girl who'd taken off in the middle of her junior year with some rich, older guy she'd met in Mykonos and flew off to Brazil for a couple of weeks. Her mother had to take their private jet and security down to find her and bring her back to school.

He'd always been the boy on scholarship and even though his parents were well-off, they had nothing like these families. He was surrounded by people who seemed to have every advantage, but Philip had something they could never have. He had a sense of values that was completely unknown to his classmates. Every day it seemed more of a struggle to retain them.

The party was in full swing as he walked in. Everything was festive and decorated in millions of little white lights and red bows with red ornaments. The music and alcohol were flowing. It appeared Chandler had spared no expense on catering and concept, which was on-brand for him.

Most of the men were in casual suits but the women looked as if they were dressed to kill, as usual. He glanced around and immediately noticed multiple celebrities and political insiders as he moved through the room to find his friends. Lucas Reinhart flagged him down. Philip grabbed a drink off a tray.

"You don't look so good buddy," Lucas said.

"I didn't sleep very well last night," Philip said.

"Worried the cops are coming for you?" Lucas laughed.

"That's not funny," Philip said.

"Have you told the police you were the last one to see Miles, yet?" Lucas asked as Jasper Sanders, another one of their friends approached.

"What's this about the police?" Jasper asked.

"I was just teasing Philip about being a prime suspect in Miles' murder," Lucas said with a wink to Philip.

"You killed Miles?" Jasper asked with his perfectly coiffed eyebrow raised.

"What do you think?" Philip asked.

"So why are we talking about the police again then?" Jasper asked. "This is a party, guys."

Apparently, none of the guys missed Miles much. Neither Lucas nor Jasper looked as if they had lost any sleep over his death. Nice friends, Philip thought.

"Philip was the last one to see Miles," Lucas said with a conspiratorial smile.

"That's not exactly what I said," Philip shot back. "And the killer was the last one to see Miles."

"Okay, but you saw him that night, didn't you?" Lucas asked.

"Yes, I saw him that night, but I left him alive and super pissed off," Philip said.

At this point, Tanner joined them with Mirabella Youngston at his side. Philip's heart pounded in his chest. He needed to change the subject.

"So nice to see you again, Mirabella," Philip said.

He usually wasn't so forward with her and she started in surprise.

"Oh, it's nice to see you too, Philip," she said but he could tell she was distracted.

"Is Stephen here with you?" Philip asked.

Mirabella made a face. Philip had asked the wrong question.

"Mirabella and I came together," Tanner said.

Aha. So, Mirabella was another one of Tanner's conquests, just as Philip suspected. He remembered how Tanner wanted to get into the film industry so he could bed gorgeous actresses. Tanner was doing very well for himself in that regard. Whether or not the actresses were married was not an issue for him.

"I heard you've had a grilling from the police," Lucas said.

Philip frowned. Lucas loved to gossip but he was usually more discreet. Tonight, he sounded like a high-school mean girl trying to drag information out of anybody he could.

"They were so horrible. There was a woman named Harper, you know that woman who got attacked by Bryan Mortimer?"

Everyone nodded. The attack and subsequent downfall of one of the biggest directors in Hollywood was still news in town.

"She came with an older policeman and they grilled me about where I was that night. Imagine them thinking that I killed Miles? I mean, I should have killed Miles. He lost all my money," Mirabella said.

Tanner squeezed her and Philip assumed it was to stop her from talking. Her speech was slightly slurred. Mirabella was obviously drunk.

"It's so good to see all of your faces," came a booming voice from behind them.

Philip turned to see Chandler, perfectly coiffed with his curly blonde hair going every which way, his tortoiseshell glasses not hiding the brilliant blue eyes behind them.

Chandler was flamboyant at best. Today, he was wearing a white button-down shirt with a gold watch and gold and leather bracelets going up one scrawny wrist. He had on a red dinner jacket with black lapels and white pants with Christmas trees on them. They were rolled up artfully to show his slim, hairy ankles. He wore moccasins with gold chains on them. He was smoking a fat Cuban cigar and grinning like a crazy man.

"My brothers! It is so good to see you all," he boomed.

As was typical for Chandler, he took over the conversation. He made sure to ask everybody how they were doing, their Christmas goals, and what they wanted from the party. Chandler then went on to tell them he was having a grab bag Christmas present thing happening at the end of the party and then invited everybody out for a swim.

Philip managed to extricate himself from the whole group and wandered away towards the raw bar. His stomach was grumbling something fierce and with the lack of sleep last night, if he didn't get something into his belly, he would be unable to drive himself home. The last thing he needed was to be pulled over on a DUI.

None of the oysters or the beautifully presented sushi did anything for him, so he wandered over to the most delicious taco bar he'd ever seen. There was al pastor and shredded chicken along with a server grilling tortillas and making fresh guacamole on request. The spread in front of him included five different types of chunky salsas, onions, cheeses, and peppers. His stomach growled with satisfaction at the smells in front of him and Philip ordered five. He gobbled them up so fast he barely tasted them and then went to get another drink.

"You don't look like you're having a good time."

Philip turned and saw a man standing next to him. He looked familiar but he couldn't put a name to the face. He was sure he had seen him before, though.

"I shouldn't have come. I'm not really in the mood to be partying," Philip said.

"It's my first time and so far, I'm pretty impressed," the man said. "My name's Ethan Hunter by the way."

"Philip," Philip said.

That's where Philip knew him from. He had been on the front cover of Wired magazine just last week. Something about a huge tech sale he'd made that had catapulted him into billionaire status.

He looked like all the rest of the Silicon Valley guys. A little geeky, a little good-looking. He was tall, around six-foot-two, with shaggy blonde hair and brown eyes. His face was tan, and he was dressed to the nines in a pinstripe jacket, a white crisp shirt, and dark blue slacks. He had that air of Silicon Valley around him. Philip noted an Apple watch on his left wrist, and he wasn't too far from his iPhone.

"Welcome to the party," Philip said.

"And how do you know the host?" Ethan asked.

"I went to college with him. With a bunch of these guys actually," Philip said.

"And what do you do, Philip?" Ethan asked.

It was the age-old question asked at every party, in every city, with this kind of group. Philip wished he had more creative friends.

"Wealth management. I run a fund," Philip said, "Didn't you just make some sort of killing?"

"Are you talking about that Wired article?" Ethan asked.

"It must feel amazing to have joined such an elite club," Philip said.

Ethan waved him off.

"It's stock valuation. I don't actually have a billion in the bank as you must know being a financial manager. It's funny money at some point," he said. "It wasn't even my own startup. I joined it as one of the investors and now here I am."

He looked around and took a sip of his beer.

"It's an honor to meet you, Ethan," Philip said.

"Hope you start having a better time," Ethan said.

Philip shrugged his shoulders and moved away. He remembered where he was and what he was in the middle of.

He really should be going home. The horrifying picture of Miles Davidson screaming flitted into his mind. Chandler having his annual party as if nothing had ever happened was too much for him.

"I'm going home," Philip said as he came upon Jasper and Lucas.

"You just got here, man," Jasper said.

"Miles Davidson was a friend of mine. It feels too weird being here right now," Philip said.

"Us, too. Our hearts are busted, bro. But life goes on, right?" Lucas asked.

Philip didn't know what to say to that.

"Any of you know the direction the police are going in?" Philip asked.

"We were talking to Tanner about that. You were there, remember? Mirabella and hubby are in the cross-fire," Lucas said, giving him an odd look.

"Can you imagine Mirabella doing something like that to Miles?" Philip asked.

"Mirabella said Stephen thinks the police think they hired someone to do it for them. Stephen swears up and down they aren't going to find anything though because he didn't hire anybody. He has his own money to boot," Lucas said.

"Ouch," Jasper said. "That's kind of throwing Mirabella under the bus, don't you think?"

"She having an affair with Tanner?" Philip asked.

They all looked over to Tanner maneuvering Mirabella out of the main living room and off down the hallway towards the bathroom.

"Sure looks like it," Jasper said.

"But the police haven't come to talk to you guys?" Philip asked.

"Have they come for you?" Lucas asked, watching Philip's face carefully.

Philip had the uneasy suspicion Lucas actually thought he might have done it.

Nice.

"No. I haven't heard from anyone," Philip said.

"I haven't heard from anyone either," Jasper said. "I bet whoever did him in took all his phones and computers and stuff. That's what I would do. It would definitely take longer for the police to track down what he'd been up to without any of his devices."

Philip nodded and finished his drink. He put it on the nearest table and turned back to his friends.

"I'm not in the mood for partying," he said. "I'm taking off."

"Suit yourself," Lucas called out behind him as Philip made his way to the door. As he opened it, Chandler slid right in front of him.

"Where are you going, buddy?" he asked.

Philip's shoulders drooped.

Great. The last person he wanted to deal with was Chandler.

"I'm not in the mood for this tonight, Chandler. Thanks for getting me out of my house but I think I'm better in it."

"It's my favorite season. I love this time of year and wanted to spread the cheer. What's eating you?"

"Uh, Miles Davidson is dead," he reminded Chandler.

Chandler's smile faded for an instant but then he plastered it back on again.

"Gotta live in the moment bro," Chandler said. "That's what Miles' death has taught me. Gotta live every day to the fullest. Who knows when the ride will come to an end?"

"Chan, remember that time you were bingeing coke, and you thought the FBI was coming for you?" Philip asked. "Remember how you were convinced they were after your dad's money and were somehow going to get it through you? Remember how paranoid you were then?"

Chandler rubbed his face at that. "Man, that's a memory. It was a lifetime ago. Why would you bring that up?" Chandler scowled.

"That's how I'm feeling about Miles. I feel like something is coming and I can't see it and it's making me crazy. I haven't done coke in close to ten years, but I feel like I'm hopped up. I can't sleep. There's something off with Miles being dead. Something about how he died." Philip said this in a rush and then immediately wished he could take it all back.

Philip closed his eyes in regret. Chandler was not the person to be confiding anything to. He used information as collateral and Philip knew that his knowing how much Miles' death affected him would be used against him at some point in the future.

"Oh, I'm sorry buddy. I didn't know how connected you were to Miles," Chandler said. "He didn't lose your money too, did he?"

"It's not about the money, Chan," Philip said.

He pushed himself away from Chandler and opened the front door.

"Thanks for the invite. Party was swell, as always. See you around," Philip said and hurried down the walk before Chandler got any other damning information out of him.

11

DAY 3 - SATURDAY, DECEMBER 1, 2018

Detective Harri Harper had a hard time getting into the office that Saturday morning. She'd hoped to be at her desk by eight a.m. but didn't get there until a little after nine. She hadn't slept well the night before and couldn't wait for Jake to come home. His flight was due late tonight.

Harri sat down and opened her email, going through the messages from the officers on the team. Detective Tom Bards appeared at her elbow.

"Want to come with me for a walk to the FBI offices in the Bradbury Building?" he asked.

"I was about to start looking into how one would acquire the services of a hitman here in Hollywood," Harri said.

"Special Agent Andrew Lou might have an answer for you," he said.

"The FBI is notorious for not wanting to share information with us," Harri said. "How did you get him to talk?"

"I'm very charming," Tom said. "I'll buy you a coffee

at Blue Bottle before the meeting. He got us for nine-thirty."

"My research can wait. Hopefully, he'll let us know," Harri said with a smile.

She was excited to join Tom for the FBI interview. Hopefully, it would get her home earlier. She wanted to clean up Jake's place before he got home. It's not that she was a mess necessarily, but her stuff was all around, and the dishes needed to be washed.

"What are we meeting with Special Agent Lou about exactly?" Harri asked.

"He was the one who reached out. Miles Davidson was picked up at one of the high-roller poker games about a month ago," he said.

"Do those still exist?" Harri asked, surprised.

"In the San Gabriel Valley."

They stopped talking as a fire truck and an ambulance wailed by them. The morning was crisp and cool and bright. There wasn't one cloud in the blue sky and a slight breeze ruffled through Harri's hair. She breathed in deep and then started coughing at the exhaust from a diesel Mercedes driving by.

"Be careful about doing that down here," Tom said.

"You're so right," Harri said, still coughing.

"If he was seen at high-stakes poker games, then it would be fair to assume he might have gambled his client's money away," she said.

Tom shrugged. "We'll see what Andrew says. My mind is pretty open as to where the money has gone. Garth found the $45 million dollars was taken out of Miles's brokerage accounts and shifted over to a bank in Switzerland through the Cayman accounts. Of course, the Swiss authorities will give us no information as to whose account that was. The money trail stops there. They were able to say it wasn't Miles'."

"Are you thinking there's an organized crime angle here?"

"If Miles Davidson was in the San Gabriel Valley, then yes. It sure looks like it."

They stopped talking about the case as they reached the Bradbury Building. They went in and ordered their coffees at Blue Bottle and then entered the Bradbury through another door that led to the inner atrium.

Harri always admired the ornate ironwork that surrounded the sky-lit atrium. The building was best known for its starring role in the 80s movie Blade Runner. Now, the building was mostly law offices, and the FBI had an entire floor there.

They took the stairs up to the third floor and turned to face the camera perched above a nondescript wooden door. They stood still, looking up at the camera until the door buzzed open. The small office area had a friendly woman sitting behind the reception desk.

"Good morning. You must be Detective Tom Bards. And who is this with you?" she asked.

"This is Detective Harriet Harper, my partner," Tom answered.

They both pulled out their credentials and showed them to her. She nodded and pressed the button underneath her desk. She smiled as the door to their left buzzed open.

"Special Agent Lou is waiting for you in Conference Room One. It will be the second door on your left," she instructed.

They followed her directions and entered a large conference room. Special Agent Lou sat at one end of a glossy wood conference table. A monitor on the wall behind him showed a paused video of Miles Davidson sitting in a dark club around four other men. On the conference table in front of him was a closed manila folder.

"Andrew, so good to see you again," Tom said. "This is my partner Harriet Harper."

Harri leaned in and shook Andrew's hand. "You can call me Harri," she said.

"Thank you for coming here on a Saturday," Andrew said.

They took seats across from him.

"This Miles?" Tom asked, pointing to the paused video on the monitor. "You mentioned you had him at one of the clubs you've been surveilling for the last six months."

"Yes, he was there every Saturday night up until four weeks ago," Agent Lou said. "He lost big and when I say big, I mean three million big."

"I'm not going to ask about your investigation, but does this have anything to do with the gangs out in San Gabriel Valley?" Tom asked.

"This game room is run by the Wah Ching and a subsidiary of theirs called the Black Dragons. They operate most of the illegal card games in that area and are also loan sharks," Andrew said.

He picked up a remote from the table and clicked the video to play. All three watched a short Asian man come up to Miles Davidson and engage in a heated argument.

"We don't have sound, but we do have intel that this man is known for giving lines of credit to people who played these high buy-in poker games. Miles Davidson had been on a losing streak the last three months and my understanding from these videos is that he was out a lot of money."

"Does this group have bank accounts in Switzerland?" Tom asked.

"They have accounts in banks all over the world, including Switzerland. You have a money trail?" Agent Lou asked.

"Miles Davidson emptied his brokerage accounts and sent $45 million to the Caymans and then to a Swiss bank account. Of course, the authorities in Switzerland won't tell us anything more than that."

"Of course, they won't," Andrew said.

"Has Miles Davidson been seen in any of your other surveillance in the last two weeks?" Tom asked.

"No, he hasn't," Andrew said. "I wouldn't have even known to call you if it hadn't been on the news last night. Sounds like his body was mutilated?"

"His eyes were gouged out," Tom offered.

Harri still couldn't believe they hadn't been able to keep that detail out of the papers.

"Do the Wah Ching do that to people who don't pay?" Harri asked.

"But he did pay, correct? Are you going under the assumption that he was killed by someone he owed money to? Could it have been his own Swiss bank accounts he moved the money into? He was ready to leave town and was caught before he could get out?" Andrew surmised.

"We're looking at all the different possibilities right now. Thank you for contacting us. It's helpful to know he was having problems with an organized crime syndicate. Have you ever heard of this kind of mutilation by their enforcers?" Tom asked.

"They usually shoot people or sometimes stab them. They don't take the time to pluck anyone's eyes out and they also like to leave behind messages saying they were the ones that did it. It keeps the fear alive," Andrew explained.

"Thank you," Tom said and stood.

"Thank you for your time," Harri said as she stood to follow Tom.

"Enjoy the rest of your weekend," Andrew said.

Harri and Tom didn't speak about the case until they were back in the bullpen at the PAB. They'd stopped for another coffee on the way out and enjoyed the beautiful Saturday morning as they walked back.

Harri set her cup down on her desk.

"Miles Davidson was a gambler," she said as she sat down. "He owed crime syndicates money which he stole from his clients to pay back. He wired the money of his own accord, as far as we've been able to ascertain, into a series of banks. We can't be certain if he was the one who made all the transactions. Maybe he did it under duress? Could someone have killed him for that money?" she asked.

"It's a definite possibility," Tom said.

"Which puts Mirabella Youngston back in play. She needs the money. If she uncovered what was happening earlier, then maybe she found a way to take some of it for herself."

Tom was deep in thought and wasn't offering much. Harri wasn't sure where his thoughts were after their conversation with Special Agent Lou. She caught herself chatting out loud to fill up the quiet. She hated when she did that.

"I'll keep looking at the professional killer for hire angle. I think it's still in play," she said.

"Miles Davidson's mom isn't coming out. I got the email from her lawyer today. We are releasing the body to him to send back east," Tom said.

"Lawyer?" Harri asked surprised.

"I was surprised too. I'll speak with her again over the phone but since she hadn't spoken to her son in weeks, I'm not sure how much information we would get from her anyway."

"You don't think his parents were involved?"

"No, I don't," Tom said.

"Going back to the organized crime theory," Harri began.

Before Tom could answer an email pinged to her phone.

"Looks like forensics has something for us," she said as she logged into her computer and clicked on her email.

"The metallic slivers recovered from Miles Davidson's eye sockets have a composition of a 92.5% base metal silver with 7.5% base metal copper. This exact formulation was found on silver spoons from the nineteen fifties."

"His eyes were scooped out with a silver spoon. That goes along with the Al Jolson song, doesn't it?" he asked.

"Does it? Money and wealth," Harri said. "The silver spoon and the song are both symbolic of wealth."

She glanced over at Tom. He was deep in thought.

"The tox screen came back, as well. He had flunitrazepam in his system," Harri said.

"He got roofied," Tom said. "What did he have in his stomach?"

"Stomach contents included whiskey and bread. The flunitrazepam was ingested," Harri read out.

"The killer roofies Miles to make him pliable. It would be easy to zip-tie him to a chair. And then his throat gets slit," Tom said. "We still have a problem with the blood."

"Do you remember that show Dexter on Showtime?" she asked.

"I don't watch mystery shows on my off days," Tom said.

"Fair enough," Harri said. "This guy Dexter would drape his killing area with plastic, and that would catch any sort of blood spray. He would then tear it down and clean up after himself that way. I was thinking our killer could have done something similar. The roofie could put Mirabella back in play. But she wouldn't be able to stage his dead body after the fact. There is no way a woman her size could drag a chair with a dead dude out to that patio without leaving some trace behind."

"I'm wondering if we're going down the wrong alley with Mirabella Youngston," Tom said.

"We don't really have another good suspect, do we?" she asked.

"You reminded me about the music. It was loud. In our face. The killer was telling us something. It was part of his fantasy. It's meaningful in some way," Tom said.

"We have a silver spoon scooping out eyes, and we have an old Al Jolson song about being on top of the world. That's talking about rich and famous and old money to me, and he's a financial advisor with a gambling problem who probably used his clients' money to pay off his debts. It feels like it has to be one of his clients. That's where all the evidence is pointing to," Harri said.

"The killer was meticulous. I spoke with the forensics team. They combed through that house a second time. The entire place was clean. There is not a hair, a speck of dust, a piece of plastic anywhere in the house. That's simply impossible for somebody without experience in forensics. The killer being able to clean after himself so well sends up red flags for me. We're being led down the wrong path," Tom said.

"I see what you're saying," Harri nodded.

Her phone dinged. A notification for an article about a big CAA Christmas party coming up in two days had arrived. She'd set an alert for any news items, articles, or blog posts about all of Miles Davidson's clients and the companies they worked for.

"Should we try to crash this party?" she asked.

"On what grounds?" Tom asked.

"All the main players should be there. Tanner is Mirabella's lover. Why couldn't he have used his connections to find someone knowledgeable who would be willing to kill Miles Davidson for her? I don't think Stephen Whitney would do it seeing as he has his own piece on the side and the leverage of the prenup. But if Tanner Asperson is having an affair with Mirabella, he might want to help her. We haven't been able to set up an interview with him yet. He's a slippery guy and I haven't even been able to find his address because it looks like he hasn't updated his DMV records. It could be the perfect time for us to speak with him."

"And how in the world would we get an invite?" Tom asked.

"How much money you want to bet that Harold Walters could get us in? He wanted to give us more information. I could feel it. I liked him and it couldn't hurt."

"I don't think I'd be an asset to you at that kind of thing. But if you can manage to swing an invite, then absolutely. Get him to talk if you can," Tom said.

"I'm on it then," Harri said.

Tom wandered away from her desk and Harri put in a call to Harold Walters.

12

DAY 4 – SUNDAY, DECEMBER 2, 2018

Harri Harper woke with a start to the sound of keys in the front door. She checked the time on her watch. It was close to midnight. Jake Tepesky's flight must have come in later than expected.

She smoothed her hair and glanced around the living room, the dining room, and the kitchen beyond. She'd had every intention to clean up after herself for his return but was so caught up in the murder book and trying to piece together Miles Davidson's last twenty-four hours that she'd completely lost track of time and then dozed off.

Apparently, she also needed sleep. She bounded off the sofa and reached the front door as Jake swung it open.

"Jake," she said and wrapped her arms around him. He dropped his bags and kissed her.

"I missed you, girl," he said.

Typically, Harri bristled at anyone who called her a girl but seeing as Jake Tepesky had known her since she was ten years old, it was fine by her. She felt elated to be his girl.

"I'm glad you're back. I wish I'd come with you to Berlin but oh my gosh the case we got."

She grabbed one of his suitcases and he grabbed his computer bag. They went inside, closing the door behind him. After saying a proper hello, Harri was thoughtful enough to ask him if he was hungry.

"I am hungry but not for that," he said and Harri grinned.

"It's a good thing I took a nap then," she said with a wink and led him up the stairs.

Harri woke up to morning sun streaming through the windows of Jake's bedroom. By the color of the light in the room, she knew they'd slept in. When she rolled over to see if Jake was in bed with her, his side was empty.

She didn't hear the shower running so she got out of bed, pulled on her robe, and slipped into slippers that were next to the bed. She padded down the stairs and found him in the kitchen making bacon and eggs. She sniffed the delicious smell of bacon as she gave him a big hug.

"I love when you make breakfast for me," she said.

"I love making you breakfast," Jake said.

They were dorky like that with each other and Harri loved it. Jake Tepesky had been a profiler in the Behavioral Science Unit at Quantico for the FBI before he retired early to go into private practice. He didn't often talk about those days, but he'd seen enough horrifying cases to be grateful for every sunny day.

Harri had gone through some of her own traumas

with cases, beginning with her sister's disappearance twenty years ago. Jake had been her sister's best friend and had initially helped search for her in the woods of Oregon. After becoming a police officer, Harri went back every year to search, and this year, they'd finally found her sister's grave, together.

They'd brought her sister's remains back two months ago and were now trying to bring to justice the man who'd funded the entire child sex trafficking operation. Jerome Wexler had boarded his private jet and vanished without a trace. She knew they would find him eventually but, for now, they kept looking as new cases came in for them both.

Harri hadn't had a chance to tell Jake more about the Miles Davidson case but as he finished up the eggs, toast, and bacon, she gave him a rundown of the case so far.

"I agree with Tom that the cleanliness of your crime scene is disturbing. It doesn't match up with everything else in the case. That's what makes it unique," Jake said.

"I figured you would say that," she said.

"And how are you finding working with Tom?"

"He's an amazing detective. He's so insightful and knows his way around the job. I know that at this stage in my career I don't need mentors per se, but I think I'll learn a lot from him. He's constantly keeping me on my toes."

"Have you had any more run-ins with Richard?"

Jake knew all about her troubles with Lieutenant Richard Byrne and how he wasn't too thrilled with her transfer into RHD.

"I've had that one meeting I told you about. Otherwise, he's kept his distance."

"Have you met any of the other members of RHD?"

Jake asked as they brought their plates of breakfast to the dining room table.

"Only a few so far. They all seem nice, but Tom and I have been so consumed with this case we've been keeping odd hours."

Jake nodded. He knew what it was like to be working on high-profile cases.

"Tell me about Jerome Wexler," she said.

"The man Interpol was holding was not Jerome Wexler. We finally got the fingerprints from the Oregon FBI Field Office and they didn't match with the man they had in custody. He was also way too young to be Wexler."

"What happened that made you want to stay the extra days?" she asked.

Harri knew already that Interpol was breaking up a massive online prostitution marketplace and had scheduled a raid on several rural homes the day after Jake arrived in Berlin.

"I wasn't part of the raid, but I was at the local station watching as they brought everybody in. The suspects were all Russians and relatively young. I didn't see anyone over thirty-five and Jerome Wexler would be close to seventy. They looked like low-level men in the organization. Interpol thought they had a line on one of the main backers of the network, but he slipped through the cracks. I was hoping he might have been our guy. The one verified image we could obtain showed a man who didn't look older than his early fifties. It wasn't him."

"It's another dead end then," she said.

She munched on her eggs and bacon thoughtfully.

"We keep looking," he said.

"I'm so glad you're home," Harri said. "Now we can start looking for a place of our own."

"Have the stairs been so bad for you?" Jake said with a grin.

"I'm getting my exercise in," Harri said. "But I also want my stuff with me. I did keep a lot of the things from my house and this feels really like your place. I want it to be our place."

"We can start looking this week then," he said.

"I was hoping you'd say that," she said.

He kissed her.

"I want you comfortable and happy, Harri," he said.

"I like that about you," she smiled.

"What are your next steps in this case?"

"I'm trying to crash a CAA holiday party so I can get close to Tanner Asperson. He's been difficult to get on the phone. I've managed to interview Mirabella Youngston and her husband Stephen Whitney. Somehow, Tanner keeps slipping through the cracks," she said.

"How are you going to get into a CAA party?"

The Creative Artists Agency was the biggest talent agency in the world. They were exclusive and precious about their guest list.

"I met a nice, old-school producer named Harold Walters. He'd been one of Miles Davidson's clients, as well. He only lost four million dollars, he said."

"Only," Jake remarked.

"He has a tight alibi, so we know he's not involved. Although, he does play poker so there is something in that. In any case, he said he would put me on the list as his guest. We'll be going together."

"Should I be worried?" Jake grinned.

"Of a middle-aged, possibly gay man?" She laughed.

"Tom didn't want to go with me. This is my operation, I guess."

"What are you trying to find out at the party?"

"Why he's been avoiding us. What he's hiding," Harri said.

"When's the party?"

"Tuesday night," Harri said. "Whatever am I going to wear?"

She winked and Jake laughed.

"I'm beginning to worry now," he said through hiccups.

"Hey now. I clean up well,' Harri said with mock anger.

"I know you can, Harri."

13

DAY 6 - TUESDAY, DECEMBER 4, 2018

Harri smoothed her chestnut hair in the rearview mirror as she waited for Harold Walters to come out of his home. She wore a black silk sweater and black slacks. Her hair was pulled back into a loose bun. She'd put on more makeup than usual and lined her green eyes and lashes in black to match. She decided on going with the minimalist look and wearing all black. She hoped she would fit in with the rest of the partygoers and be inconspicuous.

She wanted this night to be a success. For the last several days, she and Tom had tried to hunt Tanner Asperson down for an interview. He was never in his office and he didn't return any of their calls.

Tom tracked down his actual home address. Yesterday, they'd attempted to visit him there multiple times throughout the day, but he never showed. The guy was doing a good job of hiding from them.

She'd failed at putting together Miles Davidson's last twenty-four hours as well. They were still waiting on Apple to send over the details to get into Miles Davidson's cloud storage and they were dragging their feet even though the subpoena had been delivered to their offices yesterday morning.

Tom still believed that Mirabella Youngston and Stephen Whitney were their best suspects and Tanner Asperson was somehow connected. Harri wasn't as sure, but Tanner was Mirabella's alibi and they needed to pin him down to confirm that.

The passenger door opened, and Harold Walters slid into the passenger seat, grinning.

"You clean up well, Detective," he said.

"Thank you so much for doing this for the LAPD," she said.

"I'm not doing this for the LAPD. I'm doing this for you, ma'am," he said.

"What do you mean?" she asked.

"I want to option your life story," he said.

Harri laughed at that. She pulled the car onto the road and headed to the CAA party at the Beverly Hilton Hotel.

"I don't have that interesting of a story," she said.

"Are you joking?" He shot her a look. "You were attacked by one of the most famous directors in the world four weeks ago. You've brought down two serial killers and you have a fascinating personal history. A family tragedy and decades-long investigation in finding out what happened to your sister. You have a full arc, and you can't be more than forty. Is she the reason you became a cop?"

"Something like that," Harri said grudgingly.

"How much can I give you for your life rights?" he asked.

"I don't need the money," Harri said trying not to be

rude. She should have known Walter would have an ulterior motive.

"Who are you kidding? Everybody needs money," he chided her.

"You might be right but let's not talk about this tonight."

"Will you promise to at least think about it?"

"I promise I will think about it," Harri agreed.

"Who are we trying to meet?"

Harri was thankful he changed the subject.

"I'm most anxious to speak with Tanner Asperson. But I also would love to have you point out that group of men you were telling me about. The ones that swooped in from the East Coast that Miles Davidson was a part of. I haven't been able to really discover who Miles Davidson was, and that's essential to the investigation. If I talk to some of his friends, I'm hoping to piece together what he was up to that last week before he was murdered," she said.

"You mean besides embezzling from his clients to pay off loan sharks?" Harold snorted.

She'd spoken with Tom about how much she should let slip to Walter since they both knew he was a gossip. They had strategized on what information they wanted to get out to this group and Harri chatted accordingly.

"They'll all be there," he said. "I'll introduce you to everyone."

Harri smiled and pulled onto Santa Monica Blvd.

"This is something else," Harri said as she tried to keep herself from gawking.

Harri couldn't help thinking back to the last Hollywood insider party she'd infiltrated. That had resulted in her rescuing the two young women she'd been searching for and dozens of others who'd been trafficked. It was a huge bust and the follow-up investigations were ongoing. That night led to Bryan Mortimer trying to murder her in her own bedroom.

Harri pushed the memories away and focused on the present.

The grand ballroom at the Beverly Hilton had been transformed into a winter wonderland. Fresh cut trees ran alongside all of the walls with sparkling lights everywhere and the fragrance of Christmas tree was almost overwhelming. There was fake snow on the ground and ice sculptures with champagne pouring out of them.

"They always go over the top. It's for the clients, but also to give back to all the underpaid agents," Harold said.

"I've never seen anything like it," she said.

Harri scanned the room. It seemed every surface was in use to bring the area to life. There were caterers passing trays of appetizers and champagne, people dressed as Victorian carolers, and a soldier manning a toy donation station. Not to mention the glittering stars of both the big and small screen. Harri had never seen so many celebrities in one room or so many precious gems on throats, ears, and fingers.

Harold touched her elbow gently.

"See that tall, dark-haired man over there speaking to the woman who can barely stand straight from the weight of all the jewels around her neck?" Harold said in a conspiratorial whisper.

"Yes," Harri said, glancing in the direction Harold nodded.

"That's Tanner Asperson," Harold said and walked over to him, Harri in tow.

As they got closer, Harri surveyed the man she'd been trying to pin down for the last forty-eight hours. Tanner had dark hair and brown eyes. From the way his clothes hung on his body, Harri guessed he worked out a lot. He had what looked to be a constant five o'clock shadow and the smirk on his face made Harri think he knew he was good-looking.

As he lifted the champagne flute to his lips, Harri saw he wore a pinky ring on his right hand. It was gold with a black face with some sort of insignia, like a class ring. Harri did her best to hide her disgust.

"Tanner," Harold said, barreling past the woman dripping with diamonds to pump Tanner's hand. "I have a special guest wanting to meet you."

Harold had a twinkle in his eyes and Harri knew he was enjoying himself.

"Mr. Asperson. I'm Detective Harriet Harper and I've been trying to get in touch with you for days," Harri said as she shook his hand.

Harri noticed with some satisfaction that Tanner paled slightly beneath his perfectly bronze tan.

"I'm so sorry we haven't been able to connect," Tanner said.

Smooth as can be, Harri thought.

"Now we can finally talk," she said as she took him by the arm and steered him away from the woman.

It wasn't too difficult because when the woman heard Harri was a detective, she slowly backed away. Apparently, this crowd didn't appreciate a detective.

"Can't this wait, Detective Harper?" Tanner asked.

"If only you'd been able to return our calls. I wouldn't have to be doing this tonight, here, in front of all your friends and colleagues."

"Fine," Tanner said and pursed his lips.

He took another sip of champagne.

"Where were you on the night of November 29th?" Harri asked.

"If you must know, I was with Mirabella Youngston," Tanner replied with a challenging tone. Was he trying to impress her?

"And where exactly were you with her?" Harri asked.

"Is everything I say to you confidential?" Tanner asked.

"No." Harri shook her head. "I can't promise you confidentiality. But you'll be off our suspect list if you have a solid alibi."

Harri stood next to him, holding her champagne glass, but not drinking. She wanted to laugh in his face when he asked for confidentiality. Who did he think he was talking to? She watched him with casual confidence and waited for his response.

"When you put it that way. Do I have to tell you where we were?"

"We know you're having an affair with Mirabella Youngston. She's told us that. Where were you again on that night?"

Tanner nodded and smiled at someone across the room and took a sip of his champagne.

"We were at my home, in bed, most of the night and into the morning. I have no idea where Stephen was, but Mirabella did not leave my house until ten the next morning," he said.

"Did anyone else see you there that night?" Harri asked.

"No," Tanner said as if Harri didn't get it. "We're having an affair. Secrecy is a key aspect to the arrangement."

"Did you go anywhere else?"

"We were in bed having sex, Detective," he said. "It's what we like to do when we're together. We don't go anywhere else."

He glanced at Harri to gauge her reaction. Harri gave him none.

"What about in the morning?" she asked. This set seemed to have domestic help and it wouldn't be surprising if a cleaning lady caught Mirabella in his bed.

"Unfortunately for me, my cleaning lady doesn't come in on Friday mornings. That's her day off," Tanner said.

"Miles Davidson lost some of your money as well?" she asked.

"He lost me two million," Tanner said tightly. "It's not nothing, but I'm not gonna go broke without it."

"Not like Mirabella, right?" Harri asked.

Tanner turned to face her. "Look, I told Mirabella she shouldn't have her entire portfolio with Miles. I don't know what she was thinking. Stephen and I both told her over the last year to divest. I tried to set her up with Philip Townsend, but she felt bad. She thought Miles was doing a good job with it."

"Was he?"

"No. He wasn't," Tanner shook his head. "He was giving her as much growth as if she had it in one of those little funds people have their 401(k)s in. Maybe 5% growth. Maybe?"

"I take it that's not enough for you?" Harri asked.

She had a financial advisor and thought maybe she was getting 9% on her account with him? She made a mental note to follow up on that.

"The way Miles talked, he should have been getting

closer to the magical 21% ROI," Tanner said. "But I've known Miles since school. I knew he was full of shit."

"I'm assuming that's not what he was getting?"

"Not even close. No one gets that consistently. Not even Buffet. I put a percentage with him because I'd known him since college. We were frat brothers, and I understood what he was trying to build as a fund. I was one of the first people in and it helped him pull others. Mirabella invested with him because he'd collected around six million from all of us guys and could show assets."

"All of you guys?" Harri asked.

"My guys from Cornell," Tanner smiled and nodded at another party guest. "There were five of us who came out here and we all donated funds to the cause. I know Lucas pulled his percentage and so did Philip Townsend because he started his own fund. Look, Detective. Frankly, I have most of my portfolio with Philip because he has a better mind for it than Miles ever did and also..."

"Also, what?" Harri demanded.

"Also, I know Philip will never fuck me over. Ever." Tanner sighed.

"What was Miles Davidson like in college?" Harri asked.

"The same as all of us, I guess. He liked to party. He liked girls, and he was smart enough, I guess. I mean his parents weren't as wealthy as some of ours, but he had funds and he got by. He pissed people off sometimes, but he was just a fun guy to have around. Although, he was a bit of a social climber. But I guess when you're dealing with people like Chandler, then even being rich isn't enough."

"What do you mean by that, Tanner? Do you mind if

I call you Tanner?" Harri asked.

At that point, Tanner saw somebody and waved them over.

"I'm afraid you've taken too much of my time, Detective," Tanner said. "I have answered all your questions, haven't I?"

"For now, but expect a call to your office tomorrow to schedule a time when you can come down to the station and make an official statement."

"I have to go downtown? To a police station?"

"You've provided an alibi for a suspect in a murder investigation. So yes, you're going to have to come in and make a statement," Harri said.

"And what if I don't?" Tanner shot back.

"You really want to do that to Mirabella?" Harri asked. "Don't make me subpoena you, Tanner. It will only get ugly and expensive."

The side of Tanner's mouth twitched.

"Have a good night, Detective," he said and left Harri standing there by herself.

Harri processed everything Tanner told her as she watched him disappear into the crowd. Someone tapped her shoulder.

"Pleasant guy, don't you think?" Harold asked.

Harri was thrilled to see Harold. He was really growing on her.

"Show me the rest of his crew," she said.

"We're in luck because they're all grouped together around that champagne fountain. The one that looks like a dolphin," he said and gestured with his glass.

Harri looked over to see five men dipping their champagne flutes into the stream flowing out of the dolphin's mouth.

"Wait, is Ethan Hunter one of those guys?" Harri asked.

"You recognize him?" Harold asked.

"He's gotten a lot of press recently," she added.

"He's one of the Silicon Valley guys and wasn't one of the original guys I was telling you about. That blonde is Lucas Reinhart. Next to him with the reddish hair is Jasper Sanders, and then Philip Townsend is the one that's looking a little rumpled and rough."

"He does not look good," Harri agreed.

Philip Townsend stood a little behind the rest of the guys and, even from a distance, Harri could see faint dark circles under his eyes. He had brown hair and a square face that wasn't unpleasant. He was taller than the rest of his friends and solid. Like he'd played ball.

"What's his deal?" Harri asked.

"He runs a successful fund. He dropped a bundle on one of my films some years back, but mostly he's a financial consultant and manager for his buddies," Harold said.

A shorter, interesting-looking man joined them. He wore horn-rimmed glasses and his curly blonde hair was every which way. At first, Harri thought he was one of the party performers, but he approached the group as if he knew them.

His outfit was what was the strangest. He wore a purple dinner jacket with a crisp, white shirt unbuttoned down past the middle of his chest with several chunky gold chains around his neck. He'd matched it with white pants with what Harri could swear were Santa Claus heads on them. The pants were rolled up just beneath his calves to reveal skinny, hairy ankles and expensive moccasins.

"And who's that guy?" Harri asked.

"That guy is Chandler James Robert III," Harold said. "He's the king of the clique. Some billionaire's son. I don't know exactly what his father does. He owns so many different companies, it's hard to say. Daddy likes to keep things close to his chest, but his son is rich as sin."

"And why do you call him King?" Harri asked only partially joking.

"He rules over all these guys," Harold said simply.

"And he's the one who dabbled in being a director and producer? Sounds like a man who needs attention," Harri remarked.

"He wants something, but I'm not exactly sure what. When you're dealing with somebody who's lived and breathed as much wealth and privilege as he has, they act in funny ways. I don't really know what to make of him, to be fair. He's okay to do business with. He does what he says if you can get him to commit, but other than that, I keep a friendly distance," he said. "Which one do you want to meet?"

"Introduce me to Philip Townsend?" Harri asked.

"The guy who looks like he hasn't slept in a week?" Harold asked.

"Yeah, him."

Harold was smooth with the introductions and easily managed to extricate Philip from his friends. He delivered him right to Harri in the corner where she sipped soda water.

"Philip Townsend, I'd like to introduce you to Detective Harriet Harper of the LAPD," Harold said.

"It's so nice to meet you, Mr. Townsend. I noticed you're not looking so great. Are you grieving for your friend, Miles Davidson?" Harri asked.

"How did you know he was my friend?" Philip asked, taking a step back.

"Harold has been telling me about how you all arrived in town at the same time. He told me how well you've all done for yourselves here in Hollywood," Harri explained.

"That's right," Philip said looking a little bit more relieved.

This guy was certainly very jumpy and Harri wondered why.

"It's been difficult trying to put together who Miles Davidson was. What did you think of him?" Harri asked.

"He was a really nice guy," Philip said quickly. "He was a true friend who I've known since I was eighteen. We went to college together back east. We all came out here to make our way and Miles and I decided to go into the financial management business. We had a friendly rivalry, but we got along really well and saw each other at all these kinds of parties."

"When was the last time you saw Miles?" she asked.

Her question made the vein at Philip's temple start to throb. He turned slightly pale and tiny beads of sweat broke out on his forehead. Harri could see the little droplets spouting out of his skin and twinkling in the lights from the closest tree. That question sure made him nervous.

"I can't really talk about this right now. I've been drinking and his death has been difficult for me to get through. You'll have to excuse me," he said and rushed past her, disappearing into the crowd.

Harri watched him go, thoughts swirling in her mind. As far as she was concerned, he just jumped to the top of her list of people to question tomorrow.

14

DAY 7 - WEDNESDAY, DECEMBER 5, 2018

Detective Harriet Harper got the phone call at five in the morning to report to another crime scene. A body had been found in the North of Montana neighborhood of Santa Monica. It was connected to their Miles Davidson case.

Tom didn't give her too many details over the phone except the body had been identified as Tanner Asperson. Harri made excellent time driving to Santa Monica from Jake's home in Beachwood Canyon because there wasn't so much traffic at six in the morning.

She was glad she hadn't had any alcohol the night before. She would never have indulged at the party, but she'd come home to Jake waiting up for her, with a glass of wine. She'd decided against it and now driving only four hours later she was grateful she had.

She'd called Tom on the way home from the party and told him all the news. Tanner had agreed to come in the next day to give a statement that he'd been with Mirabella Youngston the night that Miles Davidson was murdered. She'd also met some of the Young Turks that

Walter had told them about. She made special mention of Philip Townsend and how he looked at the party.

Tom agreed that Philip Townsend jumped to the top of their interview list. That was last night, of course. Today, the case could be going in entirely new directions with this development.

She parked behind the coroner's van on 12th Street and looked at the artfully lit house. Tanner Asperson lived in what looked like brand-new construction. It was a home confused as to what it wanted to be. It was predominantly a weird, stark-white modern architecture while also trying to fit into the neighborhood of eclectic, older homes by featuring some terra cotta tiling on the roof. The front yard was landscaped in the Japanese garden-style crossed with California conservation of water plants.

Harri shook her head and showed her credentials to the uniform standing at the gate to the front yard. He handed her the clipboard. She signed into the crime scene log and handed it back to the uniform.

"Is Detective Bards inside already?" she asked.

"Yes, he is. Along with Dr. Grimley," he added.

"Thank you," she said.

She walked through the open front door and saw that most of the action was centered between the living and dining room. A large dog cage was set on a plastic tarp with the naked body of Tanner Asperson stuffed inside. Even from this distance, she could see that he had no eyes. His murder was definitely connected to the Miles Davidson case.

"Good morning, Tom. Good morning, Dr. Grimley," she said.

"Has the sun risen yet?" Dr. Grimley asked.

"Not quite yet," Harri said. "I saw him last night," she said to Tom.

"Around what time?" Tom asked.

"I called you as I was driving home around eleven-thirty? I last saw him as I was leaving so that would've been around eleven."

"I'm estimating time of death was closer to between one and three in the morning," Dr. Grimley said.

"He's only been dead a few hours?" Harri asked.

She looked curiously at Tom. They were dealing with a different timetable than Miles Davidson's murder. Tanner Asperson's house couldn't have been as cleaned up.

"He didn't have enough time to clean this crime scene up," Harri said.

"That's my hope anyway," Tom said. "Neighbors have been vigilant because there have been burglaries in the area. You know, holiday season. We were alerted by a 911 caller who saw a figure all in black inside the living room. They'd come home from somewhere and called it in. The layout of this place helped us in that regard. It's a lot more open to the street here than in Malibu."

"We have a witness?" Harri asked excitedly.

"We do," Tom nodded. "I just finished taking her statement."

"How'd you get here so fast?" she asked. "Were you cruising the neighborhood?"

"It was a quick shot over the 405 at this hour," Tom said.

"Did she give a good description of the guy?" Harri asked.

"Medium height, medium build, wearing all black. Black mask and black gloves. She was able to make out the skin around his eyes. It's a white guy which is unsurprising. She couldn't tell what color his eyes were from that distance."

"It's a wonder she was able to make out the skin from that distance," Harri said.

"They turned in his driveway. I'm thinking their headlights startled our guy and when he turned around is when she caught sight of him inside. He wasn't expecting that," Tom said.

A crime scene tech was photographing every angle of Tanner Asperson in the dog cage. After several more minutes, he indicated he was done. Dr. Grimley called over two of her assistants and they carefully moved Tanner Asperson's body from the cage by undoing the top of the wire enclosure.

They lifted his body out and placed it on a stretcher next to the cage. The cage was then put back together the way it had been found.

Dr. Grimley bent over the body.

"Looks like the eyes were removed by a similar instrument as before. I'm seeing the metallic slivers in the eye sockets again. There's some bruising and abrasions on his neck suggesting a three-inch wide ligature. Maybe a leather belt," she said. "Rigor hasn't started to set."

"Are you thinking cause of death was asphyxiation?" Tom asked.

"In my preliminary finding, yes. Asphyxiation because of the condition of the neck. I can do the autopsy tomorrow at the earliest."

"Thank you, Dr. Grimley," Tom said and turned back to observe the room.

"I don't think our killer would've had time to grab Tanner's electronics," Harri said.

"We should get lucky," he said.

They went in search of a home office and found it on

the second floor. This home reminded Harri of Miles Davidson's house. It wasn't a place of comfort, looked more like a place intended to entertain and impress. The décor was stark and modern. None of it looked comfortable to Harri.

Once they reached the second floor, the place became messier and more lived in. Tanner's office was originally a small bedroom. A large mirror behind the desk helped extend the space. The walls were white and bare except for a red and white graphic painting. The only furniture was the white lacquered desk and two black ironwork chairs. To Harri's relief, an iPad and MacBook Pro sat on the desk. She searched the drawers but found no phone.

"These are pretty good to start with," Tom said and put both the MacBook Pro and the iPad into separate evidence bags.

"We're thinking the same guy?" Harri asked.

"The eyes," Tom said.

"Yeah, but the method of killing is different and no music this time," Harri said.

"First on-scene uniforms didn't hear any music. The witness didn't hear anything. And there is the dog cage," Tom said.

"Which is different from slashing the throat," Harri said. "But then Tanner and Miles were old friends. Tanner was connected to Mirabella. They alibied each other. Now, Tanner is dead. Is this Stephen taking an opportunity to get rid of his wife's lover? A copycat murder? The missing eyes were in the news."

Tom didn't say anything. He just looked around the stark room and grunted.

"But not the metallic slivers inside them," Harri said.

"True," Tom said. "And our killer was interrupted. He didn't get to set up the scene the way he wanted to.

Maybe he didn't want us to find the cage. This is just the intermission of his show, Harri."

It was Harri's turn to not say anything. She stood in front of Tom and nodded. Then she remembered something.

"Wait!"

Harri rushed back downstairs.

Dr. Grimley was zipping Tanner Asperson into a body bag when Harri ran back into the room.

"Did he have a ring on his finger? On his right pinky?"

"Just a minute," Dr. Grimley said as she spread out both his left and right fingers. "I'm seeing a tan line on the right pinky, but no ring."

"Wow. Okay," Harri nodded.

Tom joined her downstairs, handing the evidence bags with the electronics to one of the crime scene techs to log.

"What is it?"

"He's missing a ring," Harri said. "Tanner was wearing a ring last night at the party. It was an insignia ring he wore on his pinky, his right pinky. It's gone. We should search the house in case he took it off before the killer got here."

Tom called over one of the crime scene techs and instructed him to look for an insignia ring. Harri quickly described the ring to everyone searching.

"He took a trophy. I'm sure of it. We could have missed that with Miles Davidson," Harri said.

"If we can't find the ring, then we should assume Miles Davidson is missing something as well," Tom agreed. "The party was a good idea after all. At least you're able to question the man before he died. How was he last night?"

"Irritated to be speaking with me," Harri said. "Wanted everything to be off the record."

Tom and Harri shared a quick chuckle at that.

"So, he didn't want to talk to you about Miles Davidson?"

"Not at all." Harri shook her head. "He denied he was avoiding our calls. His lamentations sounded hollow. He never gave me a good reason why he didn't want to speak to us. When I told him he had to come downtown to make a statement, he was pissed. He walked away from me then," Harri said. "But I saw him again briefly right before I left. He promised to come by today to give his official statement and alibi Mirabella Youngston."

"Were Mirabella or Stephen at the party?" Tom asked.

"Not that I saw," she said.

"We need to officially get them in for interviews. Have them in separately to see where they were last night. We start from there and move out. He was having an affair with Mirabella and he could potentially have been her accomplice in the killing of Miles Davidson. Stephen Whitney has a good motive for killing Tanner. The change in the manner of death is something we can't ignore," Tom said.

"Are you thinking two different killers here?" Harri asked.

"We can't discount it," Tom said. "The scene is different enough. Really the only connection so far is they knew each other. And the eyes."

"How realistic is it for two non-criminals to be involved in such brutal deaths?" Harri asked.

"This second crime scene wasn't meticulous like the last one. But again, he was interrupted," Tom said.

Tom was exploring all the angles out loud. Playing the devil's advocate was one of his specialties.

"We're missing something again," Harri said. "What are we missing?"

"I agree with you on that. Let's follow the Mirabella and Stephen thread for now. We need to dig into this boys club Miles and Tanner were part of," Tom said.

"I'll start with Philip Townsend," Harri said.

"Which one is that? The other finance guy?" Tom asked.

Harri nodded.

"If we are dealing with the same killer, the two deaths are only seven days apart," Tom said.

"We could be finding another rich guy in his fancy home next Wednesday?"

"If he holds to the schedule. This one was a lot messier, and he didn't get to engage his entire fantasy before he must have heard the sirens coming. There's still an active BOLO for him in the area."

"What if he needs to scratch that itch earlier?" Harri asked.

"I was thinking along the same lines," Tom said.

"Great," Harri sighed. "The media's caught wind already."

She and Tom watched through the large front window as the news vans parked at the end of the street.

"We need to expand our perimeter."

Harri took that as her cue to instruct the uniforms to close off the entire street. When she was done, she rejoined Tom on the front steps.

"Shall we go wake up Mirabella and Stephen?"

"I'll drive," Tom said.

15

DAY 8 - WEDNESDAY, DECEMBER 6, 2018

Philip Townsend dragged his ass out of bed at the ungodly hour of seven in the morning to go for a jog. His anxiety was going through the roof and he'd barely slept again the night before. He'd only had a couple of drinks at the CAA party and left soon after he had the misfortune of speaking with the LAPD detective.

He looked like a suspect.

The shadows under his eyes were growing darker each day, and he was swallowing Ativan at a rate he didn't like. He remembered one of his last therapists telling him the best way to relieve stress was exercise. He typically ran maybe once a week before Miles' death.

Since then, he always found a good enough reason to stay in bed. Today though, he was determined to take his life back. He would contact the police and give them the photo. He'd explain why it took him so long to hand it over and get on with his life. The stock market was still shooting up like a rocket and he was making a ton of money for his clients and himself. He'd stopped checking in on the dating app he was using the most since the news about Miles, but once he'd talked to the police, he'd check-in and see how that was going.

He put on his running shoes and glanced at himself in the hall mirror. He had a home. He had a business. He had his health. Really, his life was great. He had no reason to be this stressed out.

He had done nothing wrong.

Philip started with a fast walk down his drive and took a left onto Georgina. It had a nice curve going all the way down to Seventh Street and that's where he could cross and keep going on Montana until he reached First Street and the park.

He jogged slowly at first, his breath coming in short bursts and his chest burning. It felt good. He almost felt like himself. And then he got to Tanner's street. Tanner Asperson lived only four blocks away and as Philip turned the corner, he saw a police car that was blocking off the entire street.

Philip slowed to a walk. There were two uniforms standing guard, a coroner's van, and a bunch of unmarked cars in front of Tanner's house.

His heart skipped a beat. Tanner Asperson was dead, he was sure of it. Tanner had told him last night that he'd had a falling out with Mirabella and the affair was over. Tanner couldn't have cared less. He was getting comfortable with some starlet he'd just signed and was having a blast.

Philip forced his feet to move into a jog and used every ounce of willpower not to look back. The last thing he needed was the police being suspicious of him. Especially if that lady cop he'd seen at the party last night was also at Tanner's house.

How would it look if he was seen jogging past an active crime scene?

A crime scene at the house of one of his oldest friends. A crime scene for a guy who'd been his roommate at the frat house. He just knew Tanner was dead.

He didn't stop running until he hit Seventh Street. At that point, he slowed and doubled over to catch his breath. What in the world was he thinking going jogging so early in the morning after a party the night before? And forty-eight hours of hardly any sleep?

Was he trying to give himself a heart attack?

And how could he go to the police now?

Another one of his friends had died, and he'd sat on evidence. Christ, what was he going to do?

All thoughts of jogging down to the park or the beach had disappeared when he saw the cops at Tanner's. All he wanted to do now was get himself home and swallow three Ativan.

It was time to call Nicholas in Martin's office and tell him what he'd found in his mail and how he'd sat on it. He needed professional advice and he couldn't keep the information to himself any longer. The stress was killing him.

No longer even attempting to jog, Philip picked his way up the street while staring forlornly at all the beautiful houses. The gardeners were out mowing lawns and blowing leaves. Usually, the noise of all that activity comforted Philip, but not this morning.

He dreaded the phone call to Nicholas and what he'd say to him.

He dreaded even touching that photograph again.

Maybe he could destroy it? Pretend like it never happened? But then that would be destroying evidence and he would go to jail. His camera was still missing, too.

It's one thing to sit on evidence, it's another to destroy it. He was not going to be that stupid.

He finally made it back to his house. The first thing he did when he got inside was grab the bottle of Ativan. He popped three in his mouth and gulped them down with an entire glass of water.

He sat on the couch waiting for the pills to take effect. He leaned back and sighed. That's when he noticed something outside.

Oh no.

On the patio table in his backyard sat a brown manila envelope. They'd left another photograph.

He was sure of it.

Cold sweat ran down his back and his fingers tingled. Adrenaline flooded his system and his hands shook. He felt like he was having a heart attack.

Is this what a heart attack felt like? Because if it did, he was having one. He pulled out his cell phone and called Nicholas.

"I need you to come over here right now," he said when his lawyer answered the phone.

"You've heard about Tanner Asperson?" Nicholas asked.

Philip had been right. It was Tanner who'd been murdered next.

"I don't want to talk about it over the phone," he said. "How fast can you get here?"

"I can be there in ten minutes, but you're starting to worry me. Everything okay, pal?"

"Absolutely not. Nothing's okay. I'll tell you when you get here."

Philip didn't move from the couch until he heard the doorbell. He'd kept his eyes on the manila envelope ensuring it wouldn't disappear. When he finally opened the door to Nicholas, he was ready to do whatever his lawyer told him.

"Jesus! Philip, you look like shit," Nicholas said as he entered the house.

It wasn't something Nicholas would normally say to someone because his social skills were impeccable, as was his reputation for being the smartest guy in the room when it came to the legal field. Martin was the one who dealt with contracts, and he left Nicholas to get the clients out of hot water on the criminal side.

"I should've called you last Friday when I got the first envelope. But it was my camera, and I didn't know what to do and I just wanted it to go away. But now Tanner's dead and there's another envelope and I don't know what the hell to do, Nick. Tell me what to do!"

The words tumbled out of Philip in a rushed panic.

"Slow down, man," Nicholas said. "Calm down. I'm here now. Let's talk it through. What envelope?"

Philip led him into the dining room and pointed at the manila envelope he'd received Friday. He hadn't touched it since he'd opened it.

"It was in my mailbox," he began. "It had to be delivered by hand. Someone put it in there."

"And what's in it?" Nicholas asked.

"Something bad." Philip shook his head. "Something really bad."

Nicholas glanced around the room and then said, "I need gloves. Or some pencils. The kind with erasers on the end."

Philip left the room and returned with two sharpened pencils. Nicholas used them to open the manila envelope and pull the photograph out, only touching anything with the eraser tips.

"Is this who I think it is?" he asked.

"Yes. It's Miles Davidson. Now Tanner Asperson is dead, and I have another manila envelope sitting on the table outside," Philip said, his voice rose in hysteria.

Nicholas put down the pencils and grabbed Philip's face in both his hands.

"You need to calm the hell down," Nicholas hissed.

Philip nodded.

"I'm gonna let you go. We're going to talk this through, all right? Are you calm?"

Philip nodded again and Nicholas let go of him.

"Have you called the police?" Nicholas asked.

"No," Philip whispered. "Because the camera that took this photo is one that I own and it's missing. I have no idea when it was stolen, but I've searched all over my house and it's missing."

"You have a security company?" Nicholas asked.

"I've called them. They have no evidence of any break-ins, no alarm activity at all. I can't explain what happened to the camera. And that's the camera that took this photo."

"Hold on a second. How do you know for certain this photograph was taken with your camera?" Nicholas asked.

Philip saw the wheels in his lawyer's head turning.

"I collect medium format cameras. This photo was taken by a media format camera that has a problem with the winding mechanism. My Hasselblad, which is my favorite, had a problem with the winding mechanism. The film these photos were taken on didn't wind properly. See this red line over here?"

He pointed to the smudgy red line running along the bottom. Nicholas moved his hand away.

"Don't touch. Don't touch the envelope or the photograph again," Nicholas warned.

"My camera started doing that to all the film I used in it," Philip said. "It was cheaper to get a new camera, so I did. I haven't used that Hasselblad in ages."

"The police don't know that," Nicholas said. "There could be a lot of Hassel whatever cameras that take bad pics out there in the world. The police would have to prove that this photo could only have been taken with your specific camera and was actually taken with said camera. If you can't find the camera then what's the problem?"

The two men stood facing each other in the dining room. Nicholas had a smile on his face that was both reassuring and triumphant. Philip still couldn't find a reason to smile.

"I also saw Miles the night he was murdered," Philip mumbled.

"Jesus, Philip!" Nicholas punched the air in frustration.

"He called me in a panic. He begged to borrow a huge amount of cash to give back to his clients. I said absolutely not, and I was in and out of there within fifteen minutes. But it was the night he died. I left him alone and alive. I just want to reiterate that to you one more time."

"You're going to need a criminal attorney with experience for this," Nicholas said.

"You can't help me?" Philip started breathing fast again.

"Calm down," Nicholas said. "Calm down. Of course, I'll help you. I'm just not the guy. If you'd jacked up a client's portfolio, you know I'm your man. But this…"

"What do you think I should do? Should I call the

police? I don't want to open that other envelope. I don't want to see Tanner's screaming face with his eyes all -"

"Stop it!" Nicholas hissed. "You should've called the police last Friday," he said.

Philip looked at his lawyer and tried to suppress a howl. He agreed with Nicholas now. He should have called the police, but he hadn't.

"So now what do I do?"

"Will these photos help the investigation?" Nicholas asked. "You're a photography guy. Tell me about these pics."

"They were hand-developed in a darkroom," Philip began. "If what's in that other envelope is the same, the killer is taking pictures of the guys before they die. Feels like that could be important to the cops."

"But why is this sicko sending them to you?" Nicholas asked.

"Maybe he saw me leaving Miles' house that night and thinks he can pin this on me."

"Why would he do that?" Nicholas asked. "How does he know who you are? How does he know where you live?"

"I have no idea. I'm sure there might be people out there who don't like me. But this? Framing me for these horrible murders?" Philip tried to keep his voice steady.

Nicholas went over to the fridge and poured himself a glass of water.

"Okay, pal," Nicholas said. "Here's where we stand. From what I can tell, you haven't committed a crime yet. This is more omission than anything else. Let's walk through this. If you call them now and tell them you have the photos, you out yourself as a suspect. You'll need to tell them you saw Miles that night. You'll probably become the sole focus of the investigation at that point. So, how do we keep them from marching you straight to the gallows? Do you have alibis for last night and the night that Miles was killed?"

"I do not. I was home alone," Philip said. "I mean, I was at the CAA party, but I left before everyone else did. Tanner was still holding court when I left."

"Did you have your phone with you both nights?" Nicholas asked.

Philip nodded yes.

"Then that's your alibi," Nicholas said.

"I'm going to leave you now and put a call in to my friend, Cameron Page. He's a criminal lawyer who has experience with this kind of thing. Until then, sit tight until the police come to you."

"You don't think I should call the police with that new envelope?" Philip asked.

"Not unless you want to jump to the front of the line as their main suspect," Nicholas said. "Leave it out there on the patio. Don't touch it. Don't open it. Forget it's there for now. Leave this one exactly as it is," Nicholas said as he picked up the two pencils.

Philip watched Nicholas and tried to breathe evenly, as his therapist had shown him.

"Will you call Cameron Page today?"

"I'll call him from the car," Nicholas said with a reassuring smile. "Hang in there, pal."

Nicholas looked like he wanted to get the hell out of there and Philip didn't blame him. He wanted to step out of his life and disappear, too. He knew something bad had started, and he was in the middle of the storm.

16

DAY 8

B y the time Harri and Tom had placed Mirabella Youngston and Stephen Whitney into separate interrogation rooms down at the Pacific division station, it was closer to noon.

Harri was in a particularly bad mood because she hadn't eaten anything and the coffee she and Tom had after leaving Tanner Asperson's house had been terrible. Her stomach growled as she walked into the room. Mirabella Youngston's lawyer had finally shown up. He was an older gentleman in his sixties with a full head of silver hair and wearing what looked to Harri like a bespoke suit. This should be fun, Harri thought.

"Detective Harriet Harper of the RHD division entering interrogation room two at twelve-thirty in the afternoon on December 8th, 2018. Mirabella Youngston is present with her attorney..." Harri looked to the lawyer and sat down across from them.

"Jonathan Myers," the man said.

"With her lawyer Jonathan Myers to give a statement.

Mirabella where were you last night at around one in the morning?" Harri asked.

Harri opened her notebook as Mirabella sobbed hysterically.

"He's dead. Who could have killed him? I can't believe he's dead," she moaned, and Mr. Myers patted her gently on the hand.

"Deep breaths, Mirabella. You don't have anything to hide," he reminded her.

I'll be the judge of that, Harri thought but kept a neutral expression on her face as she waited for Mirabella to breathe normally again. When the woman had composed herself, Harri began again.

"Let's try this again. When was the last time you saw Tanner Asperson?" Harri asked.

"It was yesterday afternoon. He broke off our affair."

"And were you okay with that?" Harri asked.

Mirabella looked to her lawyer, and he nodded.

"I was not at all okay with that. He'd lied to me. He'd said he was setting up projects for me. We talked about going to Paris. I cried and screamed at him and told him he couldn't do this to me, but he was adamant." She sniffed.

"How did you two leave it?" Harri asked.

"I told him never to call me again and that I would be getting a new agent," Mirabella said.

"Did he seem concerned about that?"

"No! He told me I was overrated, and there were no projects. His plan was to have me finance the productions, but since that fucker Miles Davidson drained all my money there was nothing he could do. He said I was washed up and he couldn't find me any work. Can you believe that asshole would say that? I don't think he's been referring me to any of the projects I wanted. He just wanted to get in my pants," Mirabella said.

"He's dead now so you don't have to worry about firing him," Harri said dryly.

Mirabella sniffed at that.

"Our business relationship soured when we started sleeping together. I realize that now. That was a mistake." She said that last sentence to herself almost. "I'm devastated. In every way possible. I speak to him every day on the phone. Did you know that? We also texted a lot. Every day. He didn't really believe in me, as an actress, and he didn't want me, either. Not really. He was just packaging me like he does all his deals. I see now that without my money, he had no way of putting projects together, so he had no more use for me."

Mirabella was in shock. She kept flipping from present tense to past tense when speaking about Tanner. She was crashing down into reality and her brain was trying its best to protect her.

"You didn't see him after that?" Harri asked.

"No. I had an invite to a party last night, but I decided to stay home. Stephen was there." She stopped and looked at her lawyer again who nodded.

"Stephen was there. We got into a terrible fight when he got home. He knew all about Tanner and he told me he has some whore he's been putting up at the Château Marmont."

And with that, she started sobbing again.

"Going back to Tanner Asperson. How did you leave him?" Harri asked.

"Angry. I said some things, too. He thinks he's the best I've ever had, but I mean, I dated Pierre Vaughn before I even met Tanner." She sighed. "He was very much alive, thank you very much. One of my girlfriends told me he was hitting on some starlet at the CAA party last night," she said. "He could never stop himself when the young blood came around."

"And where were you on November 29th? That was the day Miles died?"

"I was with Tanner. I already told you that. Were you able to corroborate that with him?" she asked.

Harri couldn't imagine that Mirabella had 'corroborate' in her vocabulary. Harri smiled inwardly. Everyone watched Law & Order and thought they were experts at solving crimes. Even washed-up actresses. It wasn't a nice thing to say, but Mirabella did not seem to be the sharpest knife in the drawer.

"I know about your and your husband's prenup," Harri said.

"What does that have to do with anything?" Mirabella asked.

"That goes to motive for the murder of Miles Davidson. You were the one who was the most affected by his gambling problem. From my understanding, he lost nearly thirty million dollars of your money."

"That was everything," Mirabella said. "He made it all disappear like some kind of evil magician."

Harri could see a fire starting in her eyes.

"I trusted him. I gave him the time of day when nobody in town wanted to meet with him. He had a career because of me and look what he did to me," she cried out.

"My client is very upset, and we want to go on the record to say that she has every right to be," Mr. Myers said.

"All right, Ms. Youngston." Harri tried to calm the atmosphere in the room. "Are you telling me you were with your husband all last night?"

"We were fighting until at least two in the morning. I bet if you asked one of our neighbors, they would've heard it all. I don't think we've ever had that big of a fight in our five years of marriage."

Harri hoped for Mirabella's sake that a neighbor could corroborate that. As she watched her speak, Harri was more and more certain that Mirabella had nothing to do with these murders.

"Do you have any more questions?" Jonathan Myers asked. "You don't seem to have anything substantial implicating my client in either of these deaths."

"She has motive," Harri replied. "And her alibis are pretty weak."

Mirabella glared at Harri.

"I could never do that," Mirabella shook her head, and her voice took on a shrill tone. "I mean, they had their eyes taken out. I faint when I see blood. Have you even looked at any of their friends? Like that Chandler guy? I mean those guys are all thick as thieves, so if they're all dropping like flies now, I would think it has something to do with them, not me."

"But Miles Davidson stole your money. And Tanner Asperson dumped you," Harri said in a firm tone.

"No." Mirabella pursed her lips and looked up at the ceiling before glaring back at Harri. "No. I'm still only thirty-years-old and I have my entire career ahead of me. I'm getting a new agent and I'll get some projects, and I'll get back to where I was three years ago. I haven't done anything to anyone. Yeah, I had an affair. So what? My husband has been parking his dick at the Chateau Marmont for the last year. I haven't hurt anyone and I'm not going to jail for any man."

Harri nodded and stood up.

"Would you like any coffee or tea?" Harri asked.

"There is no reason to hold my client if you aren't going to charge her," Mr. Myers said.

"Please wait here," Harri said and left the room.

She went over to the adjoining observation room where Tom and two uniforms were observing the interrogation.

"What do you think?" Harri asked.

"Cut her loose. We don't have anything to hold her on," Tom said. "Let's get started on the husband and that temper of his. Officer Franklin here just told me Stephen Whitney's last film had a man die in a dog cage. What do you think about that?"

After Harri set Mirabella and her lawyer loose, she went back to join Officer Franklin in the observation room as Tom took a crack at Stephen Whitney. Stephen had also lawyered up, but his guy was much younger.

"Are you going to go in there with him?" Officer Franklin asked.

"No, I think I'll watch," Harri said. She liked Franklin. He was an ambitious officer who reminded her a little of herself, if she was younger, black, and a brand-new father.

She and Tom had decided to split up the interviews to see if they could get the husband and wife to turn on each other. Since Mirabella had been so forthcoming the last time, she was alone with Harri, Tom paired them up again. His plan worked well.

Stephen, on the other hand, seemed like a misogynistic narcissist, and Tom thought he knew exactly what approach might work best.

Currently, Stephen Whitney sat slouched in the chair looking defiant.

Tom went through preliminary questions and then started asking about his last film and the scene where he'd put a man in a dog cage. Stephen was indignant and couldn't believe Tom would think that he'd be stupid enough to kill somebody in the same way as in one of his films.

Harri had to agree with him on that.

As the interrogation continued Harri became convinced this unhappy couple had nothing to do with either of the murders. And from the look on Tom's face, he was beginning to come to that same conclusion.

Tom stopped the interview abruptly and left the interrogation room.

The door opened to the observation room and Tom barged in.

"I don't think he's our guy." Tom shook his head.

"What about your hitman theory?" Harri asked.

"From the rundown of his known associates, I came up with a stunt guy who's worked on all of his films that has a record for manslaughter. He's the only one I could suss out that could potentially be a connection between Stephen and the undesirable elements of society."

"And?" Harri asked.

"Rock-solid alibis both nights," Tom said.

"We're done with this avenue then?" Harri asked.

Officer Franklin left the room and Harri and Tom watched Stephen talk animatedly to his lawyer.

"I still think he's hiding something, but I don't think it has anything to do with our case," Tom said.

"When do you guess they'll get a divorce?" Harri asked.

"I wouldn't want to be Mirabella in this, but then I don't think she should have married this guy anyway. He doesn't treat her very well," Tom observed.

"But that doesn't make him a murderer."

"Did you see his face when I asked about Tanner and

Mirabella? He really didn't seem to care that she was having an affair. In fact, I almost thought he was gleeful that he'd found out. Of course, with the prenup he gets to keep all his money," Tom said.

"We're back to square one," Harri said.

"No, we have the Young Turks now," Tom said.

"I'll say my goodbyes to the Lieutenant. Thank him for letting us use his interrogation rooms," Harri said.

"Sounds like a plan."

Tom went back into the room and Harri went in search of the Lieutenant.

Harri grabbed a doughnut on her way out the door. Her stomach was about to eat itself. She took a bite and closed her eyes as the sugar melted in her mouth. She got back into the passenger seat of their unmarked car and fumbled around in her purse for a bottle of water to wash down the super-sweet, glazed doughnut.

She watched as Stephen Whitney and his lawyer came down the stairs. She wasn't surprised that he and Mirabella had taken separate cars. Tom was not too far behind them.

He got into the driver's seat and rubbed his hands together.

"At least we don't have to deal with those two again," he said.

"No. Now, we get to interview some rich boys. Lucky us," Harri said.

"I've been thinking about what you told me about those guys," Tom said. "Who would know more about Miles Davidson and Tanner Asperson than the guys that they went to college with?"

"I was going to speak to Philip first. And then Tanner got himself killed. Let's go see him," Harri said.

"About that. I checked my messages and had a note from dispatch. A Lucas Reinhart called with information about Miles Davidson's murder."

"Well, well. He's one of the wealthier ones," Harri said.

"And he came to us," Tom said. "He lives in the neighborhood. Did all these guys plan to live near each other? Are they trying to keep the frat days alive? I don't speak to anyone from college, but then I'm ancient. What about you? Do you keep in touch like that?"

"No. Definitely not. And moving cross country with a group of friends? And still being friends for all these years? And in business together? I don't know of anyone who does that," Harri said.

"Aren't you dating a guy you knew from high school?" Tom asked.

"Shut up, that's different," Harri said.

Tom chuckled as he punched Lucas Reinhart's address into a map app on his phone.

"They should all start talking to us. Two of them are dead now. There's only what? Four left? I'd be worried I was next if I was one of them," Tom said.

"I'd be thinking the same way," Harri said.

17

DAY 8

L ucas Reinhart lived in yet another exclusive
community in the Brentwood Hills. This time
they didn't have any issues with the guard at the
gate, as they were expected. The guard made the requi-
site call to Lucas Reinhart and then gave them directions
to Mr. Reinhart's estate.

"You can't really see many of the homes from the
road," Harri remarked as they drove up the heavily
wooded road. It was narrow with big shrubs on either
side. Only driveway entrance gates broke up the
monotony of the hedges.

"They like their privacy here," Tom observed.

They followed the road up the hill until they reached
a dead end. A large iron gate appeared before them with
an ornate 3251 in the center. Tom pulled into the drive
and pressed the call button.

"Is this the LAPD?" a man's voice asked.

"Yes, it is. This is Detective Tom Bards and Detective
Harriet Harper," Tom said into the speaker.

The gates parted, and they made their way up the

long drive, flanked by orange trees to the front entrance. This house was palatial. It stood three stories tall and had two wings jutting out from the central portion. To say it was ostentatious would be an understatement. Harri could see a massive chandelier through the glass two-story window above the front door.

"Have you ever been inside a place like this?" Harri asked.

"This will be my first time," Tom said.

"This place reminds me of Downton Abbey," Harri said. "Have you ever seen that show?"

"My wife was into that show. I couldn't make it through an episode without dozing off," he said with a smile.

As they left their vehicle, one of the massive wooden front doors swung open. A tall man in his 30s appeared on the front step. He had short blonde hair and glasses sitting on his forehead. He was tan and casually dressed in a white button-down shirt and jeans.

"I'm Lucas Reinhart. Thank you for coming so quickly."

"We were happy to get your call," Tom said.

He led them through the marbled foyer to the left into a formal sitting room. The furniture and décor were as elaborate and elegant as the house but did not match what Harri would think a guy in his 30s would have chosen. Harri glanced around and thought Harold Walters' mother would have very much enjoyed this room.

"Do either of you want something to drink?" Lucas asked.

Harri expected at any moment a maid would come out with a tray of drinks.

"We're fine. You called us about having information on the Miles Davidson murder?" Tom asked.

Lucas waved to several armchairs. "Please sit."

Tom and Harri took each one of the chairs and he sat in the chair opposite them on the other side of an ornate glass table.

"He hasn't come forward. I haven't seen his name in the news," Lucas said with an air of drama. "I need to do the right thing. I need to tell you what I know."

Harri wanted to roll her eyes and remind him there was no audience watching.

Tom leaned forward. "Please, tell us everything you know."

Lucas breathed in deeply as if what he was about to say was difficult for him, even though Harri could tell he was enjoying himself.

"My friend saw Miles Davidson on the night he was killed."

"And what is your friend's name?" Harri asked.

"Philip Townsend. He's also a finance guy. Manages a fund," Lucas said.

Harri thought back to the nervous man she'd met the night before. No wonder he freaked out and ran off when she tried speaking to him.

"Let's start from the beginning," Tom said. "We're looking for some background information on Miles. When did you meet him?"

"We were freshman at Cornell University. Must've been 2004. We graduated in 2008. We rushed the same frat, Sigma Phi."

"And Philip Townsend was also a friend of yours from then?" Harri asked.

"He was. He rushed that same year. Along with Chandler Robert and Tanner Asperson."

"You're all frat brothers of Sigma Phi?" Harri asked.

"Yes, and we've stayed close since college. We all decided to come out here the summer after graduation," he said.

"And why did you come to Los Angeles? Was it for a job?"

"I don't need to work," Lucas said as if he was talking to a child. "I did want to try my hand at producing films and Hollywood is the place to be."

"And what about Miles Davidson? Did he want to get into film, as well?" Tom asked.

"He was always into finance. That was his major in school and he immediately started trying to get clients for his fund," he said.

"Fund?" Harri asked.

"Wealth management. A fund manager directs a fund. He needs people to invest their assets with him so he can then invest their capital," he said. "Miles went after the Hollywood players. He figured they were never very good with their assets and he could manage their portfolios for maximum gains."

Tom watched Lucas closely. Harri wanted to ask about the gambling, but Tom beat her to the punch.

"And when did Miles Davidson start gambling?" he asked.

"Oh, we all kind of gambled in school. Back then it was mostly sports betting," Lucas said. "I didn't really get into that. Miles did, but I had no idea how bad it was until his embezzlement came to light."

"And how did you find out about that?" Harri asked.

"One of his clients discovered there was nothing left. He still had access to the fund account, and he started making phone calls. Of course, that news went through town like wildfire."

"And did you have anything invested with him?" Harri asked.

Lucas shook his head no.

"My portfolio is with Philip Townsend. I'm actually thinking now of divesting the bulk of it away from him. I'm uncomfortable with the fact that he hasn't come forward to tell you he'd seen Miles that night. This kind of publicity isn't good for business, is it?"

"And how much do you have with Philip Townsend?" Harri asked.

"That's not relevant to this investigation," he said.

Harri looked up at that and met his eyes. His expression was the same nonchalant, slightly bored, completely self-absorbed as he'd had since he'd met them at the door. His eyes were kind of dead. Nice, Harri thought.

"When was the last time you saw Miles Davidson?" Harri asked.

"Let me see," he said and looked up at his ceiling and sighed.

"It was actually four days before his death. I think it was a Monday. We were at the Malibu Beach Club. We're both on the membership committee and were going over the new applicants. It was pretty general stuff. We had lunch, had a couple of drinks, and went our separate ways."

"Who else was there at this meeting?" Harri asked.

"Around ten other members. I can email you those names if you want," he said.

"We've been trying to lock down what Miles Davidson did in the days leading up to his death. Where he went, who he was with, that kind of thing. Do you know of any of his other commitments?" she asked.

"He didn't mention anything to me," Lucas said with a shrug. "The Malibu Beach Club meeting was on that

Monday and he was dead Thursday night. I didn't talk to him after Monday, so I really can't help you there."

"Going back to Philip Townsend. How has he been since Miles Davidson died?" she asked.

"I don't know what's going on with that guy. He keeps saying that he left Miles alive, but he's not sleeping. When I saw him at the party last night, he was a mess. Something's going on with him. It's not good to have your finance guy fall apart in front of the whole world."

"And you saw Tanner Asperson at the CAA party last night, too?"

"That's correct. I heard he was found dead this morning," he said.

"That hasn't been in the media, yet. That just happened," Harri said.

"I know," Lucas said. "Philip was running by Tanner's house. He saw all the cop cars and a coroner's van. He put two and two together and texted all of us."

"All of us is?" Tom asked.

"Me, Jasper, and Chandler. Jasper has been with us since the beginning of our LA adventure. He went to USC, though. I can't believe out of the five of us there's only three left," he said.

"Chandler was at last night's party, too?" Harri asked even though she already knew the answer. She remembered seeing the man in the purple jacket and Santa Claus pants.

"He was."

"What time did he leave?" Tom asked.

"Oh, I'm not sure. We closed that party down. It could've been one in the morning? He left with some hot Asian woman," Lucas said, admiration seeping in his voice.

Chandler had an alibi then.

"Are you hiring any extra security?" Tom asked.

"I have security somewhere in this house looking over all of the cameras, so I'm not worried about myself. Nor Chandler, for that matter. He has the same set-up I do. Cameras everywhere and a company that monitors them twenty-four hours a day," he said.

"And Philip Townsend?"

"Philip was never quite in our league." Lucas leaned forward and dropped his voice as if he was divulging shameful knowledge. "Miles and Tanner weren't really, either. They were a hell of a lot better off than Philip. They come from relatively established families, and that's the only reason why they got into Sigma Phi."

"And where were you last night?" Harri asked.

"I was with Bambi Laurent," he said.

Bambi Laurent was an up-and-coming starlet from what Harri could remember.

"And were you with her all night?" she asked.

"I was," he said. "We were at her place, which was a mistake. I will never be doing that again. I can give you her number and she can tell you herself."

"Is there anything else you want to tell us about Philip Townsend?" Harri asked.

"Philip told me Miles asked him for a huge loan. He wanted Philip to borrow against his own fund."

"How much is huge?" Tom asked.

"North of forty-five million, which I wouldn't call huge, but you know. Philip said he shot him down and Miles went ballistic. Philip said he left right after that. Miles was known to get crazy sometimes, but I've seen Philip lose his temper before. It was ugly to watch. I wouldn't be surprised if those two went at each other," he said.

"Did Philip Townsend tell you that?" Tom asked.

"No, he didn't. He said there was a screaming match and then he left."

"I see," Tom said. "Is there anything else you want to tell us?"

"Isn't that enough?" Lucas asked.

"Thank you for bringing this to us. We do appreciate your coming forward. If there's anything else you can tell us, here's our direct lines," Harri said.

She handed him one of her cards and Tom gave him one of his.

"I would be careful in the next week," Tom said. "I know you have security, but your gang is dropping like flies."

"Thanks for the warning," Lucas said with a slight roll of his eyes.

They all stood, and he led them back to the front door.

"Where were you on the night of November 29th?" Harri asked.

"I was here at home," he said.

"Was anyone here with you?" Tom asked.

"No. I was home alone but I can get my security guy to send you over a video of my grounds for that whole night. I was home watching TV, and I didn't leave the house," he said.

"Thank you for your time," Tom said.

They left Lucas Reinhart standing in the doorway as they walked back to the unmarked car. They didn't speak until they left the property.

"What did you think of him?" Harri asked.

"I'm wondering why he decided to throw his friend under the bus like that," Tom said.

"Maybe he doesn't want to do business with him

anymore but couldn't figure out how to get out of it," she said. "He mentioned wanting to pull all his money out of Philip Townsend's fund."

"Could be that. Or could be he actually thinks that Philip killed Miles Davidson."

"But then does he think Philip also killed Tanner Asperson? I saw Philip at the party last night. He would've had to leave the party, gone right over to Tanner's, and wait for him to get home so he could put him in a dog cage and kill him. And why? We still don't know the motive for these killings."

"I find it interesting that all of these guys are from the same frat,"

"This case could extend that far," Harri said. "They came to Hollywood together and have remained friends for the last ten years. Maybe they all pissed off the same person when they got here. Maybe some producer who they pulled their money from? Or did something horrible to an actress and her lover is now taking revenge?"

"Could it be so far-fetched?" Tom asked.

"Maybe," Harri said. "Obviously, Miles has the embezzlement, so he's made a lot of enemies. But what about Tanner? How do they intersect outside of this group of friends?" she asked.

"That's what we have to find. All the places they intersect, whether in their little boys' club or out."

"Starting in 2004 and in another state," Harri said.

"The other thing we need to find out is what triggered this. These guys have been kicking around Hollywood for a decade. So, was the Miles embezzlement the event that kicked all of this off? Or was there something prior to that event that set our killer off on this path. Why now? That's what we have to answer," Tom said.

"I'll make sure to get that Malibu Beach Club meeting roster from Lucas. Maybe Miles talked to some of the other members about what he was planning to do that week."

"This case is centered on these guys," Tom said. "I'm almost certain they did something bad and now they're paying for it."

"Because rich white guys always get away with bad things?" Harri said.

"Exactly," Tom said.

DAY 8

Harri had Philip Townsend's address from his DMV records. He lived only four blocks from Tanner Asperson, as Lucas Reinhart had mentioned. Once they came down the hill, they had a quick drive down Sunset, then took a turn on Bundy and drove down San Vicente again. It was becoming their usual route between all the main suspects. San Vicente was a wide boulevard with a center island that ran down to Sunset Park.

The drive was pleasant and, on some days, Harri could smell the salty air of the Pacific Ocean. It would be a drive to downtown for work, but maybe she and Jake could check out some houses in these surrounding neighborhoods.

"This is such a charming neighborhood," Harri said.

"Charming, yes. Worth seven to ten million a house? I'm not so sure about that," he said.

"Is that really how much these houses go for now?" she asked.

"My wife is a realtor and has always tried to get

clients in this neighborhood because the commissions are worth the hassle."

"I didn't know your wife is a realtor," Harri said.

"Are you looking to buy?" he asked.

"I put my house on the market about a week ago. I've been staying with Jake, but we're looking to get something together," she said.

"Because of the attack?" Tom asked.

"It doesn't really feel like home anymore," she said.

"What are you selling it for?" he asked.

"My realtor thinks I can get two point five million," she said.

Tom whistled.

"I'm the last of my family. I got money from them to buy that house," she said.

"You don't have to explain to me," Tom said. "I've lived in Los Angeles for close to thirty years and what properties go for these days is insane. I don't know how people do it."

"Imagine what kind of home we could live in if we left town. This neighborhood is gorgeous. I love that it's so close to the jogging path on San Vicente. Could you imagine dropping six million on one of those small houses?"

"Nope," Tom said. "That's why we live in the valley."

"I can't live in the valley. It's too damn hot out there," she said.

"That's why we have air conditioning," Tom said as he pulled into a spot in front of Philip Townsend's house.

"This is him," Harri said.

"All of these guys have done pretty well for themselves," Tom said.

Philip Townsend's house was modest compared to the others on the block. It looked kind of like a weathered Cape house. Harri had seen pictures of homes in New England and this place reminded her of those charming cottages. There was a green lawn with roses along both sides of the home and an olive tree in front of the main large picture window.

Tom rang the doorbell, and they waited. They heard footsteps and then the door opened.

"I'm Detective Tom Bards of the LAPD. This is Detective Harri Harper," he began. "We'd like to ask you some questions about the death of Miles Davidson. We believe you were good friends with him?"

Philip Townsend looked a lot worse than when she'd seen him at the party. The circles under his eyes were deeper and darker. His hair was all over the place as if he had just woken up. He had more than a five o'clock shadow and he wore a dirty T-shirt and sweatpants.

"I remember you," he said to Harri. "What do you need to know about Miles Davidson?"

"Can we come in?" Tom prodded.

"Oh yeah," he said and moved to let them by.

Apparently, he didn't know that he didn't have to let them in, Harri thought. Her eyes ran over the colorful and comfortable furnishings. Philip's home looked nothing like Miles Davidson's or Tanner Asperson's. This home looked like someone actually lived in it.

A cream-colored tufted sofa anchored the room across from an interesting wood coffee table that was filled with books. There was a fireplace and on the mantelpiece were vintage cameras. They looked like medium format cameras, Harri thought. She had taken a photography class in college and remembered using one.

"Are you a photographer?" she asked.

"Used to be," he said. "I don't really have time for

that anymore. I've collected since I was in college. It's a decent collection."

His voice cracked when he said that.

"Are you ill, Mr. Townsend?" Tom asked.

"I'm just having some insomnia," he said and motioned to the couch. "You guys need any water or anything?"

He stood awkwardly in the middle of his colorful living room and Harri wondered if he was about to burst into tears.

"No, we're fine," Tom said.

Tom sat down on the couch and Harri sat in a chair next to it. Philip perched on the edge of a club chair and watched them expectantly.

"What do you want to know?" he asked.

"When was the last time you saw Miles Davidson?" Harri asked.

"Of course," he said and ran his hand through his disheveled hair.

Harri wondered if that was one of his nervous tics because he'd done it five times in the last few minutes.

"I saw him that night. Wednesday, I think it was November 29th. Miles had called me in a panic and asked me to come by because he wanted to talk to me about something," Philip said.

"You saw him that night?" Tom asked.

"Yes, I did," he said.

Philip ran his fingers along the arm of his chair.

"You didn't think that might be relevant to our investigation?" Harri asked.

"I assumed you would come and contact me when you saw me coming and going. I know Miles had cameras there," he said. "But you guys never came and so I thought that it wasn't important. Anyway, I saw you at the party, so I guess I've been kind of expecting you."

"What time did you arrive at his house that night?" Harri asked.

"I got there around eight-forty-five in the evening. I didn't stay any longer than fifteen minutes. I left in a hurry," he said.

"Why did you stay for such a short period of time? Did you argue with Miles Davidson?" Tom asked.

"As a matter of fact, I did," Philip said. His knee bounced up and down as he said this.

This guy was nervous.

"What was the fight about?" Tom asked.

"Miles told me he had to pay off a loan and had used all of his clients' assets. Then he had the balls to beg me for a bridge loan to tide him over. He needed a month to scrape together enough funds to replenish his accounts. He was desperate but he should have known I would never risk my clients' assets, especially to cover his gambling debts," Philip said, and his voice shook.

His fists clenched and unclenched.

"What did you tell him?" Tom asked.

"I told him no, of course. Those funds are not my own. I would never violate a fiduciary relationship. I understood he was desperate, but my hands were tied. When I said no, he yelled at me that his life was in danger. I told him that was nothing I could help him with. He's always been a risk-taker. He's always gone too far. That wasn't my problem, though. He threw me out of his house. To be honest, I was glad to leave," he said. "I wish I'd never gone."

"What time did you leave?" Tom asked.

"Didn't you see the security tapes? I think I must've left around nine o'clock. I got back home by about nine-thirty. I was pretty upset and had a drink and went to bed," he said.

"You went straight home? Didn't stop anywhere?" Tom asked.

"That's correct, Detective," he said.

"Why didn't you call to tell us this?" Tom asked.

"I already told you that I didn't think it was relevant since I left him alive and pissed off," he said.

"Where were you on the night that Tanner Asperson was killed?" Harri asked.

Philip looked over sharply to her.

"I was at the party. I remember seeing you there," he snapped. "I know you spoke to Tanner because he was pretty upset after you left. You really got under his skin."

"What exactly did he say?" Harri asked.

"He thought you were insinuating that he had something to do with Miles' death. Something about him and Mirabella getting rid of him because he lost all her money. But Tanner didn't care about Mirabella that much and he would never do such a thing. He'd dumped Mirabella that day for getting him into this whole weird triangle with her and her husband and Miles. He was off to get laid with some girl he'd started representing."

"And was that the last time you saw Tanner? At the party?" Harri asked.

"That's correct. I've had insomnia since Miles died and I was beat, and I decided to come home. I was alone for the rest of the night. I know it's a lame alibi but it's the truth," he said.

"Is there something else you want to tell us? You seem nervous," Harri said.

"Of course, I'm nervous. Two of my friends from college died within days of each other. It's disturbing and really weird. These guys were my friends. They were my best friends. That's two funerals for two guys in their thirties. And not to mention they were brutally murdered."

His face paled and Harri saw beads of sweat forming on his forehead again. This guy was not holding it together, she thought.

"You aren't keeping anything back?" Tom asked.

"No, there's nothing else. You'll see that I left Miles at nine that night. It's all in those damn tapes of his and he was alive when I left. Tanner, I only saw at the party and there should be video from the hotel showing that I left around ten forty-five."

Harri didn't think they were going to get anything else from him. She gave Tom a side glance, and he nodded at her. It was time to go.

"Thank you for your time, Philip," Tom said.

"Yeah sure, whatever," Philip said.

He looked furtively at the cameras again and Harri got a distinct impression that he was hiding something. What though, she wasn't sure.

"You're not planning to take any trips out of town are you, Mr. Townsend?" Tom asked.

"It's not any of your business, but no I'm not," Philip said.

"I hope you're able to get some sleep," Harri said.

Philip nodded and led them to the front door. When the door opened, the sunlight flooded into the hallway. He blinked rapidly and shielded his eyes.

"Have a good day, Mr. Townsend," Tom said. They stepped out on his front porch.

Philip didn't reply and shut the door on them.

Harri looked over her shoulder as they walked back to the car. The curtain shifted slightly in the living room. He was watching them go. Strange guy.

Tom clicked the doors open, and she slid into her seat as Tom started the car.

"He's keeping a secret," Tom said.

"Do you think he might have a drug problem?" Harri asked.

"Let's see what we can dig up on him. I'm getting the feeling we're finally on the right track. The whole Hollywood angle was the shiny object. This is making me feel we're finally looking in the right direction."

"Agreed. Should we get cars on him?" Harri asked.

"I'll talk to Richard. He was nervous enough to warrant a watchful eye."

"We didn't ask him if he was at the Malibu Club that week," Harri said.

"In time. We will definitely be talking to him again. I'm sure," Tom said.

19

DAY 8

When Harri and Tom got back to their desks, they split the work between them. Tom dug into Lucas Reinhart and Chandler James Robert III and Harri got Philip Townsend. As they had discussed on the ride over, Tom was going to talk to Richard Byrne about getting a surveillance team on Philip Townsend's home. They didn't have enough to formally bring him in for questioning but they both felt he'd acted in such a bizarre way there had to be something going on with him. Because of the short time between killings, Tom felt that it was urgent to start surveillance immediately, in case Philip proved to be the killer. Harri was happy to leave that to Tom.

She was grateful for the division of work because Philip Townsend had piqued her curiosity. As she started to research his life, she realized why. She reviewed his contacts on LinkedIn & read some of the recommendations from former classmates and instructors at Cornell University and the Hotchkins School, his alma maters. She ran a thorough background check on him, which came back clean outside of a couple of parking tickets. From what she'd found so far, he had a clean record in California, Connecticut, and upstate New York.

Through a search of his past addresses, she found the one he'd listed on his driver's license when he was sixteen years old. Most people didn't realize their driving records followed them from state to state.

The address she found was in Stamford, Connecticut. She discovered two names also connected to the same address at the same time. One was a woman named Sheila Townsend, and the other was a man named Seth Raskin.

When she did a background check on Raskin, she hit pay dirt. Seth Raskin had been a resident of the Northern Correctional Institute, in Somers, Connecticut. He was in for a life sentence for the murder of a liquor store clerk during a robbery in 1987. Philip had only been two years old then. He grew up without a father and he must have known his father was in prison. Harri leaned back in her chair and looked out the window, admiring the view as she wondered how the kid with a dad in prison for murder got to be part of this high-flying group of privileged boys.

Her answer came after she took a quick break and then returned to her desk with fresh coffee and researched the high school Philip attended. The Hotchkins school, which was the best rated private school in all of Connecticut and most of New England, cost north of $45,000 per school year, not including the boarding of students and supplies. Harri wondered if Philip had been one of the scholarship kids. She checked where Miles Davidson and Tanner Asperson had attended high school, and neither of them had gone to the Hotchkins School. They must have met at Cornell as

Philip said. But he had been groomed to move in the circles of status and wealth.

Each of the Young Turks was a member of Sigma Phi at Cornell, except Jasper. Harri looked to see if he'd been a member at USC, but she wouldn't be able to find out for sure until the morning. The Sigma Phi fraternity logo reminded her of the ring Tanner Asperson wore the night he was killed. That was interesting, she thought. The ring had still not turned up anywhere.

She needed to call both The Hotchkins school and the Cornell admissions offices and speak to someone about Philip Townsend, but because of the time, the offices were closed. She rubbed her eyes and noticed it was already nine o'clock in the evening. Jake would be home now. She wandered over to Tom's desk and updated him on everything she'd found out about Philip and his father.

"That makes him the black sheep of the group," Tom said.

"First thing tomorrow, I'll call the Hotchkins school and Cornell to see if they'll release any information. Doubtful without a court order but I'll give it a try," she said.

"I didn't get half as far as you with Lucas Reinhart or Chandler James Robert III. I did background checks on them and they're squeaky clean, not even any parking tickets. Their family estates are all on the East Coast. James Robert II is a billionaire industrialist. Found a lot of articles and profiles on him, but very little about his son."

"And Lucas Reinhart?" Harri asked.

"He's in the same league as Chandler. Old money going back over a century. Lucas attended a private school in Switzerland and then ended up at Cornell. His family goes all the way back to the Mayflower. They're on some register. His father is influential in politics in Boston. I'll keep digging but these guys are connected."

"As we thought they might be," Harri said.

"Calling it a night?" Tom asked.

"I am," Harri nodded.

"Oh, one last thing," Tom said. "We got a surveillance team on Philip Townsend's house. The first watch starts tonight. We can take a shift tomorrow evening?"

"Sounds good to me," Harri said. "See you tomorrow."

Tom nodded and waved her off.

Harri dragged herself up Jake's stairs, swearing under her breath. When she opened the door huffing and puffing, he was already standing there with a glass of water.

"How did you know I was here?" she asked.

"I watched you on the security camera, struggling up those stairs," he said with a smile.

"We need to start looking for houses immediately," Harri quipped.

"Give me a time and a place and I'll be there," he said.

"What are we having for dinner?" Harri asked.

She followed him into the kitchen. He served cheeseburger casserole as Harri told him about her day, focusing on Philip Townsend and the past he must have hidden from his friends to crack that upper echelon of society.

"I feel like we're missing something," she said. "Beside Philip, these two last guys in the group, Lucas Reinhart and Chandler James Robert III are blue-blood-old-money-nothing-is-ever-going-to-touch-us kinds of guys. The rules never apply to them, but Philip knows the rules apply to him. Why would he start killing them? You should have seen him. He was nervous, scared, said he hadn't been sleeping. Does that sound like the behavior of a cold sociopath who could have done these killings?"

"Are you asking me for my professional opinion on this case?" he asked.

"An unofficial professional opinion," she said and kissed him.

"Why do you think the killer is a sociopath?" he asked.

"Because of the crime scenes. They were meticulous. The second one was on its way to being meticulous. The killer was controlled, yet the damage to the bodies was specific and gruesome. Is there another type of personality that could do this?"

"Sociopaths are psychopaths who don't have feelings like normal human beings do. They lack remorse, empathy, and guilt, but they also don't fear punishment and don't take responsibility for their actions. They have a terrible time regulating their emotions and can go from calm to aggressive and violent in a split second. These individuals, in the psychological sense, are known to have antisocial personality disorder."

"Serial killers have this disorder?" she asked.

"Why do you think this is a serial?" Jake asked. His brows knitted in concern. "You didn't mention this is a serial."

"The definition of a serial is three deaths in a span of time by the same killer. We have two deaths so far, seven days apart, and I get the feeling another body is about to drop. This killer has a plan."

"Not to go off on a tangent but did you know that a

lot of the richest people in America, CEOs of major companies, score highly on the socio-pathology scale?" Jake asked.

"I'd heard that somewhere, but how is this relevant to this case?"

"I'm thinking of those two other guys, Lucas and Chandler. It's one thing to have old money passed from generation to generation. It's another thing to have a father who was a CEO and a self-made billionaire. The personality it takes to amass that kind of wealth tends toward the top of the psychopathy scale."

"Like Chandler's dad James Robert II?" she asked.

"Yes, exactly," Jake said. "Have you met with Chandler?"

"No, we have an interview tomorrow," she said.

"I'm curious what you'll think of him. The way you've described Philip Townsend is not how I would expect sociopaths to behave. Of course, people who suffer from antisocial personality disorder are highly manipulative and can hide in plain sight. Did you notice any arrogance, hostility, or aggression when you asked the questions?"

"He seemed scared and exhausted. I don't think he was lying about not sleeping for a while. He had dark circles under his eyes and looked like he hadn't showered in days. Waves of nerves were rolling off of him."

"A sociopath would have a hard time creating or mimicking those emotions. He could act them out but you as a witness would get flashes of something else behind the façade. You're a keen observer. When you sat in a room with him did bells go off?"

"Yes, but not those kinds of bells. How many sociopaths have you encountered?" Harri asked punching him gently.

She knew that he'd met one too many serial killers in his former job as an FBI profiler. He had assisted police departments in their search for unusual suspects and also studied their minds after they were caught.

"Too many. You feel something is off?" Jake asked.

"What are some of the things I should be looking for?" Harri asked.

"Sociopaths have a sense of superiority and arrogance. They're very charming and they use it as a weapon to disarm you. They tend to be disrespectful to others, they lie, and they're impulsive. They can become hostile when things don't go their way, and they don't fear consequences like we do."

"Chandler could be a good candidate because of the kind of family he comes from. Lucas as well," Harri said as she got up and put her dishes in the sink.

"His background speaks more strongly of that than Philip Townsend."

"But Philip's father is in jail for murder," Harri said,

"For manslaughter. His father killing a clerk during a robbery is a crime of opportunity. It's horrible and someone died, but it's not calculated and it's not an end to itself."

Harri sat down next to Jake. "Can't psychopaths kill if the feeling comes upon them? They don't need to necessarily have a grand master plan?"

"Oh absolutely. 'Cuz I felt like it' is what they always say. Many of the psychopaths I interviewed felt like killing women, so they did. I would say more than half of the murders were crimes of opportunity versus an elaborate scheme. Philip Townsend's behavior tells me there is something else going on there, though. He's worried. He's scared. He shows emotion. I'm not seeing the classic traits of a psychopath. Unless he's a master manipulator, of course, but the dark circles under the eyes lead me to think not. You do know that when innocent people are questioned, they tend to be a lot more nervous than when guilty people are?"

"I've taken some classes at Quantico too, you know," Harri reminded him with a smile.

They had finished their meal, and all Harri wanted to do was sleep.

"I think I gotta hit the sack," she said.

"Right behind you," Jake said.

"What about the dishes? The kitchen?"

"By the time you get out of the shower, I'll be done," Jake said.

"Let's talk about what neighborhood we want to move to tomorrow?"

"Tomorrow," Jake said.

20

DAY 9 - DECEMBER 7, 2018

Philip Townsend had called and texted both Lucas and Chandler throughout the night. When he heard nothing back, he took four shots of vodka and fell into the quiet black sleep of a drunken stupor. He didn't wake up until the next morning on his couch with drool all over his fancy pillow.

He rolled over and checked his phone for any missed calls. His heart jumped into his throat when he saw no one had called or messaged him back.

They'd never ignored him like this before. They were both always responsive, at least getting back to him with a text. Had Lucas told the police about his seeing Miles Davidson that night? The cops would have shown him crime scene pictures when they questioned him if Lucas had, right? Philip didn't know. He only knew what he saw on crime shows and he was smart enough to know that was mostly fake or exaggerated.

Why did he have the distinct impression the police had discovered he'd been there that night? Had they gone back and checked the security tapes like he'd told them? Or had Lucas said something? And Lucas and Chandler were thick as thieves. Lucas must've told Chandler and now both of them were ghosting him.

Where was Jasper in all of this?

Jasper was an old friend Lucas knew from New Jersey. He'd already come to Los Angeles a year before they'd arrived. Lucas had called him the moment they were in town, and Jasper was the one who introduced them to the first movie people. But he wasn't one of the brothers. He hadn't been Sigma Phi. Neither had he ever been particularly close to Philip.

Philip sighed and accepted what was happening. Lucas couldn't resist telling everyone his little piece of gossip. He was sure of it. He was sure Jasper was divesting from his fund too. He was out like Chandler and Lucas were out. Philip expected to be getting the paperwork from all three of them any minute.

Philip had known this day would someday come. He'd always known it was a matter of time before these guys dumped him and clawed back the funds, he'd managed for them. That's one of the reasons Philip had hustled to secure more investors, but even six years later Lucas and Chandler were still his biggest whales and made up nearly forty percent of his fund.

Things were falling apart all around him. Two of his friends were dead. The other two guys he'd assumed were his friends were ghosting him, and he was about to lose more than a third of his fund.

He fumbled around his coffee table until he unearthed his laptop under a pizza box. They were both cowards. He knew they wouldn't tell him themselves. They'd get their lackeys to do it for them.

Sure enough, as soon as he opened his email, he had notices from attorneys representing both Lucas and

Chandler. He scanned the emails and downloaded the attachments. They'd given him twenty-four hours to transfer the management of both portfolios to the attorneys.

Philip chuckled. That wasn't the safest way to divest from his fund, but if it's what they wanted. He leaned back on the couch and let out a long sigh. Then he noticed a thought in the back of his mind.

What a relief. Won't it be nice to not have to pretend anymore? To not have to put up with Lucas Reinhart who had the personality and life skills of a spoiled teenage girl? And Chandler. God, won't it be nice to not have to be constantly appeasing him? To not have to constantly be cheering on all his absurdities and assuring him he's brilliant?

Philip sighed again. All the gains he'd made them over the last five years didn't count for shit. He'd known somewhere in the deep back of his mind these guys would never be loyal to him. They could never be. They didn't even really know who he was.

And just like that, he lost a ton of revenue. They had both entrusted him with hundreds of millions. He only took twenty percent of the profit and never charged his client's fees. His trust still had over a hundred million, so he wasn't crying. It was the disloyalty. It was the damage control he'd have to do to retain the rest of his clients and rebuild.

He closed the laptop and looked over at the mantel-piece and all his vintage cameras. He still hadn't opened the second envelope he'd received the day Tanner died. He'd put on a pair of ski gloves and retrieved it from the patio. He was tempted to open it and see if there was a photo of Tanner inside, but he'd resisted and thrown it in his desk drawer, praying it would evaporate into thin air.

He groaned as he stood up and limped to his study. The photo was still in that drawer. He yanked the drawer open, put on the ski gloves again, and pulled out the envelope. He fumbled trying to get it open and then gave up. He threw it down in disgust and ripped the envelope open with his bare hands.

He shook it out, and the freshly developed photo slid out, the smell of developer wafting into his nose.

Philip forced himself to look at the photo.

Tanner Asperson screamed back at him, his naked body inside a dog cage, his eyes missing, and the sockets bloodied. He put the ski glove back on and flipped the photo over.

On the other side, 'keep all of your fame' was written in black marker. It was exactly like the other photo.

Bile rose in his throat as the image of Tanner screaming filled his mind. He ran to the bathroom and heaved until there was nothing left to come out.

Philip cleaned himself up and after gulping two glasses of water and having a piece of dry toast, he swore he'd pull it together. First, he had a phone call to make.

He sat down on the couch and called his mom. The moment her voice came through the line, he couldn't help but smile. He'd bought her a condo on the beach in Florida and she was so happy now. He had set her up with an active but low-risk portfolio, so she didn't have to work ever again. She enjoyed spending her days playing bridge and golfing with all her buddies.

"Philip, is that you? I've been so worried about you. I saw that your two friends have been killed. What's going on out there?" she demanded.

"Hey, mom. I'm not in the best shape. I'm scared and I'm not sleeping," he confessed.

"Come here! I'll take care of you," she said.

"I can't leave town now."

"Why? Are the cops sniffing around?"

"Yes."

"Did they find out about your Dad?" she asked.

"I don't know."

There was a silence on the other end.

"Do you have anything to hide?"

"No. I've done nothing wrong," he said.

His breathing had calmed, and it was comforting to hear her voice.

"Then you have nothing to fear."

"What if the police find out about dad?" he asked.

"Who cares? That man only knew you for two years. You are nothing like him," she said.

"But it looks bad that my dad was a murderer and now two of my best friends have been killed," he said.

"That's neither here nor there," she said. "Why in the world would they think you could kill your friends?"

"Miles asked me for a loan. His gambling went too far. He lost all of his clients' money."

"Oh, Lord." Sheila Townsend swore under her breath. "All that money and education. What a waste. That boy was given everything on a silver platter and all he ever did was spit on it. I hope you were smart enough not to give him anything."

She'd known Miles since they were nineteen and Philip had told her about the gambling problem a lot of his frat brothers had developed in their sophomore year. Philip had always been a scholarship kid and had no time for that kind of nonsense. He had no cash to waste, no matter how tempting their tales of fast, easy money were.

"No, I didn't give him anything. He was furious when I turned him down, but I don't know what he was thinking. He was desperate. Unfortunately, that was the same night he died."

"Oh honey, I'm so sorry to hear that." Sheila Townsend meant what she said, and Philip knew it.

"But you did the right thing, son. You've always been such a good guy. You've always been a good friend to Miles. And to Tanner, too. You've been good to all of those boys. You lift your chin up. If there's a mess you gotta get out of, then get out of it."

"I will, Mom." Philip nodded into the phone.

"You're smart, and you've come so far, honey. I believe in you. Remember what you've built with your bare hands," she reminded him.

"I love you, mom," he said.

"I love you too, honey. I believe in you. You can do this," she said.

"Thanks, mom. I love you, too," he said and got off the phone.

He closed his eyes and took several deep breaths.

She was right. He had done nothing wrong and he would not get railroaded by circumstantial evidence into being arrested.

His mother had taken him once a month to visit his father in prison. At first, she wanted to shield her son from the unpleasantness, but his father convinced her to bring him when he was old enough so that he could see the consequences of his father's choices.

His father was full of regret for his life choices and where they'd landed him. He was serving a life sentence for the life he'd taken. The robbery had gone bad, the gun had gone off, and he'd only gotten away with less than $200. His father had told him everything once he was in junior high and old enough to understand.

As he grew older, he understood more of what his father was trying to say. Don't take the easy way out. Do the right thing. Have integrity. Work hard, find a way, and don't let the bastards get you down.

No, he would not go to jail because he was innocent. The police might not believe that yet, but he would prove it to them by finding out who was killing his friends and trying to frame him for it. The photographs had to be a frame-up. Right?

He still had no idea how the Hasselblad had gone missing, but it was part of the plan, he was sure of it. His camera, with his fingerprints, would be left in some incriminating place. The photos would be found and all this evidence would trace back to him. That was the killer's plan. He wasn't next on the list; he was the last. He was the guy the killer would leave holding the bag before he threw him under a bus.

Philip had no way of knowing how much time he had to figure out what was going on. He thought back to Nicholas' question. How did the killer know he'd been at Miles Davidson's house? How did the killer know who Philip was? How did he know where Philip lived? Philip had no idea, but he knew he wouldn't be killed. His role was to take the blame.

Not if he could help it, he thought. Feeling better than he had since he'd spoken to Miles that night, he took a shower and decided he would go on a run to clear his head. He'd get a decent lunch, arrange the transfer of Lucas' and Chandler's portfolios, and then get down to the business of figuring out who'd killed Miles and Tanner and was trying to frame him for it.

.   .   .

When he stepped out of his front door, he inhaled deeply and secured the alarm behind him. He felt almost like a new man. He decided he'd take his favorite route toward Montana.

As he jogged down his street, he noticed a car parked at the very end of his block with someone sitting inside. His neighborhood was exclusive and there weren't that many people who parked on the street because everybody had multiple car garages.

Could it be a cop?

The car didn't look like it belonged in the neighborhood, either. It was a black, domestic sedan. Most vehicles in the neighborhood were foreign or flashy, except for the electric and hybrids.

If he wasn't so paranoid already, he might not have noticed the car or the person sitting inside. But he was on high alert. The cops had been there the day before interviewing him. Now, he was certain the LAPD was watching him.

Well, let them. They could look over his shoulder at every damn thing he did. They weren't going to stop him though. He had a purpose now. All he had to do was find the real killer and clear his name or die trying.

21

DAY 9

Harri and Tom checked into the PAB and found that Tanner Asperson's autopsy would be at four o'clock that afternoon. They had just enough time to go to the Malibu Beach Club and interview its president, Lewis Delmar, who had returned Harri's call that morning and agreed to meet with them. They would check in with the surveillance team at Philip Townsend's to see how the night had gone on the way to Malibu. They called the officer when they were several blocks away and he drove to meet them.

"How did our boy do last night?" Tom asked through the open window.

"Didn't leave the house," Officer Fernandez said. "I saw him in the kitchen this morning and he looked like hell. He did go for a morning jog and came back about an hour later."

"Thank you, Officer Fernandez. We should be relieving you around nine o'clock tonight," Tom said.

"Great, bring me tacos from Juan's."

"You got it." Harri laughed.

"Thank you, Detectives," Officer Fernandez said and drove off.

"We have a good forty-five minutes to get to the Malibu Beach Club," Tom said. It was still only nine-thirty in the morning.

"We should make it there with time to spare," Harri said. "If we take San Vicente down to Pacific, we can use that bridge to get down to PCH."

"Show me," Tom said and Harri directed him through the winding, tree-lined streets to San Vicente and then toward the Pacific Park and onto the bridge that brought them down to PCH. After spending so much time in the neighborhood, it was really growing on her. She saw people walking their dogs and a few women with children in strollers, but otherwise, it was quiet and peaceful.

They had another fifteen-minute drive until they pulled up to the guard gate at the Malibu Beach Club. Tom showed the guard his credentials, and he waved them through.

Apparently, people didn't go to the beach club this early in the morning because the parking lot was empty. They found a space close to the front entrance and parked.

The main clubhouse didn't look much different than the Annenberg Beach House which was down the road from this place. Of course, the Annenberg was open to the public and people only had to pay to park.

This beach club supposedly had a waitlist years-long and people left memberships in their wills. Past the main building, Harri could see the beach, a seating area, and a large pool.

The main clubhouse was an English-style manor house cut from some sort of stone that looked as if it belonged in the English countryside. It was also surrounded by palm trees. A strange style usually only seen in Southern California and sometimes coastal Florida.

"Palm trees don't fit the look," Harri remarked.

"Isn't it weird how rich people can have such bad taste?" Tom asked as they stepped inside the cooled lobby.

An unsmiling woman sat behind the front desk.

"Lewis Delmar is expecting us," Tom said.

"Of course, Detectives. He told me you were coming," she said. "Please follow me."

She took them down a plush, carpeted hallway into a large office. Lewis Delmar, a man in his seventies with close-cropped white hair and wearing a pink polo shirt with the collar up sat behind an oversized, antique desk.

Harri had done quick research on him that morning and found out he was primarily a Southern California real estate magnate.

"Thank you for seeing us at such short notice, Mr. Delmar," Tom said.

"I'm happy to assist you in any way. The deaths of Miles Davidson and Tanner Asperson have been an absolute shock to our community. We've never had this kind of tragedy here at the club in all of its hundred years of being in operation."

"Did you know Miles Davidson very well?" Harri asked as she sat in one of the chairs in front of the desk. Tom sat in the chair next to her.

"No, I didn't know Miles very well. I did know Tanner Asperson. Our legacy members vouched for both of them. Tanner and I had dinner together several times. I liked him. He was a real go-getter. Miles Davidson was part of their group of friends too, I believe," Lewis Delmar said.

"Which members?" Harri asked.

"Lucas Reinhart and Chandler Robert. Those are the kind of members we have in this club. It's a family thing, you understand. They vouched for both Mr. Davidson and Mr. Asperson."

"Is Philip Townsend a member here?" Harri asked.

"Oh yes, of course. Mr. Townsend is a new member, only joined last year. He was a bit of a wildcard, but Lucas Reinhart pushed for him and we campaigned to approve him," Lewis said.

"Lucas Reinhart and Chandler Robert have influence in this club?" Tom asked.

"I wouldn't say a lot of influence, but they're special members. Young, single, from very good families. That's the history of the club. This is a place where our members can mingle with their own and be comfortable. Our mission is to make everyone feel accepted and at ease."

Harri wondered where in the world people like Lucas Reinhart and Chandler James Robert III would not be accepted or feel at ease? Prison, maybe?

"And what is your membership fee?" Harri asked.

It really didn't have anything to do with the case, but she was curious.

"The initial buy-in is half a million. Every year after it's $250 for club privileges renewal," Lewis said.

"$250?" Harri asked.

"No," Lewis shook his head awkwardly. "$250,000 per year. This beach club is one of the oldest in town. Membership is often bequeathed."

"Did you know of any issues that Tanner and Miles

THE NIGHT BLINDER

had with any other members in the last several months?" Tom asked.

"Are you speaking specifically of member complaints?" Lewis asked.

"Complaints, or something you've seen," Tom said.

"Nothing like that. There was a kerfuffle over some memberships but that was between members. It was more of a discussion really about the future of our member base here at the club. What kind of people we want to share the facilities with, that sort of thing," Lewis explained.

"Were you at the membership meeting?" Harri asked.

"I was." Lewis nodded his head.

"Was that the last time you saw either Miles or Tanner?" Tom asked.

"Yes, it was. We had quite a heated discussion over to whom we should grant the remaining memberships available for the year," he said. "How did you know about the meeting?"

"Lucas Reinhart informed us," Tom said.

"I see. Yes, that was the last time I saw either of them. I didn't have time to go to the CAA gathering the other night. As far as their using the club, I checked our records and neither of them checked into our facilities since that Monday," Lewis said.

"We've been putting together a timeline for both men. How serious was this kerfuffle as you put it? Did either of them make an enemy that day?" Tom asked. "I know this is a private business, but two men are dead."

Lewis looked at Tom and then at Harri. He leaned towards them.

"It was to give membership to three people. As you may well know, Silicon Valley has started invading the beach

cities. Some are very welcoming to that crowd. Venice Beach is now called Silicon Beach. However, some of us are not pleased about this invasion. Three of those newly minted millionaire tech boys were hoping to get membership into the club. There were some very strong objections."

"Why?" Harri asked.

Lewis Delmar hesitated before answering. Finally, he bit his lower lip and said, "It goes to character, Detective. This is an old establishment. It has a purpose in the community. It takes a certain level of assets to buy in, of course, but it's not about wealth and status. It's about a way of life. It's about continuing the traditions of the generations that went before us. It's about creating long-lasting relationships that continue for generations. Do you understand?"

"So, new money scares you," Harri said.

"No." Lewis shook his head. "No, not always. We welcome new members who can provide a value add. We want new members who are in alignment with our values, who have the education and background that sustain our legacy. These people who've amassed quick fortunes through technology may be brilliant, but...I mean a few of them don't even have university degrees. Some of them have never traveled abroad. It's obvious they simply want to break into our community to gain clients or instant legitimacy, or what have you."

"Were Miles and Tanner on the side of wanting them here or not?"

"Miles and Tanner were on the side that barred the membership. And they were able to convince the others to join them," he said. "Although, I'm pleased it happened the way it did."

"Do your other members know that Miles and Tanner

were the ones that led the vote against letting the new people in?" Harri asked.

"Our board meetings are strictly confidential, and I would hope that none of our membership committee members would have spoken to these three candidates. However, of course, I cannot control what other people do," he said.

"Would you be able to give us the names of those three candidates?" Harri asked.

"The membership meetings are supposed to be confidential," Lewis reiterated.

"Two men have died in the last week and they both were in that meeting," Harri reminded him.

Lewis Delmar stared out the window.

"I'm an old man," he said. "I don't understand what this world is coming to anymore."

He didn't say another word. Instead, he pushed a paper toward them. It had three names on it. Ellard Menon, Ethan Hunter, Myron Linson.

Tom wrote them down and nodded to her. They had gotten what they came for.

"Thank you very much Mr. Delmar for your time and attention," Tom said. "I recognize you did not have to do this."

"It's such a tragedy," he said, and his face grew redder.

"We'll see ourselves out," Tom said.

"Enjoy your day, Detectives," Lewis said. "One never knows when it could be their last."

It was time to go. Harri and Tom left Lewis staring out at the ocean.

Thankfully, no one came to escort them out the door as Harri was feeling claustrophobic as it was.

She picked up the pace and didn't relax until they were out in the fresh ocean breeze.

"What was that about?" she asked when they got back into the car. "Not wanting Silicon Beach to invade their club."

"It's the oldest rivalry in the world. New money against old money," Tom said with a grin.

"Doesn't money always stick together?" Harri asked.

"People murder each other over ego and money. This has both," Tom said. "Looks like we have three more people to add to our list."

Tom clicked the car doors open, and they got in.

"Who would kill two men because they didn't let him into an exclusive beach club?" Harri said.

"Everyone has triggers. And we need to do our due diligence. If we really are zeroing in on Philip Townsend, then we need to make sure there are no other potential suspects."

"Ethan Hunter might be hard to get to," Harri said. "Did you see his profile in Wired?"

"I don't read Wired," Tom said.

"Well, Jake does. That's where I first saw anything about him. The only reason I looked him up was that he was at the CAA party and Harold Walters pointed him out to me."

"Which means he saw Tanner the night before he died," Tom finished.

"We can put him on the list after Chandler," Harri said.

"We have the autopsy remember," Tom reminded her.

"We can try to interview him tomorrow then," Harri said.

"Sounds good. We should be able to get back downtown and fill out the paperwork for this interview before the autopsy. Are we waiting on anyone else to get back to us?" Tom asked as he started the car.

"Waiting for callbacks from Cornell University and Hotchkins school. I'm trying to get some background information on Philip Townsend."

"And what about this Jasper Sanders," Tom said. "I've seen his name in the notes, but he seems to have fallen off the radar."

"We should interview him, too. He was at the CAA party, but he wasn't one of the original group. He didn't go to Cornell. He was out here at USC. He seems to be connected to Lucas Reinhart," she said.

"You're thinking the reason for this crime is extending back to their college days?" Tom asked.

"I'm stuck on that missing pinky ring from Tanner Asperson. I think it might have had a Greek symbol, for their frat. Could the murders have something to do with the fraternity?" she wondered aloud.

"Bit of a stretch. That was so long ago," he said.

"I don't know, Tom. You hear so many stories about hazing gone wrong. It's the first thing that jumped to my mind when I noticed all the guys were in a frat house together," she said.

"It's a theory," he said.

He didn't sound convinced, so she let it go. There might have been another reason for the signet ring going missing.

A ring was an easy trophy to take though, she thought.

22

DAY 9

Philip Townsend hopped into a hot shower after his long run. The stress his body had been storing had nearly dissipated. As he toweled off, exhaustion came over him. He collapsed on the bed and fell fast asleep.

When he awoke, Philip felt more refreshed than he had since this horrible business began. He could finally think straight.

He dressed in his favorite soft button-down shirt and comfortable shorts. He didn't want to put on his t-shirt and sweatpants to plunge him back into the depression he'd been fighting all week.

He padded downstairs and went straight to his study and the two photos the killer had sent him. He flipped over the first one and read the phrase again.

'Keep all of your fortunes and keep all of your fame.'

He typed the phrase into the browser and hit search. The first result was lyrics by Al Jolson to a song called 'I'm on Top of the World'.

A far memory floated to the fringes of his brain. He

opened his Spotify app and typed in the song name. There were several entries, but only the first one was by Al Jolson. He clicked play and sat back in his chair.

The old song played, and the hair stood up on the back of his neck. Of course, he knew that song. It was playing on that awful night.

Holy shit, Philip couldn't believe this was actually happening. It had taken him days to find an all-white tuxedo, but Lucas insisted there was no way that he could get around without wearing one. He and Lucas had gone down to Ithaca commons to a tuxedo store, and the owner knew exactly what they were looking for, and why. The Sigma Phi all-white party was famous around Cornell, partly because of the exclusivity, partly because of the stories about what went on that became legend and lore.

He would finally find out if he'd been chosen for the frat. And Amber Lila, the girl he'd been crushing on would be there. Her sorority had been chosen as their escorts for this year. Every year the top sororities competed to join them at the annual event. After the girls left, the final initiation would happen and the next morning either he would be Sigma Phi or not.

"Are you ready yet?" Lucas asked.

Philip had been trying to tie the knot on his white bow tie.

"I wish he'd just given us clip-ons," he said.

"Clip-ons." Lucas snorted a laugh. "Leave it then. It doesn't have to be perfect."

"We're walking there, right?" Philip asked.

Chandler had talked about getting a car, but they all lived on West campus and Sigma Phi was not up Lib slope. The frat house was only a short walk away, and they didn't need a car.

The gang was going together: Lucas, Chandler, Tanner, Miles, and himself.

Philip took Lucas's advice and left the bow-tie pieces draped around his neck.

"I'm ready," Philip said.

"Finally," Lucas said.

They left their dorm room and found the rest of the guys waiting outside. Philip noticed the excitement on his friends' faces. None of them appeared doubtful or apprehensive in any way. He was. Philip was always acutely aware he was different than his friends. He didn't have a trust fund. He was on scholarship and had been even in prep school. They were shoo-ins, but Philip wasn't. Whatever he achieved, he'd had to work for. Whatever connections he made, he had to maintain. Whatever opportunities came his way, he had to take.

"Anyone's Patsy still left?" Chandler asked.

The older Sigma Phi brothers had come up with another terrible hazing game for this year. All of the pledges had been instructed to find a guy who would never be let into Sigma Phi and convince him that he could be and get him to pledge. Whoever's Patsy was left by the end of the night would be crowned king. Philip had chosen a guy named Billy but had told him what was going on after the first night of humiliation they'd all endured. He didn't want Billy going through it for no reason. Billy had been pissed to find out it was all a humiliation game and quit the same day, right after Philip had given him a free portfolio evaluation and shown him how he could increase his gains by over thirty percent by repositioning his investments.

His friends hadn't been as kind to their pledges and last Philip had heard, Chandler's Patsy was the only one left. Chandler was determined to be crowned freshman king. He had convinced his roommate, a guy named Danny Sadowski, to pledge.

"Mine quit a week ago," Philip said.

"They all dropped out this week," Tanner said.

"Not mine," Chandler gloated.

"What is it with you wanting to be king?" Miles muttered in irritation.

"Because I am the king," Chandler said with a wink.

They had reached the frat house in minutes. Jazz music played from inside the old home that was lit with twinkle lights outside. Sports cars lined up in front of the entrance and beautiful girls wearing white gowns streamed in.

"Holy shit," Philip said under his breath.

Lucas had a grin on his face while Miles jumped up and down in excitement.

"I am so ready for this," he said.

Chandler grinned and led them all in.

The party was going off. The place had been restored to its original glory years before and this night was decorated with party lanterns, bunting, and banners welcoming the rushes. There was a jazz band playing at the end of the grand hall. Servers bearing silver trays of champagne and appetizers weaved through the crowd and dancing couples. Philip had only seen these kinds of parties in the movies.

He grabbed a champagne flute off one of the passing trays and swallowed the alcohol in one fell swoop. His hands shook slightly as he put the empty glass down and grabbed another flute. He needed to fortify himself for this.

Philip pulled himself out of his reverie of that long-ago time. He didn't want to remember exactly what happened, nor could he really.

He remembered talking and making out with Amber

Lila, the girl he was madly in love with and ended up dating for that freshman year. She left with the other girls around midnight and that's when it all went downhill.

He'd drunk a lot and hadn't eaten enough. He could barely keep himself on his feet. The rest of the night was somewhat of a blur. He remembered Chandler being crowned king.

Philip had a fuzzy memory pulling Danny Sadowski aside and telling him it was all a joke. Danny told him to go to hell. Philip tried to convince him that he needed to leave. Danny had responded by swinging a punch at him. Danny was drunk, too. The punch didn't connect, and Lucas had pulled Philip away from him. Philip had blacked out after that and didn't remember a thing.

No one mentioned what happened that night again. Philip had been sick all the next day. They had all become brothers of Sigma Phi. Except for Danny Sadowski. Then midterms came and he and Amber Lila got closer and he forgot about Danny Sadowski and what his friends might have done to him.

Philip had no idea what happened to Danny Sadowski after he swung at him. Danny Sadowski disappeared, and the only thing Chandler ever said about him was that he couldn't hack school and had dropped out.

Philip remembered that Danny was a lot like him. He was a scholarship kid with ambition and drive, and the smarts to get where he wanted to go. He was a nice guy and Philip remembered how horrible he'd felt in the weeks after the party.

The guilt gnawing at him made Philip want to drop out of the frat, but Lucas Reinhart told him he was a fool for even thinking of it. He lucked out in being invited to pledge in the first place. Philip consoled himself by saying how drunk he was.

But in the back of his mind, he knew he could've done more. If only he hadn't passed out. If only Danny had listened to him. He'd blocked that whole time out of his mind and focused on his girlfriend and his studies. Then the next year, Amber Lila had met someone else and the gambling started and then school got really hard and Philip forgot all about Danny Sadowski.

That was his name.

Sadowski.

Could that be why Miles and Tanner were dead? Could whatever had happened that night be coming back to haunt them?

Kill them?

He closed his eyes again and tried to remember.

Were Miles and Tanner part of that?

Chandler had been the one who invited Danny to be a pledge.

So why did Miles Davidson and Tanner Asperson die first?

And why was he getting their death photos?

He didn't remember a thing.

Could he have participated in something he didn't remember? Could Chandler and Lucas also be involved?

Would they get themselves involved in that kind of scheme?

No. They would hire people to do it for them.

What if Danny Sadowski had proof or evidence of what they'd done to him and was about to go public with it? Would Chandler and Lucas hire goons to get rid of anyone who had participated in whatever had happened?

No. Philip wouldn't put it past either of them to hire hitmen, but then why weren't other brothers of Sigma Phi dropping dead?

Whatever it was, Philip had to figure out what happened that night and he was running out of time. He couldn't trust any of the guys to tell him the truth. Did Jasper know anything? He hadn't been there that night.

He'd never trusted Chandler.

And Lucas? What about Lucas?

They'd been roommates.

Business partners.

Philip fell back in his chair. Lucas was like Chandler. They never experienced the consequences of their actions. He couldn't trust Lucas, either. Not after he'd told the cops about his being at Miles' house the night he died. Not after they'd all just ghosted him.

He was truly alone. What kind of life had he been leading to have friends as duplicitous as these?

"Stop it," he said aloud to the quiet room. He was smart enough to get out of this. He would find Danny and get the story from him.

He was not his father.

Philip had done nothing wrong and he would make sure that everyone knew it.

He opened up a new tab on his browser and got to work.

23

DAY 9

Chandler Robert's home was the grandest of them all. He lived in Brentwood, off Saltair Avenue which ran above the hills of Santa Monica. It was a massive French Normandy manor home in an L-shaped pattern. The main house had three floors with a gabled roof. The grounds were immaculately kept, and the drive sloped through an orange grove to the main house. As they drove past a five-car garage Harri saw a new Tesla parked next to a vintage Maserati.

"How much do you think this one went for?" Harri asked.

"In this neighborhood? I'm thinking close to thirty million probably," Tom said. "This case has brought out the real estate agent in me. What is with these houses? Should we care how much they cost? That such wealth exists while people in this same city live in tents? People kill each other whether they're destitute or rich as Croesus. They all have the same reasons for doing it."

"True on all counts. Although I'm beginning to

wonder if this case isn't entirely about wealth and status," Harri said.

The doorbell was answered by a woman in her fifties in a maid's uniform.

"May I help you?" she asked.

"We're here to see Mr. Chandler Robert," Tom said.

"And who is calling?" she asked.

"LAPD Detective Tom Bards and Detective Harriet Harper," Tom said.

They pulled out their credentials and she peered at them closely reading the names.

"I'll go get Mr. Chandler now," she said.

She closed the door and they looked at each other as the sound of her footsteps faded. They stood at the door for another five minutes before it opened again.

The man himself opened the door this time. Chandler was shorter than his friends. Harri guessed he couldn't have been taller than five feet, seven inches. He sported wild, curly blonde hair and piercing blue eyes behind tortoiseshell glasses. He wore a vintage zip-down Fila tennis jacket in blazing orange. The jacket was only zipped up halfway, leaving his hairy chest exposed. He'd completed the ensemble with paint-encrusted chino pants rolled to his calves, showing his slim, tan ankles and bare feet.

Ethan Hunter stood right behind him. This was a surprise, Harri thought. Were they going to get two for one today?

"It was brilliant chatting with you, Chandler. I'll reach out," Ethan said and stepped past the two detectives.

Harri was about to call out to him, to set an appointment for an interview when Tom shook his head. She kept her mouth shut and focused back on Chandler.

"We need to ask you some questions," Tom said and showed Chandler his credentials again.

"I know who you are, Detective Bards. My housekeeper told me you were at the door. You can come in," he said and turned his back on them and walked to a room to his right.

Harri closed the door behind her and they followed him into a large sitting room featuring French doors with a view of a manicured lawn. From the outside, Chandler's home looked like a traditional, French Normandy estate. Once Harri was inside, she realized his wild taste in clothing extended to the home's interiors.

A red-lacquered grand piano was staged in the corner and two bright green Chesterfield sofas centered around a clear Lucite coffee table. Harri glanced around and noted what appeared to be authentic Roy Lichtenstein paintings on the walls and a Pac-Man arcade game in the corner opposite the piano. She glanced up at the brightly-colored glass flowers hanging from the ceiling and knew they must be original Chihuly pieces.

Chandler sat down on one of the sofas, crossed his legs, and looked up at the detectives.

"So, what is it you want?"

He was fully in control of the situation. They were going to need to change that. She sat down opposite him on the other sofa and Tom sat in a chair that Harri could only describe as a huge, fuzzy, grey ball.

Tom was tall and looked ridiculous in the chair, but he played it off as nonchalantly as he could. Chandler looked from one to the other without saying a word.

"I think you know what we want, Mr. Robert," Tom began. "We're here because we are investigating the murders of two of your associates, Miles Davidson and Tanner Asperson."

"Associates?" Chandler pouted.

"Friends, then?" Harri asked.

"That's right. I've known them both since we were still in our teens. We all went to Cornell," Chandler said.

"That's where you all met?" Harri continued.

"Yes," Chandler sighed as if he couldn't be more bored. "I mean, no. I've always known Lucas from the registry."

Harri noticed Chandler's demeanor was similar to what she observed when they'd interviewed Lucas Reinhart. He had that same, nonchalant, somewhat bored, so-above-it-all attitude. As if he wasn't being interviewed by two LAPD Robbery-Homicide detectives about the brutal murders of two of his closest friends.

"And what is that?" Harri asked.

Chandler closed his eyes for a moment as if he had to gather inner strength to continue the conversation. When he opened them again, he spoke.

"Lucas Reinhart and I are both descendants of passengers on the Mayflower. You've heard of it? Our genealogy is verified. There's a registry. It's a whole thing."

Harri copied him by closing her eyes for a moment. When she opened them again, she looked him directly in the eyes and said, "How special for you."

"Where were you on the night of November 29th?" Tom asked.

"I was here planning my annual holiday party. It's the premier event that launches the holiday season. I always hold it on the first Friday of December. I was dealing with a catering issue and had to discharge the company that was scheduled and engage another company. One that knows how to follow directions," he said.

"Did you know Miles Davidson was having money troubles?" Harri asked.

"Miles and I weren't that kind of friends. He wasn't managing any of my assets. I knew he couldn't handle himself back in college. We were in the same fraternity and he was out of control, even back then. Gamblers are weak-willed and lazy people."

"Did Miles ask you for any money?"

Chandler waved that off.

"He knew better than that. He knew that I don't give, I only lend. And Miles certainly couldn't have afforded to borrow from me, even if I would've. I don't bet on losers."

"When was the last time you spoke to Miles?" Harri asked.

"Let me see. You know, Miles and I were not as close as we'd been in the past. I relate more to Lucas and Jasper. Miles was a bit of a, shall we say, tag-along to the three of us. I'd say I saw him maybe about two weeks before his death. We all decided to go get drinks at the Bel Air Hotel and he was there. We didn't talk much, though," he said.

"What about Tanner Asperson?" Harri asked.

"What about him?

"Was he with you and the others at the Bel Air Hotel?" Harri asked.

"He was. For drinks with the guys. His job kept him busy. You know those Hollywood stars are quite demanding on his time." Chandler smirked.

He cocked his head at Harri. "Where have I seen you before?"

"There must be some perks to having a friend who manages such big names in this town?" Tom asked. "I'm sure the parties must be something else."

"I don't need Tanner to access that scene," Chandler balked.

Harri inwardly smiled.

Tom had found a sore spot.

"My party is the event of the year here in Hollywood. It always has been since I arrived. People in this town line up to kiss my ass all year long in hopes of even being considered for the fucking waitlist. My parties are where careers are made. Just getting through that door," he pointed to his front door, "is a huge accomplishment for all these little people. They think it's talent and determination that gets them anywhere in this town, but it's not. It's the connections and I'm the guy who makes those connections."

His arrogance was bursting out, Harri thought. She wanted to see how many characteristics of a sociopath Chandler exhibited. So far, he was running a ten on arrogance.

"So, when did you see Tanner last?" Harri asked, imitating Chandler's previous tone of boredom and nonchalance. She knew he wanted them to be impressed and intimidated, but she just didn't have it to give.

"I saw him the night of the CAA party. The whole gang was there. Jasper Sanders, Philip Townsend, Lucas, and myself. I mostly spent time with Lucas. Tanner was busy with his latest squeeze," Chandler said already looking bored.

Harri had seen Chandler there and remembered how he'd been surrounded by so many people. Now she knew why.

"And what did you do after the party?" Harri asked.

"I came home. I was alone and went to bed," Chandler said.

"You came home alone and went to bed," Harri said

as she wrote it in her notebook. "And what time was that?"

"I don't know." Chandler sighed. "One? Two?"

Hadn't Lucas told them Chandler left the party with a gorgeous Asian woman? Harri looked over at Tom.

"Then you don't have an alibi for the night of Tanner's murder?" Tom asked.

"And why in the world would I need an alibi?" Chandler snapped at Tom. "I definitely didn't kill Miles. I have an alibi for his death. I'm pretty sure that whoever killed Miles killed Tanner, so I don't see why you're even asking me these questions."

"Why would you believe it was the same killer?" Harri asked.

"Are you seriously asking me that?" Chandler asked. "It's all over the papers. They are all calling him The Night Blinder now. Stupid name, I think. I'd be pissed if I were him."

Aggression flashed from him. It was time to try and throw him a bit off.

"We have witnesses who saw you leaving the CAA party with an Asian woman on the night of December 5th. Why are you lying to us?" Tom asked.

That grabbed Chandler's attention. He unfolded his legs and leaned forward.

"Who told you that?" he demanded.

The nonchalant attitude was gone. Chandler now sat up straight, leaning forward, his hands on his knees. His mouth was set in a line.

"If this woman is your alibi, why won't you give us her name?" Harri asked.

"I'm not obligated to even speak to you," Chandler hissed at Harri. "You are only here because I allow you to be. I let you into my home in good faith. Obviously, that was a mistake."

"What is her name?" Harri asked again.

"It's time for you to leave," Chandler said and stood up.

His eyes had narrowed to slits and Harri could feel the hostility he directed mostly at her.

"It's unfortunate that you don't have an alibi." Harri shook her head. "We came here to cross you off our list of suspects so we can get on with this investigation."

"I have nothing else to say," Chandler said in a threatening tone laced with anger. "If you want to speak to me again, arrange it through my attorney. I'm done."

Tom and Harri both stood up to go.

"Show yourselves out," he said. "And don't even try wandering around my property. I have cameras everywhere."

He stomped off into his lush green lawn leaving Harri and Tom standing in the sitting room.

"That shook him up a bit," Harri said.

"Wonder why?" Tom chuckled.

"An affair? The lady's married?" Harri asked as they headed for the door.

"Think someone like him cares about that sort of thing?" Tom shook his head.

Harri followed Tom to the car.

"The Night Blinder is a silly name," she said. "I hadn't read that yet."

"Some blogger coined it, it caught fire on the internet and the LA Times picked up today," Tom said.

"Glad I'm not dealing with the media on this," Harri said.

"Same. Wonder what Ethan Hunter was doing here?"

"It could be a coincidence," Harri said.

"He wasn't part of the main gang, was he?" Tom asked.

"My research hasn't brought Ethan Hunter up at all," Harri said. "Although seeing as he was blocked from joining the beach club maybe he's coming to Chandler to see if he could help him out in that way. Looks like one word from him and they'd let Ethan in with arms wide open."

"These people are so strange," Tom said, and they got back into the car.

They headed back Downtown. It was time for the Tanner Asperson autopsy.

DAY 9

P hilip Townsend struck out with his search. There were very few people who matched Danny Sadowski on the internet. He'd been unable to find any social media accounts or any other mentions of the guy. The guy was a ghost.

He'd found Sadowskis on Facebook but none of them looked like they could be his family. He'd finally remembered that Danny talked about being from Braintree, Massachusetts.

Philip went looking for his old yearbooks from Cornell but couldn't find them anywhere. He'd torn through his study, his bedroom, and had even searched the boxes in the attic space to see if he could track them down, but they were nowhere to be found.

His mother still had some boxes of his with her. They had to be there. If they hadn't been stolen when his Hasselblad camera was. The thought made Philip's heart sink. If that was true, the killer had gone through his entire house. The yearbooks weren't displayed out in the open, on the mantelpiece. They were put away somewhere. The killer would've had to have gone through everything. And Philip had never noticed.

He pushed those thoughts out of his mind and decided to do a reverse people lookup search for Danny. He paid fifty dollars to see if he could find anybody with the last name of Sadowski in Braintree, Massachusetts. He finally lucked out and found a woman by the name of Gail Sadowski who still lived there. The service also provided a phone number.

Philip tried calling the number twice and nobody had picked up, not even a voicemail. It was a dead end. If Gail Sadowski was still alive and living in that house, she didn't have a landline in service.

Why would she? Everyone used cell phones for everything now. Philip ate lunch and stared out into his yard. Another memory rose in his mind and he slipped back into the past.

"Still drinking champagne?" Lucas yelled over the raucous noise the guys were making. The exclusive all-white party had come to an and. Philip hadn't been able to find Amber Lila anywhere, even though he could still taste her berry lip balm on his lips. He couldn't believe he'd finally made out with her. It had been his dream since he'd first seen her two weeks before. She was the most beautiful girl he had ever seen. He got up to walk and swayed back and forth. He was good and drunk.

"Drink this. More manly than champagne," Lucas quipped.

Philip grabbed the shot glass and threw it back. He tasted Jägermeister. Gross. He hated Jägermeister.

"Why did you give me that?" He laughed.

He started back in the direction of the open bar, but Lucas grabbed him by the shirt.

Where was his jacket?

Wasn't he wearing a jacket to this thing?

Yes, it was a tuxedo jacket and he needed to bring it back.

Christ, where did he leave it?

"Where are you going?" Lucas said and pulled him back into the main room. A bunch of guys stood around in a circle with a DJ playing loud rap music. A chanting began about someone being king and the DJ stopped playing the music. He put on that old-timey jazz song with the guy singing about how he's on top of the world.

"What's going on?" Philip asked.

"It's time. We're going to crown the freshman king," Lucas said, barely containing his glee.

The guys stood in a circle, surrounding two people. Philip tried to see what was happening, but he was having a really hard time focusing.

"Who is that?" Philip asked.

"You all have to prove to us that you're worthy of becoming our brothers," said a voice coming from somewhere to Philip's right.

"But you're my brother already, man." Philip leaned toward Lucas.

When he turned to see him, Lucas was gone.

Philip tried to steady himself. He looked around and saw a lot of the guys were walking away. Two guys stood in the middle of the room. The shorter one looked like Chandler? Who was that standing with him?

The world started spinning, and he felt himself hit the ground.

Philip started in his seat. The memory was so vivid he almost felt the pain from hitting the ground. More fragments of that night were coming back to him.

Where had all the brothers gone? Did all the freshman pledges have to do something horrible?

He searched in his memory for anything else, but it was a gaping black hole. He breathed in and out as he felt the panic rise in his throat. He tried to swallow the big lump down, but he couldn't.

Philip gulped down a glass of water.

If the water was going down, his throat wasn't closing up. This was another panic attack. He got to his feet and managed to get up the stairs to his bathroom by clutching the handrail and pulling himself forward. A hot shower might help, he thought.

Adrenaline shot into his bloodstream and his hands shook. This was going to take a while to get under control. It was turning into a bad one.

He stripped off his clothes and turned the water on so hot that he could barely stand it. Steam filled the bathroom. The water stung his skin as he sat down in the tub and rocked back and forth. Back and forth.

Back.

And.

Forth.

He was going to be okay.

He was going to be okay.

Everything would be okay.

The wave of panic crashed over his head and left him gasping for breath. Philip sat like that for a time. When he was sure the anxiety had passed, he dragged himself out of the tub, toweled off, and put on fresh clothes.

He sat on the edge of his bed and did a five-minute meditation breathing exercise. It was hard to focus, but he pushed through it. He wanted to lay on his bed and let the world drift away, but he couldn't. He knew he couldn't let himself get dragged down.

Still feeling weak, he got to his feet. He was going to beat whoever was doing this to him or die trying.

He stumbled back down the stairs to call the Sadowski household again.

This time, a man's voice answered the phone.

"Excellent. Oh, I'm so glad you picked up. I've been calling this number for the last couple of hours and I thought maybe I had the wrong number," Philip said without giving any indication of who he was or why he was calling.

"And who is this speaking?" asked the gruff man's voice on the other end.

"I'm sorry. My name is Philip Townsend, and I went to Cornell University with a guy named Danny Sadowski. I've been looking to get in touch with him and I found this number. Are you a relative of his?" Philip asked.

"What did you say your name was again?"

"Philip Townsend. We were in the same dorm together freshman year," he added helpfully.

"That's my wife's son. My name is Ruben, and my wife Gail is who you're looking to speak to. I personally have never met Danny," Ruben said.

That didn't sound good.

Was he dead?

"Something happened to Danny?" Philip asked.

"We lost touch with him. My wife isn't here to speak with you. She's in a convalescent home right now doing physical therapy after a serious car accident," he said.

"I really need to find Danny. Is there any way your wife might be able to speak to me?" Philip asked.

"Why are you looking for Danny so many years later?" Ruben demanded.

Philip heard the suspicion in the man's tone. He had

to think fast and said the first thing that popped into his head.

"I'm in AA. I'm working the program, working on the steps. I wanted to find Danny to make amends to him for something that happened in college. I know it seems like it was a long time ago, but it really affected my life and I want to tell Danny that," Philip said, trying to sound as sincere as possible.

All Philip heard on the other end was a sigh.

"I've been there," Ruben confessed. "Congratulations. It's been seven years, four months, two weeks, and one day since I had my last drink."

"Wow," Philip said, genuinely impressed. "Wow, congratulations on that. It's been one year, six months, one week, and four days for me."

He felt terrible for lying to this man, but at the same time, he needed to find Danny.

"Where are you located?" Ruben asked.

"I'm in Los Angeles. But I can fly out to Braintree tonight if you think your wife might be willing to talk to me?" Philip asked.

"Sure. I think she'd like to help you. I don't know exactly what happened between her and Danny. She does like talking about him though and I'm sure she would have no problem with me bringing you to her. Might cheer her up."

"Thank you so much, Ruben. I can't tell you how much I appreciate this," Philip said.

Ruben remained silent for a second.

"I'm happy to be able to help a fellow traveler."

Philip confirmed the address and got Ruben's cell number, promising to call when he arrived in Braintree. He hung up the phone and sat down at his laptop to book a flight that would get him to Boston by morning.

He booked the flight and reserved a car, then went upstairs to pack.

Maybe, if he got lucky, Gail Sadowski would have a picture of her son. A picture and contact info so he could find Danny and talk to him about what had happened that night. And if his friends were murdering each other because of it.

DAY 9

"All right, let's get this done," Harri said as they entered lab number two.

"Good afternoon detectives," Dr. Grimley called out as she prepared to start the autopsy on Tanner Asperson. Tanner 's naked, unwashed corpse was laying on the metal table with a sheet over his private parts. She hadn't opened the chest cavity yet or removed the top of the skull.

"Thank you for expediting this one, too," Tom said.

"I'm hoping I can give you something to catch this guy because he's working fast," Dr. Grimley said.

Harri and Tom moved over to the table and looked down at Tanner. His neck was mottled with black and blue bruises, as was the side of his cheek.

"So, I wanted to inform you that we were able to match the composition of the metallic slivers we found in the eye sockets of Miles Davidson to the ones found in Tanner's sockets. They were also 92.5% silver with 7.5% base metal copper. Both sets of eyes were scooped out with an antique silver spoon," Dr. Grimley said. "How is that for a statement?"

"A silver spoon?" Harri asked.

Dr. Grimley nodded.

"It appears so," Dr. Grimley said. "I had the techs rush the tox screen on Tanner's blood. He also had fluni- trazepam in his blood."

"Anything found on that cage?" Harri asked.

"Not so far," Dr. Grimley said. "No fingerprints, no DNA, just some carpet fibers from inside the room."

She pointed to Tanner's neck. "This appears to me as ligature strangulation. I have measured the bruising and it looks like it came from about a 2 1/2-inch object. Perhaps, a belt. Death most likely was caused by cerebral hypoxia caused by blood vessel compression going to the brain."

Dr. Grimley turned her recorder on and officially began the autopsy by stating her credentials and the date and time. As she worked, she explained everything she was doing to both Harri and Tom and for the benefit of the recording.

Dr. Grimley opened Tanner's mouth.

"I found the hematoma on the left side of his tongue," she started again. "He also has subcutaneous hemorrhages on the neck muscles on the right side and the back of the neck," she said and pointed to the bruising.

"Did you find anything under his fingernails? Did he put up a fight?" Harri asked.

"No, his fingernails were clean. The dose of the drug was too much for him to defend himself. I'm not seeing any visible indications that he put up a struggle," Dr. Grimley said.

"What about the time of death?" Tom asked.

"I've narrowed it down to between one and four in the morning. My approximation of TOD was close at the scene," Dr. Grimley said.

She opened the chest cavity and then weighed and inspected all his organs.

"This was a healthy male. I see no disease on any of these organs. His stomach appears to be empty. He hadn't eaten in the hours before his death. His blood-alcohol level was .10% which is more than legally drunk. He was incapacitated," Dr. Grimley said. "I stand by my ruling as death by ligature strangulation causing cerebral hypoxia."

"That gives us enough to work with," Harri said. "Any DNA found on Miles Davidson?"

Dr. Grimley shook her head no.

"Miles Davidson had no foreign DNA on his body. He was cleaned thoroughly. We found soap residue under his fingernails. I've taken swabs of all the usual places. I can't see how Tanner could have been cleaned once he was in the cage. We might get lucky this time in finding evidence in the home," Dr. Grimley said.

"Did he die in that cage?" Harri asked. "Or did he get stuffed in there after death?"

"The way he was positioned I'd say before death because of how difficult it is to maneuver a dead body. I'm still hoping we'll find something on that cage. He doesn't have any bruising to indicate he was shoved inside post-mortem."

The autopsy came to an end. Harri and Tom thanked Dr. Grimley and left the room.

"You did pretty good in there," Tom remarked.

"Mind over emotion, right," Harri said. She grinned at him.

"Whatever gets you through it, Harri." Tom nodded.

As they stripped out of their protective gear, Tom's phone buzzed. He read the text and grimaced.

"Richard Byrne wants an update," Tom said.

Harri walked with him out to the car.

"I'm not surprised. We've had two high-profile murders in the last week. I'm more shocked he's not all over us," Harri remarked.

"They're having a real fun time with that huge burglary ring," Tom said as they got into the car.

"Do you mind if you update him on your own?" Harri asked as he drove out of the parking lot.

"Sure, I can do that, but you need to tell me why. Outside of the obvious."

"I want to dig further into Chandler," Harri explained. "I had a conversation with Jake last night about sociopaths and he told me specific things to look for when we were interviewing him today. Mainly aggression and arrogance and some lying smattered in. He hit all three. With the kind of life he's led, I want to see if there's anything in his past we should look at. Something that might've been covered up."

"He's a wealthy dabbler in crime?" he asked.

"I don't want to make any assumptions, but guys like Chandler tend to be in the center of their peer groups. He's a leader with his minions. They do his bidding. The way he spoke about Miles and Tanner gave me the impression that he deigns to have them around, but never considered them his equal. Not like Lucas Reinhart and all that registry stuff. And did you notice how he didn't really mention Philip Townsend either? If the start of this began years ago, my money is on Chandler having been the instigator of whatever happened back then. He's that guy."

"Yeah. The shit starter. He's not a follower nor would he ever take suggestions from his minions, like you said. He likes to control and when he loses control, he throws a tantrum like he did with us. He couldn't keep it together, which makes me think he wouldn't be able to handle having his rule questioned. I agree that if we're looking at something that happened at university with these guys, then he's at the center of it."

"Then why wasn't he killed first? Why wasn't he the primary?" Harri asked.

"Maybe our killer is working up to him. Think he'd be nervous about someone coming for him? Stalking him? I didn't see it," Tom said.

"He didn't look afraid to me, either. He did mention he had cameras all over that mansion of his so maybe he thinks he's protected." Harri stopped talking for a moment. "What if he's our guy. He's our killer. What if whatever happened back then threatens his position and he's cleaning up the mess?" Harri wondered aloud.

"It's a theory. I agree his shift from uncaring to aggressive was fast. And he lied to us. And his arrogance is off the charts. But, he has an alibi for the night of Miles murder."

"He doesn't for the whole night though? I'll try to poke holes in that alibi of his," Harri said.

"That's a good enough reason not to go and get chewed out by Richard," Tom said.

"I think so," Harri grinned. "I can't believe we aren't getting much from the security camera's all these people are supposed to have. They'd be shocked to see how unprotected they really are."

"We still have the uniforms looking for footage from Tanner's neighbors," Tom said. "They've been knocking on doors and people seem happy to give them what they have. I told them to give us a call as soon as they find anything out of the ordinary. That was twelve hours ago, and we still haven't gotten any updates."

"That's odd. How is this guy such a ghost?" Harri mused.

"He had a lot less time with Tanner. When there's so little time, mistakes happen. Only a matter of time before we find that mistake," Tom said.

"You're right. I'd love to be able to get ahead of him instead of constantly trailing behind. I have a bad feeling that someone else is going to die soon," Harri said.

"Yeah," Tom sighed. "He's not done. If he came for one of them, he's coming for them all."

"You're not gonna tell Richard that, are you?"

"Harri, if there's one thing I've learned about Richard in all these years is that he doesn't want anyone's opinion but his own. So, I'm only giving him the facts," Tom said.

He parked the car and they parted ways.

Harri got a cup of coffee before going back into the PAB. She kept going back to their conversation with Chandler and wondering if his tantrum was also an act. It was a small lie to tell them and he didn't necessarily look surprised that he was caught in it.

So why would he lie about going home alone after the party?

And why would he throw a tantrum?

Could it be a way of throwing them off?

Maybe he did have way more control over himself and wanted to keep that hidden. But he had an alibi for the Miles Davidson murder. If he said caterers would be able to give him that alibi, she was sure that they would.

He hadn't given them the names of the said caterers, but she'd call his lawyer to get them as soon as she got back into the office. That's what she would do first to make sure Chandler knew they were verifying his entire story. And she would puncture a hole in that alibi if she could.

26

DAY 9 - 11PM

Philip had two hours to get to the airport and he'd come up with a plan to lose his police shadows. The last thing he wanted the cops to know was that he was leaving town. Something that the big cop warned him not to do. His red-eye flight was leaving at one in the morning from LAX and no one would stop him from going. His life depended on it. His only luggage was a backpack, which included a change of clothes, his wallet, and his cell phone.

On his run earlier, he'd seen two cars parked with two men inside each. One was at one end of Marguerita Avenue and the other sat on Carlyle Avenue. He figured his best bet was to go through the rear alley and hop into his friend Marcus' backyard, then come out on 11th Street. He'd already made sure there was no surveillance on that block.

He texted Marcus on the pretext of returning some books he'd borrowed months ago. Marcus had texted back saying he wouldn't be home and to leave the books on his back porch. That was exactly what Philip was hoping he'd say.

He grabbed the two books, swung his backpack over his shoulder, and set the house alarm. He opened the back door and waited for the familiar chime. The countdown to get out started. He breathed in deeply and set off.

Philip hurried through his backyard with his heart thumping. He opened the back gate and peeked his head out. The alleyway was clear, and no cars were visible from this vantage point.

He wanted to sprint but decided if any of his neighbors saw him on their security cameras, he might look suspicious. All of Santa Monica was on edge after Tanner's murder, especially his neighborhood. Instead, he stepped out of his yard and calmly walked across the alley to the darkness of the adjacent garage.

He held his breath as he reached his arm over the top of the gate and released the latch.

The door squeaked open. He froze.

Should he look to see if anyone noticed? If he was just returning books, he wouldn't look. It was hard not to turn his head and he resisted. He stepped into Marcus' backyard and closed the gate behind him.

His heart beat wildly in his chest as he walked up the brick path to Marcus' back porch. He put the books on the bistro table next to the back door. Now, he just needed to get out of the neighborhood somehow.

Instead of going out the way he'd come, Philip went through the side yard and out the side gate. He stood in front of the gate and looked out onto the street. He hoped the cops hadn't decided to move since his jog that afternoon. He guessed the surveillance teams thought they had a good view of Marguerita and Carlyle Avenues from how they'd set up earlier in the day.

He glanced up and down the street but didn't see anything out of the ordinary. He wished he'd parked his car away from his home. But he hadn't figured out a way he could drive his car somewhere and then come back without it. He was sure they would have noticed that, and he didn't want anything generating suspicion.

Philip decided he would call for a rideshare to pick him up at Marcus' house. He could wait in the side yard and pretend like he was leaving out the side gate when the ride arrived. He made the call.

He watched on the app as the car took a right off of Montana and headed in his direction. The app said it would be there in three minutes. The white Toyota Camry arrived in two.

Philip nonchalantly came out of the side yard and waved at the driver. He got into the backseat and told the young woman he was going to LAX. She pulled out and took a left on Marguerita Avenue.

He saw no cars following them.

No cop cars pulled them over.

No sirens followed them out of the neighborhood.

He'd made it.

He'd successfully evaded his shadows.

He'd been able to execute this leg of the trip without a hitch, at least.

Philip had set the interior and exterior lights at his house on timers to shut off and on with the time of day. Computers could do an amazing job of pretending someone was home if they were programmed right. He hoped the cops wouldn't figure it out. How could they if they were just sitting in cars and watching from the street?

Santa Monica flashed by as they got onto Lincoln and then on to the I-10 freeway. Philip was relieved to be out of his house and away from the watchful eyes of the LAPD. Maybe he should stay in Massachusetts indefinitely, he thought.

But no, that would mean he was running away from this whole mess and he wasn't doing that. He hadn't done anything wrong and he would prove it.

27

DAY 10 -DECEMBER 8, 2018 -
MIDNIGHT

"It doesn't feel good to be right about this," Harri said as she stood next to Tom Bards in Lucas Reinhart's home. His security staff had found him in his living room and immediately called 911. The room was the site of a bloody massacre.

Blood spray had gone everywhere. The sharp metallic smell filled Harri's nostrils as she looked down at the man they had interviewed two days ago. A champagne bottle had been rammed down his throat, grotesquely deforming the head and neck. His eyes were missing like the others, and he had been zip-tied to his own dining chair.

The same Al Jolson song, "I'm Sitting on Top of the World" blared from the speakers. One of the techs finally turned it off and everyone visibly relaxed.

"No, it doesn't feel good to be right about this. I asked Richard to put details on Lucas and Chandler, but he said city resources shouldn't be used to protect people who already had an army of security available to them. Guess he was wrong," Tom said.

"Where was his security anyway?" Harri asked.

"Lucas sent them away for dinner they said. He was having a special guest over and didn't want a record of it. Told them to turn off all the cameras."

"You've got to be joking," Harri said. "He knew he was a target. You told him to be careful."

"Yeah, well," Tom sighed. "The security guy I spoke to, his name is James Aquino, said Lucas has done that before. He had a liaison with a woman who refused to be on camera and didn't want to be seen at his home. They all thought he was having an affair with some married celebrity who was paranoid about being caught."

"How long were they gone for?" Harri asked.

Tom had arrived at the scene before her and had taken the statements of both of the security guards who had found the body. Uniforms were milling around and Dr. Grimley was preparing to examine the body. She arrived right after Harri.

Harri had arrived home around eleven that night from a day researching Chandler. His alibi was solid until two a.m. the night of Miles' death. She'd failed to nullify his alibi much to her chagrin. She really thought he was good for these crimes. She'd stepped through her door and greeted Jake when she got the phone call. It had been an easy enough drive to Santa Monica, but it still took her forty-five minutes. She'd arrived there right before midnight.

"I'm sorry to have to see you guys again so soon," Dr. Grimley said.

"Likewise," Tom said.

"He wasn't very clean this time," Dr. Grimley observed.

"He didn't have enough time. We have a strict time-frame of six to ten-thirty in the evening. His guards found him at ten-thirty so that should at least help with our time of death," Tom said.

"The body is starting to cool down," Dr. Grimley said as she took Lucas Reinhart's body temperature.

"This time we have the blood splatter that we assumed we would find at the Miles Davidson scene," Harri said.

"I was thinking the same thing. However, the champagne bottle is a bit of an overkill."

She examined the large slash wound on his neck and then the stab wounds all over his chest.

"I think the throat laceration is what probably killed him, although one of these stab wounds could've gotten him in the heart around the same time and still caused this kind of spray."

Dr. Grimley peered closer at his slashed neck.

"I can see this cut was created by the same type of instrument that was used on Miles Davidson. It was extremely sharp and makes me think of a scalpel again. It's also a right-handed attacker, like with Miles Davidson."

Harri took note of the zip-ties binding Lucas to the chair. Harri walked around to his back and saw sweat staining the back of his white shirt.

"He could have been tortured in this chair too," she said. "He sweated so much that he's still wet."

"There's so much blood that it's going to be difficult to tell you right now what's been done to this body. But like the others, I'll try to get this done for you as quickly as I can. Hopefully tomorrow."

Harri turned away from Dr. Grimley and conferred with Tom.

"Have you called the detail on Philip Townsend?" she asked.

"Yes, I have. They were going to bring him in for questioning and found that he was not answering the door. I have a warrant to search his home request with a judge as we speak. He's given us the slip," Tom said.

"Are we bringing him in and charging him?" Harri asked.

She didn't think they had enough to charge him. Apparently, Tom agreed with her.

"I want to bring him in for formal questioning and search his house. The evidence we have right now is a bit weak for the search warrant. He has a motive and possible means for Miles and had seen both of the deceased before they died. Except for Lucas, of course, because we don't know yet. But no evidence has put him on any of the scenes as of right now."

"He only had three hours here. He had to leave something behind," Harri said.

"His rage got the best of him this time," Tom said. "People don't realize that stabbers usually cut themselves as they're stabbing their victims. All the blood coming out of the victim makes the weapon slippery. It's our best shot at getting DNA evidence this time."

They both looked around the room at all the blood everywhere.

"It's gonna take days to process the scene," Harri said.

"He left us something to work with this time," Tom said.

The rest of the coroner's team arrived and were helping Dr. Grimley catalog the body and prepare it for transport to the coroner's office. The crime scene techs arrived and ushered Harri and Tom out of the room.

They had been careful, wearing booties and hair protectors to make sure they didn't contaminate the scene in any way. Tom ordered the uniforms to lock down the scene outside as concerned neighbors were gathering at the gate.

The one good thing about crime scenes and rich people's homes was that no reporters could bother them. Lucas Reinhart lived in a gated community with lots of Hollywood elite and the gatekeepers were exceptionally good at keeping the media out. The uniforms wouldn't have to deal with that, at least.

Tom joined Harri out on the front lawn.

"We need to find Philip Townsend," he said.

"What about Chandler? We should protect him. Are we positive it's Philip Townsend? If we bring in the wrong guy while Chandler is being killed..." Harri trailed off.

"You don't think that Chandler is the killer anymore?" Tom asked.

"I couldn't dent his alibi for the Miles Davidson death. He's not the Night Blinder."

"Oh, you are using that name now for him?" Tom asked.

"No. I was thinking of how pissed the name would make Chandler if he was the killer. But, no. He was with four employees of the catering company until two in the morning. So, Philip Townsend then?" Harri asked.

She was having a hard time reading Tom and what he actually thought.

"The officers will keep us updated on his status. We don't have the search warrant yet for Philip's house, but he's our prime suspect right now."

"Agreed."

"We'll get the warrant and bring him in," Tom said.

"I'm with you on the questioning. I don't want to find another body tonight is all."

"I'm with you on that. But our guys can protect Chandler better than he can."

"What if he doesn't open the door to them? What then?"

"We call the security company and have them do welfare checks. He doesn't strike me as the type to turn his cameras off," Tom said.

"Or send his security detail away? What in the world was Lucas thinking?"

"He wasn't." Tom sighed. "Dumbass thought he was invincible. The teams have this crime scene covered. I called Richard Byrne on the way over here and asked for another detective from RHD. He's sending Jennifer Martinez to oversee this crime scene as we track down Philip Townsend. I tried calling Chandler while I was waiting for you, but he didn't answer. That worries me."

"Or he could be choosing not to pick up the phone," Harri reminded him. "How likely is it for the killer to strike twice tonight?

"The scene inside was frantic and unhinged. It was like a different killer in there. Gone was the meticulous control. If it wasn't for the eyes gouged out again, I'd think this was another killer entirely."

"Or his rage went so out of control that he could be shifting his timetable? Moving onto Chandler immediately?" Harri asked.

"We'll find out either way and we can go from there."

Harri thought about what Tom said as they watched an unmarked car pull up. Detective Jennifer Martinez waved at them and got out of the car.

"And our help has arrived," Tom said.

Harri walked up to her and stuck out her hand. "I don't think we've formally met. My name is Harriet Harper. Harri, for short," she said.

"Welcome to the team," Jennifer said. "I've been wanting to take you out for welcome drinks, but this burglary ring is taking up all of our time."

"I totally understand and thanks for helping out here," Harri said.

"Hi, Tom. Looks like you caught another serial then, didn't you?" Jennifer teased.

Jennifer was a full-bodied Latina woman with big brown eyes, a generous smile, and a thick mane of black hair.

"What can I say?" Tom shrugged. "Must be the law of attraction, huh?"

"I don't think that's how that works." Jennifer laughed.

They gave her the rundown of everything that was happening inside and left separately to Philip Townsend's home.

The tide had changed in their investigation. Harri could feel the adrenaline pumping through her. This case was breaking. She wasn't entirely sure how, but it was. She wasn't sure yet if Philip was their killer, but they were close to finding who was.

Hopefully, they could protect Chandler because she was sure that he was next.

28

DAY 10 - DECEMBER 8, 2018 – 2 AM

Harri and Tom arrived at Philip Townsend's house at close to two in the morning. The uniforms who'd been sitting at both ends of the street watching the house had moved their cars to the front of Philip's home. The quiet neighborhood was empty of cars passing by or people out walking their dogs, which was good for their purposes.

"How many times have you knocked on his door?" Harri asked Officer Nolan.

"Every hour, detective. He has to have the lights on a timer. The living room lights went off at eleven-thirty and the bedroom light went on eleven minutes later. We haven't seen any movement through the windows. No one answers the door and there've been no sounds from inside," Officer Nolan said.

"Did you have eyes on the rear alley?" Tom asked.

"Off and on," Officer Ramirez said. "We'd do random walk-bys as well as move the cars every hour as to not alert the neighbors. It's a quiet neighborhood. Not many cars come and go during the day. I'm not entirely sure we haven't been made."

"We had eyes on the alley most of the time on both ends. However, if he crossed through the alley to a home behind and came out on the other street, we wouldn't have seen him," Officer Nolan said.

"Thank you, officers," Harri said.

"Are we going to be here all night then?" he asked.

"We're waiting for the search warrant to come back from the judge. When that comes through, then we'll have our own team do the search. At that point, you'll be able to leave," Tom said. "Getting to the end of your shift?"

"That's correct, detective," Officer Nolan said.

"We should be getting the call in the next fifteen minutes," Harri added.

They left the officers at their cars and went up the walk to Philip's home. The lights in the bedroom were still on. Apparently, the timer had malfunctioned.

"His timer got confused and didn't turn off the light in the bedroom," Harri said.

"His cover's blown," Tom said.

"This doesn't look good for him, does it?" Harri asked more rhetorically.

"He knew we were watching him, and he evaded us. There could be different reasons for that now, but none of them look good."

They knocked on the door one last time and waited.

"Could he be home and ignoring us?" Harri asked.

"It's possible, but I doubt it. I'm sure the officers would've had some indication."

Tom's phone buzzed in his pocket. He pulled it out and read the text message.

"Warrant is on the way. They should be here in twenty minutes," he said.

Within the first hour of the search, Harri and Tom discovered envelopes with photos of Miles Davidson and Tanner Asperson in Philip's study. Another manila envelope taped to his back door had a photo of Lucas Reinhart.

The photos were gruesome.

Miles Davidson was screaming, his eyes empty sockets. On the back was written in all block letters the phrase 'keep all of your fortunes'.

Tanner Asperson was photographed screaming in the dog cage and that photo had a similar phrase on the back. It said, 'keep all of your fame'.

The manila folder which held Lucas Reinhart's photo, a similar graphic image of him right before death, had the words 'I'm quitting the blues of the world' on the back.

Harri searched each of the phrases on her smartphone and the results were lyrics to the Al Jolson song "I'm Sitting on Top of the World".

"And there's the song again."

"I'm sure he would've had it playing at Tanner Asperson's home if he hadn't been interrupted," Tom said.

"Philip Townsend collects cameras," she said.

She pointed to the mantelpiece in the living room filled with old medium format cameras.

"These photos are square, and they're hand-printed."

"A square frame doesn't always mean a medium format camera. The printer could have cropped it," Tom said.

"You've done some photography?" Harri asked.

"Some. Never hand-developed photos, though," he said.

"This photo of Lucas still smells like developer," Harri said, sniffing at the print.

"Developer?" Tom asked.

"The chemical used to develop the film. I'll bet this photo was developed in a home darkroom. You can't rent a darkroom in this city anymore. Haven't been able to in years," she said.

Tom waved over one of the crime scene techs.

"Have you found a darkroom anywhere in this home?" he asked.

"What do you mean a dark room?" the crime scene tech asked.

"The kind you develop photos in," Tom said.

"Like an editor's station?" the crime scene tech asked.

Tom shook his head and sighed. "Either you're too young or I'm too old. It would be a fully-enclosed room, with a sink, a red light, and three plastic bins. And it would smell."

"Nothing like that, Detective. This is just a house. Just bedrooms, bathrooms, a kitchen. Are we looking for a secret room?" the crime scene tech asked.

"Does this place have an attic or basement?" Tom asked.

"No, just crawlspace up there and down below," the crime scene tech answered.

"What about the garage?" Harri asked.

"It's a garage. There's no secret room in there."

"Thank you," Harri said.

The scene tech went back to work and Harri turned back to Tom.

"How did Philip get the photos developed? It's not

like he could send them out to a lab. Could he rent an apartment and have it there?" Tom asked.

"Or another idea? Was he even the one who took them?" Harri asked.

"Could he have a partner?" Tom wondered.

They'd never explored the angle of a team committing the murders. The possibility hadn't been on their radar. Only of a hit man, but even then a loner working on his own.

"These murders don't feel like a team effort. If two men were working in tandem, then why roofie the victims? They wouldn't need to, I would think," Harri said.

"Agreed," Tom said. "So, what does that mean? Philip is a person of interest, but he didn't take these photos. Unless he has a rental somewhere with a working darkroom? Why put the phrases on the back? And Philip may have already been gone when this last envelope was delivered."

"Okay." Harri nodded. "Okay, well then why leave the other two behind? Why not burn them in his fireplace or something?"

"Why didn't he bring these to us if he is innocent?"

"He was the last person to see Miles Davidson. He must have realized he would've become our prime suspect and we would go through his entire life," Harri said.

"Like we're doing right now, Harri?" Tom asked. "And he is our prime suspect."

Tom's phone rang.

He groaned when he saw who it was.

"It's Richard."

Tom answered the phone and listened. Harri heard Richard yelling on the other end of the line. She caught snippets of "disaster" and "where are you in" and "you understand who was just murdered tonight."

Harri stood quietly listening as Tom explained about the search at Philip Townsend's house and the photos they'd found. Tom told him Philip had somehow evaded their surveillance teams. Tom listened. Richard had stopped yelling and Harri couldn't hear what was being said.

"I don't think we have enough to make an arrest," Tom said.

Tom listened some more. Richard had apparently calmed down when he heard the photos had been found.

"He's a person of interest, yes," Tom said.

Finally, she heard Tom say "understood" and he hung up.

"He didn't sound happy," Harri remarked.

"He wants us to arrest Philip Townsend for all three murders. You heard me say we don't have enough, but he's insisting we bring him in. He's putting out a city-wide alert for him as a person-of-interest. He thinks the photos are trophies. I'm thinking he's getting pressure from above to make an arrest."

"If we bring him in on weak evidence, we'll just have to release him again. I'll bet he's already got an expensive defense attorney lined up," Harri said.

"Philip's not the guy. He's falling apart at the seams. He's not a psycho," Tom said.

"I agree with you. But like you said, Richard doesn't care about anyone's opinion but his own. We need facts and we're low on those. What if Philip is next on the killer's list?" Harri asked.

"Police custody could save his life then."

"It'll give us time to get the results back from Lucas

Reinhart's crime scene. We won't have to worry where Philip is," Harri said.

"We need to find him in time though," Tom said.

Harri stared at a picture of Philip Townsend and Lucas Reinhardt at the beach club. They stood next to each other in the pool, tanned, fit, smiling at the camera. Was Philip already dead somewhere? Or was he really the one who was killing all his friends? For what reason though?

Philip didn't have a clear motive for any of this. In their investigation, they still hadn't come up with any reason for Philip killing them. They hadn't uncovered the key yet.

"We still don't have the key yet," she said.

"What key?" Tom asked.

"What drives this killer to do this?"

"Feels like revenge," Tom said. "The eyes. That's some vengeful shit right there. Payback for something that happened. Something they saw? You know, each one of the crime scenes made me think of shame. The killer desecrated each of these men. And the way they were killed showed rage, but he's organized. He's not frenzied. Until tonight."

"Will all these friends die then?"

"If we don't catch him before that," Tom said.

"We will catch him," Harri said.

Tom nodded in agreement.

"Have we heard anything from the team that went to Chandler's for the welfare check?" Harri asked.

Tom shook his head no.

"Let me go call them now."

29

DAY 10 - DECEMBER 8, 2018 –
BRAINTREE, MASSACHUSETTS
MORNING

Philip's red-eye flight from LAX into Boston's Logan Airport arrived a little after seven that morning. He picked up the rental car and drove the forty-five minutes down to Braintree. The cold winter air refreshed Philip as he drove.

The sky was gray and hung low. When Philip lived on the East Coast, he'd hated these long gray days. But after living in Los Angeles for close to ten years, with its blue sky stretching on for months without a break, he welcomed the gray, the cold, and the barren trees stretching their naked branches into the sky. It fit his mood perfectly.

Gail Sadowski's husband, Ruben Miller, was to meet him at the nursing home at nine that morning. Philip had about an hour to pass before then. He pulled into a diner right outside of Braintree for breakfast. Philip smiled. The diner was reminiscent of one he used to go to in high school with his buddies. He knew exactly what would be on the menu and it was exactly what he needed.

He had eggs and toast and drank two cups of coffee

while he waited for his meeting. After his breakfast, he felt better than he had in months. Why had he stayed away from the East Coast since moving out to Los Angeles? He had no roots here any longer. His mother lived in Florida. He hadn't seen his father in years.

There was no one to come back to here, but the place felt like home, even if it was Massachusetts. It was similar enough to Connecticut to make him nostalgic. For the boy he'd been before Cornell. Before his friends had changed the course of his life.

If he survived this, maybe he would move back. He'd never lived in Boston, but if he did, he wouldn't have to wake up at the crack of dawn anymore to catch the morning market.

As the time for his meeting grew closer, Philip checked his watch and practiced what he would say in his mind. He'd mapped the drive to the convalescent home, and it was nearby.

Ruben told him that Gail Sadowski had been in a bad car accident nine months before and was in a coma for a month. She was in daily physical therapy to restore her mobility and Ruben had assured him her mind was in perfect shape.

Philip pulled the rental car up to the charming brick building with white shutters and saw a man in his sixties standing outside. He assumed that was Ruben. Philip was glad he'd showed up ten minutes early. He got out of the car and joined the man at the front steps.

"Are you Mr. Ruben Miller?" Philip asked.

"I am. You must be Philip Townsend?"

Philip shook hands with the man.

"Thank you so much for meeting with me here on a Saturday morning," Philip said.

"Sure thing. Gail doesn't know anybody here who

knew Danny back then. I think she'll enjoy talking to you about him," he said.

Philip's gut clenched with guilt. He hadn't known Danny back then. Not really. And he could very well be responsible for hurting her son. He'd gone over all of his interactions with Danny and they numbered on one hand. He'd spoken maybe ten sentences with the guy, and he hated himself for using the ruse of being in addiction recovery, but he had to get this meeting.

What kind of man was he becoming? He never believed the ends justified the means. He had to step lightly here.

"Thank you again," was all Philip managed to say.

Ruben opened the door for him, and they went inside. Ruben spoke to the nurse at the front desk about seeing Gail.

"You'll need to sign the register," the nurse said and indicated the sheet to the right of Ruben's arm.

"Sure thing, Angie," Ruben said and signed.

Philip followed suit.

"She's been awake for some time now," Angie said.

"Is she in a good mood?" Ruben asked.

"The best," she said. "She's excited to meet her guest."

Angie smiled at Philip.

Hearing that made him feel like a complete asshole.

"Glad to hear it," Philip managed to choke out.

Philip followed Ruben down a corridor to their left. The place looked like a mid-priced hotel. Nothing too fancy, but everything was clean, and the people seemed friendly.

Ruben stopped at room number twelve. He opened the door to a sunny, relatively large bedroom. A gray-haired woman with brown eyes sat up on a hospital bed staring out at the lawn outside the window.

"Gail, I brought Danny's friend here. Philip Townsend," Ruben said.

Gail turned her head and smiled at the both of them.

"Hi honey. I've been up for hours waiting for you both," she said.

"Thank you for agreeing to see me, Mrs. Sadowski," Philip said.

"Call me Gail," she demanded.

"Yes, ma'am," Philip said.

"You knew my Danny at Cornell?"

"I did, ma'am. We were in the same dorm freshman year," Philip said.

"I'm gonna go grab a coffee at the diner," Ruben said. "Are you okay if I leave you two to talk?" he asked his wife.

He went over and kissed her on the forehead. "How are you feeling today?"

"I'm feeling so much better. I really think I should be able to go home in the next week," she said.

"That's terrific news honey," Ruben said. "All right, let me leave you guys to talk and I'll see you in about half an hour?"

"Sure, honey," Gail said.

Ruben left and Gail turned to Philip.

"Has he done something to you? Why did you come all the way from Los Angeles to see me?" she asked.

Philip was taken aback by her question. Warning bells went off in his head. He had to be on the right track. And Ruben had been right. There was nothing wrong with her brain.

"I'm not sure what you mean. I haven't seen him in

years. I do need to find him though, which is why I'm here. Do you know where he is?"

"I do. What do you want to see him for?"

"As I told Ruben, I'm here to make amends. I'm in AA and there was an incident that happened our freshman year I really wanted to talk to Danny about," he said.

"So, you were a part of that?"

"I was," Philip said and pulled a chair over so he could sit and be at eye level with her.

"Did you know Danny before that happened?" she asked.

"I did. He was smart and ambitious. I was a scholarship student as well and we bonded over that," Philip said.

"That's what Danny had in spades. Ambition. He was always the smartest kid in the room when he was growing up. I was a waitress and couldn't give him what the other parents could, the tutoring and the summer camps. But we always lived in Massachusetts. We have an amazing public school system here and he worked his ass off to get into Cornell."

"I heard he dropped out of Cornell?"

"He never told me exactly what happened at that party. He called me crying after that night. Never said what happened or who did it to him. I knew he was excited about some party at that frat he was pledging. I put two and two together that something awful must have happened that night."

"He never gave you details then?" Philip asked.

"No. His grades went to hell after that and they put him on probation. Most of his grants were contingent on keeping his grades up, so he lost those. When he came home at Christmas, he'd lost so much weight and he'd changed. He was mean and short-tempered. Nothing I said to him was right and it was impossible to have him in the house. When he lost the grants, he couldn't go back to school," Gail said.

"That must've been really tough for him. Especially after how hard he'd worked to get there," Philip said.

Gail frowned. "He was a different person. I don't know what happened to the Danny that went to Cornell. The Danny that I got back was another version of my son. He was cold and hateful. When he couldn't go back to school, he ended up getting landscaping work around here and saved all his money to get the most ridiculous thing."

"And what was that?" Philip asked.

"A nose job. Whoever heard of a man getting a nose job?" Gail asked. "When I asked him about it, he said he didn't want to keep looking in the mirror at a loser. He needed his face to be different. He no longer wanted to be Danny Sadowski. Can you imagine? And he really meant it. He learned how to speak without his accent."

Gail smiled at that.

"I couldn't hear his accent. Sounded normal to me. His new way of talking sounded like he had an accent. Anyway, he ended up going to a community college around here and changed his major to computer programming. He excelled, of course, as he had done in everything else. When he finished, he went out West," she said.

"Out West? Is he in Silicon Valley?" Philip asked, quickly putting things together.

"He became ruthless. Do you know what I mean? He became someone who you knew would do anything to win. I guess that's what it takes to be successful," Gail said.

"When was the last time you talked to him?" Philip asked.

He could sense there was more to this story than the woman was telling him, and it was something that was causing her quite a bit of pain.

"I haven't spoken to him in about eight years. He said I was part of his old life. He didn't want anything to do with the past, including me. He threw me away like he did everybody else," she said.

"If you haven't spoken to him in eight years, you don't have a way of reaching him?" Philip asked.

"No, I don't have his phone number. Everybody knows who he is now. Under his new name," she said.

"What do you mean?"

Gail's eyes fluttered to the window. "He's famous now."

30

DAY 11 - DECEMBER 9, 2018 – 5 AM

Detective Tom Bards had called Chandler Robert every hour on the hour from two in the morning until now. The moment it was morning on the east coast, he called Chandler's father to find out the name of the new company Chandler used for security. They were meeting with the head of the firm at eight at Chandler's to get inside and do a welfare check.

Philip Townsend's house was still being searched by the crime scene techs for any sign of photography developer chemicals. Richard was insisting they keep trying to tie Philip to the photos. Harri didn't think they'd find a connection because she didn't believe Philip took or developed the photos. Tom knew they had to rule it out, one way or another.

They pulled up behind a black Range Rover. The property looked the same as when they were there last. The Maserati was parked in the exact same spot, but the Tesla was gone. Harri wondered if that had been Ethan Hunter's car.

A man wearing a black suit came out of the Range Rover to meet them. Harri noticed he wore the kind of earpiece security professionals preferred. She guessed he was ex-military.

"Mr. Robert called me as soon as he got off the phone with you," he said.

"You must be Allan Duqus?" Tom asked. "From Cantwell Security?"

"Yes. Detective Bards? And Detective Harper?" Allan asked.

"That's us," Harri said and pulled out her credentials. Tom showed his, as well.

"I've called the two staff members in charge of this account. One of them was out sick last night. We haven't been able to contact the other man."

"Is that normal?" Harri asked.

"No, it's highly unusual," Allan said.

That didn't sound good.

Harri and Tom followed Allan as he opened the door to the mansion and turned off the alarm with a wireless device.

"Mr. Robert? Are you home? It's Cantwell Security," Allan called out.

No one answered.

"There was a housekeeper here when we spoke with Mr. Robert two days ago," Harri said.

Something was off.

"We need to clear the scene," Tom said. "Duqus, stay here."

"Wait a minute!"

Whatever Allan Duqus was about to say was interrupted by Tom.

"We haven't been able to make contact with anyone at this address for the last twelve hours," Tom said.

"You don't have a search warrant. I have a verbal directive from Mr. Robert to check on his son," Allan pushed back.

"I don't need a search warrant if I have reason to believe someone in this residence requires emergency aid," Tom said.

The two men stood glaring at each other until Harri intervened.

"Go ahead then and check for Mr. Robert," Harri said. "If you run into any trouble, we'll be right here for you."

Allan Duqus shot Harri a look she could tell was meant to put her in her place. Little did the man know, Harri was right where she was supposed to be.

This house felt too still. Like it was waiting to reveal its secrets. Something bad had happened here. Harri could feel it. It felt like another crime scene. It didn't take long for Allan Duqus to call out to them.

"Detectives! In here," he shouted.

Harri and Tom followed the sound of his voice to the enormous kitchen. The housekeeper who had opened the door for them before was lying on the kitchen floor, a bullet hole in her forehead. She looked peaceful, as if she hadn't seen her killer coming.

Harri called it in, asking for the crime scene techs and coroner. When she hung up, she turned to Tom.

"They should be here in ten minutes," she said.

"Give me some gloves and a bag," Tom said.

Harri pulled a pair of latex gloves and an evidence bag from the bag she always carried.

Tom nodded a thank you and then turned to Allan Duqus.

"Put your firearm in the bag," he said.

"You can't be serious!" Allan yelled.

"You have complete access to the premises, and you were on scene before we arrived," Tom said in a neutral tone. "Put your firearm in the bag so we can check for ballistics and rule you out."

Allan Duqus pulled a Glock from his shoulder holster and glared at Tom as he placed it in the evidence bag.

"Is that the only firearm you have on you?" Tom asked.

After a few moments, Allan sighed and pulled a smaller firearm from his ankle holster. "I'm licensed to carry concealed," he said as he held it up.

Harri pulled another evidence bag from her jacket pocket and Allan dropped the smaller gun inside.

"How about you go wait in your car until the cavalry arrives," Tom said.

Harri placed each of the guns in their evidence bags back into her bag. She pulled her own firearm and followed Tom as they cleared the first floor. They didn't see any signs of struggle nor anything obviously out of place. The second floor looked like it hadn't been lived in after it had been decorated. All the rooms were bedrooms and bathrooms.

The third floor was where the action happened. Blood was smeared on the walls and a dark-haired man wearing a security guard uniform lay dead in the hallway leading to what they assumed was Chandler's suite.

The door to the master suite was smashed. It had probably been kicked in and the room inside was a mess. Clothes were strewn everywhere, as was broken glass. The smell of whiskey permeated the air.

"He grabbed Chandler," Harri said as she searched the huge closet and bathroom and then an office past another walk-in closet.

"Got anything?" Harri asked as she came to a broken mirror with blood on it. There was more blood on the carpet below.

"He knocked him out," Tom said. "Look. Drag marks."

From their angle, they could see bloody drag marks on the carpet.

"Two people dead, another missing. The killer has completely destabilized," Harri said.

"He's never taken any of his victims out of their homes," Tom said.

"Where in the hell is Philip Townsend?" Harri asked.

"He could have done this," Tom reminded her.

Harri bit her lip. Could she be so wrong about the guy?

"Or he's somewhere tied up with Chandler," Harri said.

31

DAY 11 - LOS ANGELES, CA

P hilip's flight back from Boston arrived after two in the morning Los Angeles time. Instead of getting a ridesharing service, he rented a car at the airport. The whole process took him another hour and a half, so he didn't get back to Santa Monica until four in the morning.

He was frustrated at how much traffic was on the I-405 so early in the morning. The city was becoming a town that never sleeps. Philip was hoping the cops watching his house were exhausted, or maybe were even asleep in their cars.

On his drive back from the airport, he made a plan to do a drive-by and see what the situation was. He chose to go up Marguerita Avenue because it had the best vantage point to his house.

When he arrived in his neighborhood, the lights were obvious from blocks away. The police cars had taken over the street in front of his house. Their lights were blazing, and teams of people were going in and out of his door.

The detectives must have gotten a search warrant for his home. He was in their crosshairs now. They must've found the photographs. He would be suspect number one, just as Nicholas had predicted. They would be looking for him. They'd arrest him. They'd bring him in on murder charges for three men. His friends of the last ten years.

On the flight back, his anxiety had peaked for just this scenario. He had made arrangements to stay at one of his client's places in Topanga Canyon.

Jason Adams, his client, was in Europe. Philip texted Jason to ask if he could use his home as a getaway for the holidays. The killings of Miles Davidson and Tanner Asperson were all over the international news too. Jason had already told him he could use his home whenever he wasn't in town and had texted back that it was no problem.

He'd also asked how Philip was holding up. Philip lied and said he was hanging in there and needed some peaceful, hippie canyon time. Jason had laughed at that. At least, he had somewhere to go tonight. Or really, this morning as it was almost five now.

Philip drove out of his neighborhood as calmly and quickly as he could, taking the next available left and going down San Vicente to reach Pacific Coast Highway. He could get to Topanga along the coast.

As he drove, his mind ran through all the different outcomes of his predicament. He didn't have proof yet, but he was sure Ethan Hunter was Danny Sadowski. Also, he was sure Ethan Hunter was the killer of his friends.

Friends? Could he really even call them that anymore? Philip didn't know. All he knew was that Danny Sadowski had killed them. However, at this moment, the police were apparently convinced it was him.

Ethan had taken those photographs on Philip's camera to plant them at an opportune time as the final frame. He wasn't sure how it would play out now that the police had found them at his home. The envelopes were dropped off at his house and now that he'd read that Lucas Reinhart had been found dead, he was sure another manila envelope had already been delivered.

He should have brought the photos to the police immediately. That would have given him an edge on this plot against him. He shouldn't have listened to his lawyer, either. What did Nicholas know? He only dealt with white-collar crimes. Cameron Page, the high-powered defense attorney Nicholas had sworn he'd call, hadn't reached out. Philip had known he never would. Nicholas probably hadn't even called the guy.

And then there was Lucas.

He hadn't even thought about Lucas Reinhart in the last twenty-four hours. His best friend since they'd been roommates at Cornell. Philip winced at the thought of never seeing Lucas again.

He shook his head to clear it of the memory of Lucas laughing. Lucas had always been laughing at something. Even when the moment was serious, Lucas couldn't be. Not entirely. He always had to find something to laugh about. Philip couldn't believe Lucas was also dead. They'd done so much together, and now?

Lucas turned on him. Philip still didn't know why. Did Lucas really think he'd killed Miles? And Tanner? If so, then he must have been surprised when it wasn't Philip who came for him.

Philip hated himself for that thought. Lucas had been his friend, just not a very good one. He didn't understand why Lucas had turned on him. And now he would never know. Like he would never know what happened at that fraternity party all those years ago.

He'd hoped the memories would keep coming back, but he hadn't gotten anything new. There was a black hole where the rest of the night should have been. He was sure Danny Sadowski had suffered through some awful humiliation. They'd humiliated the real pledges plenty. He couldn't quite stomach what they must have done to Danny.

Even so, none of them deserved to die these horrible deaths. And he sure as hell wouldn't be taking the blame for any of it. He needed to make Ethan confess to what he had done.

By force if necessary.

Philip had researched the different ways to get something admissible in court. The easiest way would be to record the conversation on his iPhone. That would also have all the metadata connected to the recording. The time, the date, and the location.

His plan was a terrible one. He knew that. Everything could go wrong, and most likely would. The plan sounded like something out of a bad thriller movie. But what other options did he have?

Should he go to the police and turn himself in? Tell them the whole story?

No. That ship had sailed.

He hadn't gone to them at the beginning and now when there's probably a warrant out for his arrest, he was going to turn himself in?

He'd be able to get a good lawyer and go to trial if it came to that. He could afford a bulldog attorney. Someone who wouldn't care about being on a front-page case like this. Some attorneys liked being on cases that dominated the media. It was good for business to get their name out there.

But what if the trial didn't go his way? He didn't have a rock-solid alibi for either of the deaths. At least for Lucas, he might have been out of town. And the prosecuting attorney would bring up his jailed father. The man who had murdered a twenty-year-old kid for two hundred bucks.

They'd say the apple doesn't fall far from the tree and he'd be convicted for the murders, even though he was innocent. And that was exactly what Ethan Hunter wanted. He was punishing the guys for whatever happened to him that night, and Philip going down for crimes he didn't commit was his punishment.

Philip still didn't understand what he'd done to Ethan, or Danny as he constantly kept thinking of him, to deserve this punishment. Maybe like how Gail Sadowski had said, her boy had changed so much after that night, he had become a different person. Maybe Philip Townsend was convenient.

Or maybe he hated him the most because Philip was the most like him. But unlike Danny, Philip had managed to break into the social and professional circles they'd both worked so hard for.

He opened the windows to take in the night air. The salty smell of the ocean calmed him as he drove along Pacific Coast Highway toward Topanga Canyon Boulevard.

Jason had a gun at his home with ammunition. He'd shown Philip on the day he'd given him the keys and tour of the house. He'd also given Philip the code for the gun safe, along with the alarm system. A gun might convince Ethan to tell the truth about what started all of this in the first place.

Danny Sadowski had made good, even after dropping out of Cornell. He'd changed his looks and become Ethan Hunter. He was the newly minted billionaire, and his new face was on the cover of magazines. Why would he choose to kill instead of using his funds to get the best therapy he could afford? What could have happened for him to go on this gruesome rampage?

Philip wouldn't have the answers until he asked him. Philip had reached out to his network to find out Ethan's contact info.

They'd met, again, at Chandler's party. It wouldn't be unreasonable for Philip to reach out to him, maybe invite him over to the beach club for a drink. Hopefully, Ethan would think Philip was pitching his fund and wealth management services.

The articles he'd found spoke of Ethan Hunter recently buying a home in Los Angeles. There were only a certain number of realtors who worked in the price range he assumed Ethan bought into.

Babs, his realtor, would have the info. She kept her finger on the pulse of real estate all over town. She'd know exactly which property he purchased, and for how much. If Babs hadn't returned his email by early morning, then he would call her. He kept checking the internet to see if his name was in the news yet, and so far, it wasn't. He needed to talk to her before it got out that he was a wanted man.

He needed that information. It was the only way he was going to make it out of this thing alive. And with his freedom.

32

DAY 11 - LOS ANGELES, CA

T he crime scene techs and Dr. Grimley, the coroner, had moved from Lucas Reinhart's place to Chandler Robert's home. They'd cordoned off both the kitchen and the hallway on the third floor and the bodies had been processed at the scene and removed.

Dr. Grimley put the time of death at approximately within the last five hours and the cause of death was a lot simpler than Lucas Reinhart's. Dr. Grimley had given the cause of death as gunshot wounds to the head in both cases. The killer had shot each of these victims in the forehead. They'd seen his face.

In the case of the housekeeper, it appeared close-range. Harri guessed she was facing the sink when she heard something, turned around, and bang. When it came to James Halter, the Cantwell Security employee on the third floor, Dr. Grimley had also found gunshot wounds in his back. It appeared he'd been shot twice in the back but had tried walking, running, stumbling down the hallway before the killer also shot him in the head.

As the crime scene techs continued to gather whatever evidence they could find in both locations, Tom called in the news that Chandler Robert was missing. Lieutenant Richard Byrne had called the press conference for that afternoon to explain to the citizens of Los Angeles what was happening in this investigation.

"The media are crawling all over these crime scenes," Dr. Grimley remarked as she was packing up her equipment.

"Have they uncovered the Philip Townsend connection yet?" she asked.

"Absolutely," Dr. Grimley said. "They're staked out on his street. I also saw media vans as I was leaving Reinhart's place and they're already clustered around the gates outside."

"With the press conference scheduled, hopefully, they'll move downtown," Harri said.

"It's been a bad night," Dr. Grimley said.

"Three bodies in the span of what, eight hours?" Harri shook her head.

"A very bad night," Dr. Grimley said.

"Could you prioritize Lucas Reinhart?" Harri asked.

"I was going to do that anyway. These two autopsies will be straightforward, I imagine. Lucas Reinhart is still a mystery. All that blood and the stabbing. I'm thinking we might find some foreign DNA on him," Dr. Grimley said.

"Let's hope we do," Harri said.

Dr. Grimley said her goodbyes and left with her team.

"Richard is demanding I go downtown for this press conference," Tom said, appearing at her elbow.

"He's making sure he has a scapegoat around?" Harri asked and frowned.

"And that would be me," Tom said.

He hadn't slept well in days, either. He was ragged and he looked it.

They both desperately needed to destress, unwind, and get a good night's sleep.

"I can hold down the fort here," Harri said. "This damn place is so huge, it's gonna take us a couple of days to collect all the crime scene evidence."

"We need to figure out where Chandler is being held," Tom said.

"With the amount of blood we found, do you really think he's still alive?" she asked.

"Probably not," Tom said. "But until we have a body, we have to operate under that assumption."

His phone buzzed in his hand.

"I can only imagine who that might be," Harri said.

Tom frowned at the screen.

"It's Richard again. I have to take this," he said.

Harri nodded and waved him off and watched him take the call as he walked out the door to his car.

Poor guy, thought Harri. She wouldn't switch places with him, though. She was perfectly happy to stay here and figure out how the killer got Chandler out of this fortress.

First, he would've had to get to the gate and sign-in. Same story as the Lucas Reinhart crime scene. How had the killer accessed the properties? As they were leaving Lucas Reinhart's place, they'd confirmed with the security guard at the gate that there'd been no visitors for Lucas, and no traffic on his street in the timeframe for his murder. Harri expected it would be the same here.

The killer had to get Chandler out of here somehow. He had to have a vehicle somewhere close. He could have slipped out of Lucas' home, but not with a body. Unless Chandler was buried somewhere on the grounds.

But then why didn't he leave him inside the house like he'd done with all the others?

He had to have a vehicle. He had to have access without going through the security at the gate. Who could come and go like that, undetected?

She went outside and sat on the front steps, her notebook open on her lap. She jotted down all they knew so far.

Philip Townsend went missing last night.

Lucas Reinhart's body was discovered by eleven last night.

Chandler disappeared that night, too.

The killer didn't have to drive far because all of the victims lived in the same neighborhood. Traffic cameras would need to be checked. Cameras were still active at some of the intersections here.

A lot of cameras had been removed when the law allowing their use in issuing traffic tickets had been reversed. Some had survived the purge, however.

They would need to get footage from all of the neighbors' cameras. Nothing had been found on the cameras surrounding Miles Davidson's home, however. They were still tracking down security footage for Philip Townsend's street and there were calls out to all of Lucas Reinhart's neighbors.

This estate was so large and spread out the only way they would get any sort of camera footage is if the killer went through the front gate. She knew who to call about security footage.

She and Tom had sent Allan Duqus away after they'd found the first body. He'd given them a statement and his card. Tom had logged both of the man's firearms into evidence.

Harri bit her lip, then breathed in deeply and called him.

"Allan, hi this is Detective Harper. I wanted to say that I am so very sorry about your employee being found like that," she said.

"Thank you for that, Detective Harper. He was a good man," Allan said.

"I wanted to follow up and see if you had a chance to look over the security footage for the last twenty-four hours?" Harri asked.

"That's what I've been doing since I got back to the office," he said. "You know, without either of my firearms."

He let that hang in the air a moment.

"I understand," she said. "We've asked ballistics to clear them both as soon as possible."

"Uh, huh." Allan said. "Okay, well here's what we have so far. There were only two vehicles that drove by overnight. One was a white paneled-van with no visible plates and the other was a dark-colored, late-model Mercedes four-door sedan. When I ran the plates for the Mercedes, the registered owner came back as one of Chandler Robert's neighbors, Clyde Hofstetter. Lives in the property exactly left-adjacent. The white van would be perfect for transporting a body, but it only drove by. The van didn't stop within our camera's range."

"Is there another way into this property?" she asked.

"When we inspected the property initially, we found a garden gate at the far northwest end. It's behind the guesthouse."

"Are there any security cameras there?" she asked.

"Yeah, we put in a camera there but when I checked, it hadn't been working the last few days. I don't really know how our team missed that, but I don't have the footage for last night," he said.

"Thank you, Mr. Duqus," she said.

She put her phone in her pocket and walked outside the entire length of the mansion. She stepped past the rosebushes and walked alongside the hedges until she came to a garden with a two-story guesthouse along the back wall. The gate was supposed to be behind it.

Harri found a dirt path leading to the back of the guesthouse. She followed it to a rusty gate that stood open, nearly falling off its hinges. She was sure the killer had come out this way. It was the only way he could have. She called Kevin, the head crime scene technician, and told him to bring someone with him.

She gave him the instructions and stepped out onto the street. She didn't see any other back gates nearby. Across the street was a wall of tall, green hedges. The street curved right and if the estate next door had a back gate, she couldn't see it from where she was standing. It was a perfect blind spot to load a body into a van.

Harri realized the van must have rammed the gate to get through. That's why it was hanging on its hinges. Excitement ran through her as she rushed back to Chandler's property.

She pointed to the gate and explained her theory to Kevin and Tony, the crime scene technicians. They unpacked their equipment and began processing the gate, looking for viable surfaces for fingerprints, or paint chips from the white van.

She left them to their work and went to interview the security guard at the front gate.

33

DAY 11 - PHILIP

P hilip Townsend sat parked in his rental car on San Vicente Blvd observing Woodacres Road. His realtor, Babs, had gotten back to him with Ethan Hunter's new address. She gossiped with Philip about introducing Ethan around town, knowing Philip would love to have him as a new client for his fund.

Babs knew so many beautiful, charming young ladies who would love to meet the new bachelor in town, especially now that he was settling into his new home. Philip knew all about his realtor's side game as an unofficial matchmaker. He'd nearly become one of her victims but shied away when he realized all the available beauties Babs knew could only be described as gold-diggers.

Ethan bought an estate dating back to the 1920s at the end of a cul-de-sac that had only one entrance. He'd been staking out the entrance to Woodacres Road for the last hour to make sure no LAPD units were watching Ethan Hunter's new home.

Ethan wasn't part of their original crew, so Philip assumed he wasn't on the LAPD's radar. Seeing as he was about to illegally enter Ethan's home with a gun, Philip wanted to make sure he wasn't being observed. After an hour of sitting in silence and seeing no suspicious activity, he made his move.

Philip had studied the property on several high-end real estate websites that featured detailed photos of the property from its listing. Philip scrolled through them all, viewing the interiors, exteriors, and floor plans. The estate had a lush expanse of lawn with lots of trees which looked to him like a perfect cover to get in and sneak up on his quarry.

An architect built the estate as his own home in 1921 and it had showcased his designs for decades. Fortunately for Philip, the home had been featured in architecture magazines and blogs, so it wasn't hard for him to plan how he would access the property undetected. He memorized the floorplan as best he could. From what Babs had told him, Ethan hadn't started renovations yet, but security was on his list because the realtor who'd sold him the place had called Babs for her security company's contact information only yesterday. Security hadn't been installed either, she believed. Philip hoped she was right, and from what Philip had gathered in his interactions with Babs, she always was.

Philip walked along the edge of Woodacres Road as if he belonged there until he reached the front gate to the property. Two large brick pillars stood on each side of a wrought-iron gate spanning the rough, asphalt driveway. Philip saw no pin-pad or cameras. He pushed at the gate. It opened with a creak. He stepped onto the estate.

That was easy enough, he thought. Was he walking into a trap?

Probably?

Did it matter?

Not anymore. He wasn't sure if he would get what he needed to prove his innocence, but that wouldn't stop him from trying. Even though he was sweating and could hear his heart thumping in his ears, he felt strangely calm. He'd made up his mind. There was nothing else he could do. Ethan had seen to that.

Philip stepped to his left and behind the trees. He walked along the inside perimeter of the brick wall between bougainvillea bushes and the tall pine trees that grew on the property. From the aerial photos he'd seen, the estate also had a guesthouse, full-size tennis court, and an Olympic-standard swimming pool. The most impressive of all was the two-story Spanish Revival main house.

He'd mapped out a path along the wall to the guesthouse and then along the side of the pool toward the main house. The aerial photos had been crucial to his plan.

As Philip crept along, he kept scanning his surroundings for cameras, but he didn't see any. He wondered if Ethan had gotten a chance to install a security system, but maybe he'd been too busy killing Philip's friends to get on that.

The Gen 3 Glock 19 in his pocket kept hitting his thigh as he walked and made him think he was about to shoot himself. He'd shot this gun exactly one time, at a gun range with Jason Adams months ago. Philip was far from an expert and he was a terrible shot. He'd hit the paper only three times out of an hour session with numerous rounds.

The brief conversation he'd had with Ethan Hunter at Chandler's party gave Philip the impression Ethan was another geeky Silicon Valley hotshot. But he wasn't.

He was Danny Sadowski, deep down inside. Even if

he'd changed his face, and changed his name, he was still Danny and if he was capable of killing Philip's friends in such brutal ways, Philip knew he was in danger coming here. The gun was his only protection.

Philip brought a ten-round magazine and hoped it would be enough.

If someone had told him he would be in this situation a month ago, he would have thought they were insane. Instead, here he was creeping on some billionaire's estate with a gun in his pocket and a plan to force the psycho to admit to murdering his friends. This whole situation was ludicrous. Doubt flooded his brain. He wasn't some secret agent spy who could force a confession and turn the guy in.

He stopped walking. He could still turn himself in.

Stop this craziness.

The photos of Miles and Tanner screaming, their eyes missing, flashed through his mind. He squeezed his eyes shut and shook his head to clear it of the horrific images.

And now Lucas Reinhart was dead, too. He'd seen that on the morning news.

He wasn't going down for their murders. Philip would rather die than go to prison.

The news had called him a person of interest in the case and said he was wanted for questioning.

Philip knew what that meant. All of these murders would be pinned on him.

The thought made his feet finally move.

Philip went around the guesthouse and sprinted alongside the pool to get to the ivy-covered wall of the main house.

The French doors were open, and Philip could see the living room was empty.

He hadn't come up with this part yet.

Should he wait for Ethan to appear or go searching for him?

Neither option made Philip happy. He felt exposed out here, but he'd be at a distinct disadvantage inside.

He closed his eyes and breathed deeply.

What was it going to be?

34

DAY 11 - HARRI

Detective Harri Harper had just reached her car to drive down to the gatehouse when her phone buzzed. It was Jake.

"Are you coming home?" Jake asked.

"I'm on my twelfth cup of coffee and I've been up for the last forty-eight hours. I need to talk to the gate guard again. I have a potential lead," Harri said.

"It's been a busy night for murders," Jake said.

"What's the news saying?"

"Lucas Reinhart was found dead. Lots of police activity at Philip Townsend's place and now breaking news that several people were found dead in yet another estate. The Night Blinder has struck again, they said. They haven't released any names yet," he said.

"That's where I am right now. The last estate. We have a potential kidnap victim. Glad they didn't get wind of that yet," Harri said dryly.

"Give it fifteen minutes," Jake said with a laugh.

"True enough."

"When can you get some sleep?" Jake asked. "You sound beat and your voice sounds like it's about to go out again."

Harri was straining her vocal cords dangerously now. Her throat ached something terrible and she felt a large lump on the side of her neck. She worried she'd set her recovery back weeks.

"We found evidence at Philip Townsend's house. And now with the potential of finding a victim alive, I'm not sure what time I'm coming home."

"Do you have someone to drive you around, at least?" he asked.

"Tom hasn't slept, either. And no, I'm driving myself."

"That's not safe, Harri," Jake said quietly.

She quashed the flash of irritation that flared inside her. She knew he cared about her and she wasn't used to this kind of affection. She wasn't going to bite his head off for telling her the truth.

"I know. Tom was called back downtown for a news conference with Richard Byrne about the latest death and how Philip Townsend is a person of interest. We're closing in."

"Is he your guy?"

"My gut is saying no, but I don't have any evidence telling me otherwise," she said.

"You sound exhausted," Jake said.

"I am," she said, her voice turning into a scratchy whisper. "I should save my voice."

"Call me again in a bit. I'm worried about you," he said.

"This case is breaking all over the place. I'll try to rest when I can," Harri said.

The call-waiting beeped.

"I have another call coming in," she said.

"Call me back when you can. Harri...I," Jake began to say but Harri's finger slipped and she cut him off in mid-sentence.

"Is this Detective Harriet Harper?" a woman asked on the other line.

"Who is this?"

"Police dispatch, Ma'am," the woman answered.

"What's wrong?" Harri asked pushing her voice even more. She was going to lose her ability to speak soon.

"You flagged five addresses. We were supposed to contact you if any of them had any suspicious activity. One of the addresses has alerted," the woman said.

"Which address?"

She'd flagged both Chandler Robert's address and Lucas Reinhart's. She'd also flagged Ethan Hunter's, as well as the other two men who'd been rejected for membership to the Malibu Beach Club. She'd already been to the first two in the last twelve hours.

"This is the address on Woodacres Road in Santa Monica."

"What was the call for?" Harri asked.

"Security called us. There's been a breach to the perimeter, and they've been unable to reach the resident. The security company called 911 and have their own units en route. You were my next call."

"Thank you so much," Harri said and hung up.

Her hunch that Ethan Hunter was next proved correct. She mustered up the last bit of energy she had and yanked her car door open.

She was down the street from the address, and it was a five-minute drive, tops. She screeched down Chandler's driveway and called in for backup units.

She was firing on all cylinders as she barreled down

the road toward San Vicente. If she could get there in time, maybe she could at least save one of these men.

35

DAY 11 - PHILIP

Philip had been wrong about tripping the alarm. From somewhere deep in the house, he heard a beeping noise and a phone ringing. Soon after, Ethan Hunter appeared in the living room. It was now or never, Philip thought. He turned on the record function on his phone.

He stepped through the French doors into the living room, putting his hand in his pocket to take the safety off the gun. He gripped it tight, ready to pull it out. He hoped he was wrong about this whole thing. And if he was, he didn't want to come out guns blazing.

Ethan turned to look at him, his eyes narrowing.

"I know who you are," Philip said, his voice shaking slightly. "I know what your real name is. You are Danny Sadowski."

Ethan didn't acknowledge anything Philip said. Instead, he cocked his head at him and smiled.

"You broke into my house? Why?" Ethan asked.

"You have blood on your hands," Philip said and

took a step back. His vision tunneled and a roar filled his ears.

He had been right all along.

Ethan Hunter was Danny Sadowski and Danny was a killer.

"Whose blood is that?" Philip asked and pulled out the gun.

Ethan laughed.

"What are you doing with that? Are you going to shoot me now?"

His lack of fear was unnerving Philip.

"Do you have Chandler here somewhere? He's the last one left. You killed Lucas and the others."

"I cut myself. This is my blood," Ethan said.

"I don't see a cut on you. That's a lot of blood," Philip said.

The gun was getting heavy and he could feel a slight shake in his hand.

They stared at each other from a good ten feet apart, the gun in the middle. Philip had to get him to admit he was Danny.

"I don't remember what happened that night, Danny. I had a full-on blackout because I was so drunk."

"And what night was that?" Ethan asked.

"I went and saw your mother, Gail. She's a nice lady. Did you know she was in a car accident? She almost died. She was in a coma, but she's getting better now. She still has her mind, though. She told me all about you."

That finally made something in Ethan's face twitch.

"You were always the clever one," he said, his friendly mask disappearing.

Philip could now see Danny Sadowski.

He recognized him.

"None of the others remembered you, did they?"

"No. Not a one," Ethan said. "Danny is dead. I killed him off long ago. He was a pathetic wannabe. I'm not him. Not anymore. Not for a long time."

"Why did you come out here then? Why did you start hanging out with us?"

Anger flashed across Ethan's face.

"Should I call you Ethan or Danny?" Philip needled.

"Danny is dead," Ethan said evenly. "I remade myself. There is nothing left of him."

"Except for his shame," Philip said.

Ethan stepped forward threateningly and Philip pulled up the gun higher.

"Don't come any closer," he said.

Ethan glanced down at Philip's pants.

"Are you recording me right now?" Ethan chuckled. "I can see your cell phone in your pocket."

"Is that Chandler's blood? He was the one who invited you. I'm sure he was the one who instigated what happened to you that night," Philip said.

"I saved him for last," Ethan said and shrugged.

There it was. He had gotten him to admit it.

"What happened to you that night? I don't remember any of it. Is that why you decided to pin this all on me? Is that why you're framing me?"

Ethan stood eerily still, his face pale and his eyes dilated. He was scaring the shit out of Philip. He didn't look human. More like an animal.

A predator.

Philip gripped the gun tighter in his hand and pulled out the phone, still recording.

"I'm calling the police now."

"No, you aren't," Ethan said,

This stopped Philip dead in his tracks.

"Why wouldn't I?"

"You broke into my home. You're holding me at gunpoint. How do you think that's going to play out? You know cops shoot first and ask questions later," Ethan said.

His creepy smile returned.

"I did record you. You said you left Chandler for last," Philip said.

This cracked Ethan's facade somewhat. He took a step closer to Philip.

"I don't think you're going to shoot me. I don't think you have it in you," Ethan said, taking another step closer.

"Go ahead do your worst," Ethan said with a sneer.

They both heard a scrabbling sound coming from the kitchen.

Holy shit, thought Philip. Who was that?

36

DAY 11 - HARRI

Harri parked the cruiser in front of Ethan Hunter's wrought iron gate and got out. She used her radio to call in and get an ETA for the backup units and was given a five-minute window. She didn't think she had that much time and told the dispatch she was going in to see if the resident was in any danger.

She pushed on the gate, worried to find it open, and ran up the drive. The two-story Spanish-style mansion was a surprising choice for a tech entrepreneur like Ethan Hunter. The place needed work and looked as if it had been neglected for years.

Harri didn't want to announce herself before her backup arrived but needed to find a way inside, nevertheless. She tried the ornate wooden front door.

It was locked. She unclipped the strap holding her weapon in her holster, pulled back the safety. She put her hand on it, ready to pull it out.

Harri turned the corner and headed to the back of the

house, checking in the windows for any movement inside. She saw no one in the main part of the house.

Coming around the back, she heard voices coming out of a set of open French doors. She crept closer to get a better listen.

A gunshot exploded from inside. She jumped into action, pulling out her gun and speed dialing dispatch.

"Gunshots heard from 1118 Woodacres Road, Santa Monica. Where are my backup units?"

Her voice came out raspy and not very loud.

"I'm going in." The last word came out a whisper. She needed her voice now more than ever.

She ran toward the double doors at an angle attempting to limit her exposure. When she reached the threshold, she shielded her body with the wall and peeked around.

Philip Townsend stood holding a gun on Ethan Hunter, while Chandler Robert lay at both men's feet. All of the men were dripping with blood.

Harri stepped out into the doorway.

"Drop your gun, Philip. Drop it." Her voice cracked. She strained her vocal cords to get out the sound and winced with the pain.

She trained her gun at Philip's head. "Now."

37

DAY 11 - PHILIP

Chandler shifted at Philip's feet. He was still alive.

"It's not me, Detective Harper. Ethan Hunter is behind all of this," he said.

His hand shook, but Philip kept the gun pointed at Ethan's head.

"You need to put the gun down," Detective Harper said.

"I can't do that, Detective," Philip said.

"You need to put the gun down," she said again.

"You're not listening to what I'm saying," Philip said. "This man's real name is Daniel Sadowski. We all went to school with him at Cornell. Something happened to him. Something terrible happened."

Ethan burst out laughing.

"You're holding a gun to my head and telling that stupid story? Are you hearing this, Detective?"

"Philip, I will listen to you if you put the gun down," Detective Harper said.

Philip was losing her.

"He broke into my house. He threw this man down at my feet. I don't even know these guys," Ethan said.

"That's a lie," Philip yelled.

He was losing his cool, and the detective hadn't moved. She still held a gun on him.

"Philip, listen to me. You're holding a gun to this man. In his own home," Detective Harper said. "We can't talk until you put the gun down."

Her tone was making Philip even more nervous. He was sure he was seconds from being shot.

"Chandler came out of the kitchen and the gun went off. I'm a terrible shot," Philip confessed. "The bullet ricocheted, and Chandler was hit in the leg. He's bleeding."

"Which is why you need to put the gun down. I don't want to shoot you, Philip," Detective Harper said.

Philip glanced from Ethan to the detective. Her hand never wavered. She held the gun steady and it was still pointed at him.

"He's going to kill me. He's framing me with those fucking photos. I didn't do any of this and I'm willing to die to prove it," Philip said, rising hysteria in his voice.

"We don't need to do it that way," Harri said. "If I put my gun down, then you can put your gun down and we could get your friend help," she said.

Philip heard sirens coming closer in the distance.

This was it.

This was his last chance. If he couldn't convince Detective Harper Ethan was the killer, then she would shoot him, and Ethan would get away with everything.

"He sent me photos. I know you've been inside my house. Did you find them? Did you see what he did to Miles and Tanner? Why would I send myself photos of my dead friends?" Philip heard himself pleading with her.

The sirens were getting louder.

"We can't have this conversation until you put that gun down," Harri said. "Listen, do you hear that? The cavalry is here, and when they come in here and see you holding a gun to an unarmed man with a bloody man at your feet, there's going to be trouble. I don't want you to get hurt."

"How can I get you to believe me?" Philip begged.

"By putting the gun down," she said again.

38

DAY 11 - HARRI

H arri was losing control of the situation. Philip was still holding a gun to Ethan's head. Harri questioned what she saw in front of her. She had mere seconds to decide what to do.

Blood pooled underneath Chandler Robert. He was no longer moving.

Philip was losing it. Sweat dripped down his face, his eyes appeared crazed, and the hand holding the gun was shaking. Harri noted there was no blood on Philip's hands.

Blood dripped from Ethan's hands. A lot of blood. Why would Philip kidnap Chandler and bring him to the home of someone he barely knew to kill him?

Ethan's story made little sense.

"Why do you have blood on your hands, Ethan?" Harri asked.

Her question changed Ethan's posture for a half-second. If she hadn't been watching closely, she would have missed it. She also would have missed the sparkle of gold on his pinkie finger. Was that a ring he was wearing?

"I checked to see if Chandler was okay. After he was shot." Ethan said.

Alarm bells went off in Harri's head. Had Ethan wore a ring the last time she saw him?

"With a gun on you?" she asked.

Ethan changed tack.

"I don't think this man here wants to shoot me. He wants to frame me for what he's done to his friends," Ethan said.

"Are you kidding me?" screamed Philip. "Don't gaslight me like that. You are the one doing that exact thing to me."

"Philip, they're almost here. If you don't put the gun down, they will shoot you even if I don't," Harri warned. Her voice was nearly gone. It came out in a raspy croak and the pain seared her throat. She needed to see Ethan's right hand again. It was blocked by his body.

"You don't understand, detective," Philip hissed. "This guy is a psycho. They did something to him that night. That's what this is all about. He's insane and he's punishing us. There's no way I'm putting this gun down. He's crazy. He'll kill me somehow."

Shouts were coming from around the house. Harri could hear at least four distinct voices. She had to get him to put the gun down before the uniforms entered the room.

"Philip, do it," she yelled, but nothing came out. She'd lost her voice.

39

DAY 11 - PHILIP

Philip gave up. He couldn't control the shaking of his hand and it was hard to hold the gun. He'd tried to convince Detective Harper, but she wasn't listening. He couldn't get her on his side. No matter what he said.

He looked into Ethan's face and a cold realization hit him.

His eyes before looked worried and anxious.

Now, they were glittering, glassy, and blank. He was about to do something. Something to save himself.

How could he signal to the detective that something had changed? Something was about to happen.

He knew if he didn't put the gun down, she would shoot him. That's when he looked past Ethan into the kitchen. There was blood on the wall, marring the all-white kitchen.

On the counter sat his camera. The one Ethan had stolen from his home. His favorite Hasselblad camera. Ethan had defiled it by taking pictures of his tortured friends before he killed them. Philip could see blood all over the camera.

"I can prove I didn't murder anyone. My camera, the medium format Hasselblad those photos were taken with, is sitting right there on his kitchen counter. There's blood all over it too," Philip said.

He met Ethan's eyes.

Ethan's cheek twitched.

"His story can't be true. If he got blood on his hands checking on Chandler, how did blood get on the camera?"

Philip turned to Detective Harper as the gun wavered in his hand.

DAY 11 - HARRI

H arri watched in relief as Philip pointed the gun he was barely holding at the ground.

With movement quick as a cat's, Ethan jumped back toward the kitchen. Harri heard Philip pull the trigger. Harri shot and clipped Philip in the shoulder.

Philip crumpled next to Chandler's body.

The uniforms swarmed all around her.

"Check them for pulses," Harri croaked out. "I'm going to look for the other one."

She ran for the door Ethan had disappeared through.

The kitchen was empty.

Swipes of blood were the only thing on the kitchen counter. She didn't see the camera. The only way out of the kitchen was through a door near the fridge.

"We have a pulse for the both of them," one uniform yelled from behind her.

"I'm going after him," Harri said, but a hoarse whisper came out.

She heard the uniforms call for an ambulance and crime scene techs.

She needed to find Ethan.

Harri walked through the door by the fridge, gun at the ready. She stood in a small hallway.

To her left, the hallway extended back into the house, but to her right, it ended at another door leading to the lawn outside.

She checked the handle and saw it was unlocked. Ethan's hands were covered with blood and this handle was clean.

Could he have gone back toward the house? She followed the hallway down toward the living space. She came out back into the living room. Two uniforms were trying to stop the bleeding on Phillip's shoulder wound while another uniform checked Chandler's naked, bloody torso. Blood, dirt, and grime seemed to be everywhere.

Where had Ethan disappeared to? She retraced her steps into the kitchen and stood next to the island. The kitchen was all white cabinets and Carrera marble. Except for all of the blood. She looked at the blood smears. Why were they only in the kitchen and not in the hallway? There was no other way out of the kitchen. Where had he gone off to?

She heard more voices in the other room and walked out to see Chandler Robert and Philip Townsend being lifted onto stretchers by medics. They were both still alive.

The crime scene techs had arrived. She whispered instructions to Kevin when she saw him. He got to work with his team, and she turned to see Detective Tom Bards had arrived. That was fast, she thought.

She'd been on her feet for more than two full days. Everything was starting to feel hazy. She stood in the living room where she'd shot Philip Townsend and looked at Tom Bards.

"How did you get here so quickly?" she whispered.

"It wasn't so quick. You've lost your voice," Tom said. "Are you okay?"

"I'm not sure," Harri whispered.

He gestured to have her sit on the couch. She did and rubbed her face with her hands. She needed sleep. Her body felt like it was breaking down.

"Harri, how did you even get here?"

Harri whispered to him how she'd received the call from dispatch about the security alarm at Ethan's home and what she'd walked into.

"Philip was the one holding the gun, but Ethan had blood all over him. Especially on his hands. Some blood looked dry and not fresh. I told Philip to put down the gun repeatedly. When he finally pointed it down, Ethan jumped for cover and Philip shot at him, and I shot Philip."

"They're both alive?" Tom asked.

"I clipped Philip on the shoulder. Chandler was so bloodied I don't know what happened to him before I got on scene," Harri whispered.

"Ethan went up and disappeared?"

"Panic room?" Harri muttered. "Oh, the camera."

"What camera?"

"Philip said he saw the camera that took the photos. He said there was blood on it," Harri whispered.

If she kept talking, she would lose her voice completely. How in the world was she supposed to do her job?

"Press conference?" she squeaked.

Tom drew his head closer to hear.

"The press conference?"

Harri nodded.

"Didn't make it. I was almost downtown when I heard the call for all nearby units to this address. Your name was mentioned. I doubled back and got here as fast as I could," he said.

"Richard?"

"He's livid. You and I are here for the duration. He wants us to close up this crime scene and not come back without Ethan Hunter."

Harri shrugged and shook her head. She showed Tom her empty hands.

"I know," Tom said. "We've got units in the area and the uniforms are searching the grounds. We'll search this house from top to bottom. We'll find him."

Harri hadn't slept in too long and the world around her was blurring. The crime scene techs were on hour six of gathering evidence. The uniforms had been searching the house, grounds, and buildings on the property for nearly seven hours and still hadn't located Ethan Hunter.

Finally, the crime scene techs were done with the blood in the kitchen and the scene in the living area. They recovered both bullets Philip had fired and had dusted for fingerprints in both rooms.

The hospital called to inform Harri that both Philip Townsend and Chandler Robert survived. Chandler was out of surgery for the knife wounds to his torso and the gunshot wound to his leg. Philip had a through-and-through gunshot wound to his right shoulder, and Harri was relieved to hear the bullet had missed all the major arteries.

"We're finally done," Kevin the crime scene tech said.

Some of the crime scene technicians had been on call

for the last twenty-four hours processing three crime scenes. Everyone had survived a crazy night and day.

Harri gave him a thumbs up.

"Anything interesting?" Tom asked.

"We found some droplets of blood on the kitchen floor. They seem different than the blood that was smeared on the walls and counter. Those seem consistent with the victim who was stabbed, you know like he was pulling himself along. The drops of blood are from someone standing in one place. They're more consistent with some of what we found in the living room, where the homeowner was standing," Kevin said.

"Disappeared," Harri rasped.

"Right, detective," Kevin said with a nod. "Honestly, I don't know how you're still standing on your own two legs."

Harri smiled wearily. She didn't know, either.

She waved goodbye to them all and watched the sun set over Ethan Hunter's grounds. She finished putting up the yellow police tape across both doors.

She and Tom hadn't found the camera nor the darkroom in Ethan's house. He looked like an innocent man on paper, except for blood. And what had Philip said about Ethan really being someone else?

What a mess, Harri thought.

Tom came out of the kitchen as the rest of the uniforms drove off. They were alone in the house. Harri sighed without making a sound. Her throat was burning and each time she turned her neck, pain seared through.

"We'll find him, Harri," Tom said.

She pointed to her eye and then shook her head. She was trying to say 'I know' in her own strange sign language.

A scraping sound emanated from the kitchen. Harri

pulled out her gun and released the safety as, out of nowhere, Ethan rushed Tom with a scalpel in his hand.

Tom's eyes widened, and he dropped to the ground.

Harri opened her mouth to scream, but the only sound she heard was the shot she fired.

Ethan jerked back and then lay still on the kitchen floor.

Harri rushed over to Tom and helped him stand.

"Are you all right?" she tried to ask, but nothing came out. Tom went to check on Ethan.

"Got him square in the chest, near his heart, Harri," Tom said as he kicked the nasty-looking scalpel away and then leaned in to check for a pulse.

"He's gone," he said.

Harri shook her head and pointed to her own shoulder.

Tom nodded, understanding she was trying to say she'd aimed for his shoulder. She touched his hand with her shoe. His pinkie showed a gold band on it. She was certain they'd find Tanner's ring on that finger.

Harri turned to the kitchen. Where had he been hiding?

They stepped over Ethan's body and entered the kitchen. A door had been hidden behind a cabinet. The cabinet door was open, and the shallow shelf of canned food was also a door. Stairs led down to another level.

"Found his hidey-hole," Tom said.

They both had their guns out as they went down the stairs. The smell coming back at them made Harri wrinkle her nose. She tapped Tom's shoulder and when he turned to her, she tapped her nose.

Tom nodded. "I smell it too. Developer chemicals. I'm also smelling blood."

They came out into a low concrete room. Three large

dog cages ran along one wall. In the center of the room was a chair. Used zip-ties hung on the legs and arms. Blood was everywhere.

One entire wall was covered with photos. Some were in color, some were black and white. They looked like surveillance photos. Harri looked closer and saw Miles Davidson, Tanner Asperson, Lucas Reinhart, and Chandler Robert. There were only a few photos of Philip Townsend. Every single photo had each of the men's eyes scratched out in black marker.

Tom opened another door on the opposite wall. They'd found his amateur darkroom. Harri followed Tom in and turned on the red light. They saw more photos hanging of all the murdered men in different states of torture and death.

"Here's our case. Made for us," Tom said.

Harri shook her head and held up her hands to gesture 'why?'

"Chandler and Philip will have to tell us that," he said. "They're the only ones left."

DAY 12 - DECEMBER 10, 2018

Harri took a deep gulp of the hot coffee and then a bite of muffin. She'd spent all night at Ethan Hunter's house providing information of what happened to Dr. Grimley and directing the crime scene techs to the kitchen and the basement of horrors they had uncovered. It was slow-going because she really had lost her voice. She was grateful for how patient and understanding her team was about that.

Tom had gone back downtown to do another press conference with Richard Byrne, where they unmasked Ethan Hunter as the man, as The Night Blinder, who had killed Miles Davidson, Tanner Asperson, and Lucas Reinhart. He made sure not to mention Philip Townsend or Chandler Robert yet.

After the conference, he joined Harri at the hospital to get statements from both Philip and Chandler.

Both Harri and Tom had gone past two full days without sleep. Tom had requested a five-hour break, but Richard demanded they get the statements before Chandler or Philip had a chance to lawyer up.

And that's where they were. At the hospital, trying to survive on what felt like the fifteenth adrenaline rush and copious amounts of coffee.

"I have a surprise for you," Tom said.

Harri smiled.

"I spoke with Jake. He's picking up your car from Ethan Hunter's residence. Then he's coming here to pick you up."

Harri wanted to hug Tom, but she smiled and saluted him instead.

"Who should we talk to first?" Tom asked.

Harri wrote down C in her notebook and showed it to Tom.

"He's on the second floor and no longer in intensive care. The lacerations to his stomach and chest were shallow," Tom said.

"Lucky," Harri wrote and showed Tom.

She stood up and immediately felt lightheaded. She grabbed the table and straightened herself.

"Steady now," Tom said.

Harri smiled and nodded.

"Okay, so let me do all the talking this time," Tom teased her.

Harri rolled her eyes at him but was grateful she wouldn't have to use her voice. Her throat felt tight and a dull pain throbbed from the side.

They found Chandler in his bed, finishing up green Jell-O.

"Mr. Robert, we're pleased to see that you're making a recovery," Tom said.

"Detectives," he said.

Harri noted the bored tone in Chandler's voice had returned. As if being kidnapped, stabbed, and shot was ever so tedious.

He looked small and scrawny in the hospital bed. His face was bruised, and his wiry, blonde hair was going in all directions. The bottom portion of his torso was wrapped in gauze and otherwise, he was bare-chested.

"We need to ask you a few questions while everything is still fresh," Tom said.

Chandler nodded. "If you must."

"What happened at your home?" he asked.

"I really have no idea," Chandler said. "I was up in my room, tinkering. I didn't hear any shots or anything, and he took me by surprise."

"Why do you mention shots?" Tom asked.

"Because of the security guard."

"You weren't knocked out?" Tom asked.

"He jabbed me with something," he said. "It must have been some kind of drug because I got really fuzzy,"

"When you say he, who do you mean?" Tom asked.

"The killer," Chandler said in exasperation.

"Was it someone known to you?"

"Yes," Chandler said. "I mean, no. Not really. It was Ethan Hunter. I only met him a few times. I don't really know him."

"Then what happened?" Tom asked.

"He put me on a blanket or bedspread or something that he dragged me on. I was going in and out. That's how I saw the security guy in the hall. Is he dead? He looked like he was dead."

"Yes, James Halter and your housekeeper, Encarnacion Sanchez, are both dead," Tom informed him.

"Oh," was all Chandler said.

"What happened next?" Tom asked after a moment.

"He dragged me down the stairs and across my lawn. The last thing I remember was being put in the back of a van. He put the blanket on me, over my face. Then I woke up in that basement staring at all the pictures of us. What was up with our eyes?"

"Were you put in that chair? Did he zip-tie your hands and feet?"

"He had started to and then the alarm went off. I think that's when Philip broke into his house," he said. "He managed to get my feet tied up. I pretended I was out of it. He left my arms untied because he thought I passed out. The minute he left me down there, I started getting myself free."

"Do you remember how he knifed you then?" Tom asked.

"I don't remember that part. I woke up with all these cuts on my lower belly," he said, gesturing to the white bandages.

"Then what happened?" Tom asked.

"I got free," Chandler said smugly. "I escaped. I went up the stairs and I was in a kitchen. I heard them in the other room and then I saw Philip had a gun. I tackled Ethan. I was a lot weaker than I felt. I fell into Philip and the gun went off. The next thing I felt was a sharp pain in my leg. Then I must have passed out again."

"And then?"

Chandler looked up at him with a grimace on his face.

"I woke up here," he said.

"How did you know Ethan Hunter?" Tom asked.

Harri watched Chandler's face closely.

He kept his face neutral.

"I just told you that I didn't," he said. "I had some meetings with him because he wanted me to invest in this tech company he was starting. That's as far as I knew him."

"Do you have any idea why he targeted you?" Tom asked.

"No. Isn't that your job?"

Harri wanted to lean in and slap the self-satisfied look off Chandler's face. He knew exactly why he'd been targeted. He knew why three of his friends were dead, why his housekeeper and a security guard had been killed.

"Have you ever heard the name, Daniel Sadowski?" Tom asked.

"Maybe. I vaguely remember a guy from college with that last name," Chandler said.

"You might remember because Daniel Sadowski was the name of your roommate at Cornell University your freshman year," Tom said. "According to University records."

"Like I said." Chandler sniffed. "I vaguely remember the guy."

"Didn't you pledge the same fraternity?" Tom asked.

"I don't remember that. We weren't friends, and that was a long time ago," he said. "I'm sorry but they've given me morphine and I'm getting really drowsy. Can we do this another time?"

He closed his eyes and Tom looked at Harri.

Harri shrugged, and they both stood up.

"When you're feeling better, you'll need to come downtown and provide a formal statement about what happened," Tom said.

Chandler didn't answer. Harri looked over at the grown man playing possum, pretending to be asleep. She and Tom looked at each other and shook their heads. How pathetic. They left the room and went to find Philip Townsend.

• • •

Philip Townsend's demeanor differed greatly from Chandler's.

"Did you find the camera?" he asked the moment they entered his room.

Harri nodded and Tom said, "We recovered a camera in the basement."

"I told you. I told you. You should've believed me. You shot me," he said.

"You shot at an unarmed man," Tom reminded him.

For the first time, Harri was glad her voice was gone. It prevented her from apologizing to Philip for shooting him. She was sorry but apologizing to him would be problematic. She had sympathy for everything Philip had been through since the night he'd gone to Miles Davidson's house to see if he could help his friend out.

"Mr. Townsend, why don't you tell us how you got here?" Tom asked.

Philip then told them how he'd found the first and second photos. How he'd been too afraid to tell them about them because he knew the photos had been taken with his Hasselblad. He told them how he felt the only way he could clear his name was to find out who was framing him. He told them about connecting the Al Jolson song to something that happened at Cornell.

"What happened, Mr. Townsend?" Tom asked.

"I don't know. I swear I don't know," Philip replied. "I've tried to remember what they did to him. I don't know."

He told them how he'd found Danny Sadowski's mother and gone to Braintree, Massachusetts, to speak with her. He explained how he learned that Danny had become Ethan Hunter. He told them he hadn't recognized Danny because of the rhinoplasty and lack of a Massachusetts accent. He explained that when he got back from Braintree and saw how the police had descended on his home, he'd panicked. He tried to get Ethan Hunter on a recording saying he was Danny Sadowski and was responsible for all these deaths so that Philip could take that to the police with the photographs. He got some of that on his phone.

"And you thought bringing a gun to this man's house would do it?" Tom asked.

"I know it was a stupid plan, but I was desperate. You guys were about to haul me in for murdering my friends and I was scared shitless," he said.

"How did you break into Ethan's house?" Tom asked.

"I didn't. It was all open. I walked right through the gate and onto his property. The gate wasn't even latched. His alarm went off, but I didn't know that. I was desperate to prove myself innocent. I was willing to die trying," he said.

"What happened with Danny Sadowski back then?" Tom asked again.

"You mean why did he do all this?" Philip asked. "I just told you I don't remember the whole night. Chandler didn't tell you?"

He looked at the both of them.

"Of course, he didn't. Whatever they did, pushed him somewhere dark and ugly."

"We still don't have a complete motive for any of this carnage," Tom said. "What do you remember?"

"He was tortured that night. I don't remember all of it because I was passed out drunk for a good portion of the evening," Philip began. "It was one of those white-tuxedo parties and this fraternity was the most prestigious on campus. I'd been asked to pledge and so had Danny, but Danny was the Patsy. They were playing a cruel joke on some of the pledges. They'd told the real pledges to get Patsy pledges to go through rush week and then whichever real pledge had his Patsy still standing at the end would be crowned king. Of course, Chandler Robert had to be king. He was the one who convinced Danny to pledge."

"And then what happened?" Tom asked.

"All the rest of the Patsy pledges had dropped out. I'd told mine the same day I asked him to pledge that it was all a big joke and he quit. Danny was the only one left and after they crowned Chandler king, that's when it happened."

"What happened?" Tom demanded.

"I don't know. I swear. I heard things after that night. There were rumors on campus. I think they stripped him and did things to him. Again, I don't remember much of it, but I know alcohol was involved. It always was."

"What were the rumors you heard?" Tom asked.

Philip closed his eyes and winced as if he was in pain. Harri wondered if it was from where she'd shot him, or from what he was remembering.

"He might have been treated like a dog. They might have stripped him, chained him up, put him in a dog cage, made him eat dog food, beat him. I heard rumors there are still photos at the frat house."

Neither Tom nor Harri could hide their disgust. Harri made a mental note to contact the University Police. If those photos existed, she wanted them.

"Okay, well that's a nightmare you told us," Tom said. "But that was ten years ago. He became a billionaire. So, what started this whole thing off? Why did it take ten years for him to get revenge on all of you?"

"I think maybe," Philip began and then shook his head.

"Out with it, Philip." Tom used his dad voice. "I want everything you know or think you know."

"I have a theory. He applied to join the Malibu Beach Club. It made sense now that he had his billions, but Miles and Tanner and Chandler convinced the committee to not approve his membership because he was from Silicon Valley. I think that second rejection did it to him. I mean the guy got a new face, a new name, a whole new life. He got the money and they still rejected him. I think he finally snapped," Philip said.

"Why didn't he kill you?" Tom asked.

"Because he was setting me up," Philip said, his voice laced with bitterness. "I think he hated me because I was like him, a scholarship kid. Maybe he found out that I'd warned my Patsy off but didn't warn him. I did try, though. I tried to tell him at the party, but he didn't want to believe it. I don't know, but he broke into my house and stole my camera. So he could take those horrible photos of the guys. I think in some weird way he was trying to tell me what happened to him, what they'd done to him. I swear, if I hadn't passed out that night, I would have stopped it. I would have. I would have never joined that fraternity."

"Tell me about the camera," Tom said.

"I'm sure it was supposed to be found next to Chandler with my prints on it. I know my fingerprints must be inside the mechanism because it was broken. I still have no idea how he got into my home. He hacked me somehow," Philip said.

Harri thought of how Philip's programming of the lights in the home had gone haywire and alerted the surveillance team that he couldn't be inside. Had Ethan done that, too?

Philip leaned back on the pillows and sighed. He was

exhausted, too. They had gotten what they needed from him for now.

"We need you to make a statement downtown when you're out of here," Tom said.

"You guys will be my first stop," he said.

Harri stood up when Tom did. She smiled at Philip and gave him a thumbs up to say get well soon. He smiled back weakly.

"I'm sorry I made you shoot me," he said. "I didn't know what else to do."

She smiled and nodded and waved her hand to say, 'forget it.'

"Philip," Tom said. "What you did, going over there with a gun, that was incredibly stupid."

"I know," Philip said.

"You saved your friend because of it," Tom said.

"Yea," was all Philip said to that.

Once they were out in the hospital lobby, Tom sat down with Harri on a bench outside of the gift shop. He sighed deeply. Harri looked over to him and put her hands together next to her cheek to say, 'time for sleep.'

"I just got off the phone with Richard and there's another media circus down at the PAB. He's having the time of his life because we caught the guy. He'll enjoy sticking that feather in his cap. He's ordered both of us to stay home and rest for the next couple of days," he said.

"What about the eyes?" Harri wrote down.

"He kept them all in a jar in his basement. They were all witnesses to his humiliation. But we'll never know for sure."

Harri nodded.

"What about IA in my shooting?" Harri wrote in her notebook and showed him.

"There's an investigation already open. I'm supposed to take your gun, Annie Oakley."

Harri gave him a look and handed him her gun.

She was ready to go home and sleep.

A horn honked and she saw Jake pulling up in her car. She'd never been so excited to see him. She stood and waved.

"Your chariot awaits," Tom said.

She walked out into the sunshine to Jake's car. She slid inside and Jake gave her a kiss on the lips. Her smile faded as she saw the look on his face.

"What is it?" she whispered.

"You should get some sleep first," Jake said.

"Tell me," she whispered again.

"I think Jerome Wexler contacted us," Jake said.

Where does Detective Harri Harper go next? Find out in The Skin Hunters on pre-order!

ABOUT DOMINIKA BEST

Dominika Best is the author of the Harriet Harper Thriller Series and the Los Angeles Ghosts series.

For more information:
www.dominikabest.com
hello@dominikabest.com

Made in the USA
Monee, IL
30 July 2022

10571731R00184